HUNTERS IN THE SNOW

HUNTERS IN THE SNOW

DAISY HILDYARD

JONATHAN CAPE
LONDON

Published by Jonathan Cape 2013

2 4 6 8 10 9 7 5 3

First published in Great Britain in 2013 by
Jonathan Cape
Random House, 20 Vauxhall Bridge Road,
London SW1V 2SA

www.vintage-books.co.uk

Addresses for companies within The Random House Group Limited
can be found at: www.randomhouse.co.uk/offices.htm

The Random House Group Limited Reg. No. 954009

A CIP catalogue record for this book is available from the British Library

ISBN 9780224097444

The Random House Group Limited supports the Forest Stewardship
Council® (FSC®), the leading international forest-certification organisation. Our
books carrying the FSC label are printed on FSC®-certified paper. FSC is the only
forest-certification scheme supported by the leading environmental organisations,
including Greenpeace. Our paper procurement policy can be found at
www.randomhouse.co.uk/environment

MIX
Paper from
responsible sources
FSC
www.fsc.org FSC® C013604

Typeset in Sabon MT by Palimpsest Book Production Limited,
Falkirk, Stirlingshire

Printed and bound in Great Britain by CPI Group (UK) Ltd, Croydon, CR0 4YY

For my parents and Luke and Rosanna

Author's Note

Although this novel uses some conventions of non-fictional writing, it is fiction.

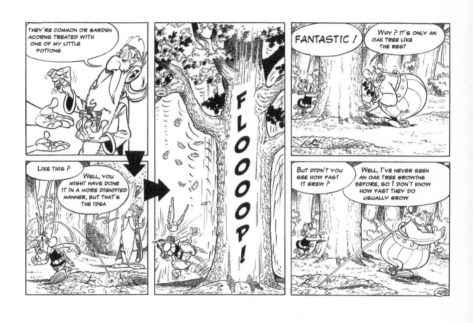

List of Illustrations

I will tell you in three words what the book is.—It is a history.

Laurence Sterne, *Tristram Shandy*

Foreword

My grandfather's name was Thomas James Thompson, but he was known to everyone as Jimmy, and we still called the room in the porch Jimmy's study, despite the fact that a year had passed since his death. His study was the first room in the house: a single approach ran from the York road along half a mile of potholed drive, through ploughed fields and into the stackyard, which was a ridged cement court, and what they called the porch projected over it: a low construction with a slate roof on which a ceramic cat stalked a ceramic single-winged bird. My grandfather told me that he had bought these figures, but I do not know how the bird lost its wing. Perhaps a slipped tile or a storm. This entrance to the house was the front entrance but it was known as the back door, while the door at the rear of the house – neat, white, porticoed and opened only occasionally to the lawn – was known as the front door on the instructions of my grandmother Liv, whose sheepskin coat still hung on a hook by the door. As a child I imagined that this fleece, which Liv wore for foddering, was supposed to let her pass unnoticed among the sheep. I had seen the men disguising orphaned lambs, and saw no reason why the principle shouldn't apply to my grandmother.

Other than Jimmy's desk, the porch was given over to

muddy boots, farming implements and a defunct cooking range which was sealed shut. Damp ash and apple logs were piled up by the wall. A butler's sink shelved a piece of cracked lemon soap tigered with mud, a couple of clods of dirt that may have contained potatoes, and a bowl of chicken-shitty eggs awaiting the wash. There was a hook from which dead game hung in the season: splotches of blood dripped intermittently into the sink, then spread, then flowed slowly towards the plughole. Dirt was the theme of the room, and dirt is matter out of its element. The room being the element of dirt, it was recognised that it should not be cleaned.

The bureau reached the full height of the room: glass-fronted, Victorian-Gothic, and locked after Jimmy's death, my uncle, who had inherited the house, had not found it useful. Some of its holdings were archived in Manila envelopes contained within small cardboard boxes which Jimmy had stacked and filed, unlabelled, in the deep desk drawers. Most of these papers were connected to ancestry: in the largest lower drawer there was a manuscript which drew a line passing through a sequence of Thomases and the Annes and Elizabeths they married. Then a sudden elision projected the family into the branches of another tree, and dominoed Abraham – Lameth – Methuselah – Enoch – Mahaliel – Canan – Enos – Seth – Cain – Adam. GOD. The trees were drawn by hand, one turning root to head, depicting Jimmy as the single descendant of enlarging tiers of ancestors which culminated in the eighteenth century with 128 great-great-great-great-great-grandparents, most unnamed. Another traced us, via a late-seventeenth-century Catherine, to Neptune of the Sea and his wife, who was a fish.

I think that the papers were notes towards a family history that was never finished, or begun. But the trees were wishful. The family is old but not illustrious; historians would probably call us landowners, or gentry at a push: farmers with bookshelves. My grandfather had told me some of the stories, of course, but he wrote, many times, that the study of history was the study of great men and great events. He thought family histories were solipsistic as well as dull, and he said that they were usually full of lies. Each of his thirty-two histories focused on the major European dynasties and although he maintained that everything in the universe had a history, not one of his publications could be said to have brought ordinary people into the foreground. Some things, he argued, were more historic than others. Because of this I found it difficult to know what to make of these papers, and how to deal with the rest of the disorganised rubbish that had collected in his desk: receipts, clippings, pictures and quotes; journal entries or memoranda on loose notepaper; Walnut Whip wrappers, which were probably hidden from my grand-mother – he was a diabetic – and other bits and pieces drawn in from his environment.

To the right of the bookshelves above the bureau was a sash window looking out across the farm. First the old barn that my grandmother called the undercroft and my grandfather called the justice hall. Then a lawn with an apple tree on it, at its end a path with bricks in a herringbone pattern leading to a leaning white wrought-iron gate guarded by two clipped yews, which picturesque entrance gave abruptly onto a ditch, and beyond that bare fields running to the foothills of the Wolds which kept the horizon at a low, familiar, uninterrupted grey-purple line. This was the edge of the visible world. It fell dark early in the afternoon at that time of year, and it was extremely cold – a draught came in at the window – which was why I was wearing two jumpers, a coat, and several pairs of socks pulled up over my jeans. When I took off my boots my toes were cramped and purple.

I describe the room, the desk and its contents because my grandfather began each of his works with a description of the archive, so that, it seems to me, all his history books are stories of their own sources. I have always followed in his footsteps and I still try, but it seems hard to follow any further and I'm not yet old enough to make my own way. An artist is born, Jimmy wrote, and a poet or a novelist may become so at a young age. But a historian must be old. Old, and not only because the scope of his subject is unlimited, and familiarity with such a range of material requires so long a length of time, but also because his work calls for great events to develop, complete their course and collapse; and for new forms to be attempted before his own eyes. (The historian, for Jimmy, was always 'him', but in the absence of grandsons he decided that I should follow him into the profession.) My body acted in sympathy – I grew my first grey hair aged eight.

I was his successor and it was logical that I should be the one to deal with the papers when the farm was to be put on the market, while I was still working on my doctorate – as my uncle pointed out, it wasn't like I didn't have the time.

There were short obituaries of Jimmy in the national papers and a longer piece in the *Echo*: 'LOCAL HISTORIAN DIES'. The headline would have appalled him; he hated local historians. These obituaries were written by journalist acquaintances, but a while later I was invited, by email, to write a memorial essay for a historical journal. I turned down this invitation, and three other similar requests from different print journals. I wouldn't have been able to put together a proper chronology, only a few anecdotes, and most of them are remembered from my own childhood.

Instead of a memorial, then, it seemed better to complete the unfinished work on his History of Modern England. Seven volumes had been planned but there was not much left: four box-files with some notes and pictures relating to traditionalist watersheds converging on the present – the Wars of the Roses (Edward IV, rather than Henry VII, was for him the first modern English king, but that was partly because he hated Henry and was loyal and devoted to the misunderstood Richard III). Then the scientific revolution, the abolition of the slave trade, the advent of industry, the Great War.

The longest and most truthful biography of my grandfather exists of course in his books. To separate the historian from the history, he wrote, is to dismiss the dancer, then call for the dance to come back. He is omnipresent, as it were, in his accounts of a past in which he never lived. But little actually happened in his life – he didn't have any history of his own.

Memories of my grandfather came back, naturally enough, when I looked through his last work. But they came in the wrong order, and some of them seemed to have changed – these memories of my own seemed at least as old as, if not older than, the proper historical content, and it made me realise that my adult life was completely cut off from my childhood, not only by the distance between Yorkshire and London, but also by the expensive education which began when I was eleven, for which my grandfather had, at least in the first instance, paid.

He said that it was good for a historian to stand distinct from his past. Childhood to the grown man, he said, is as history to the nation. Good for a historian to be an outsider; gives him a comfortable perspective. Nonetheless it was unsettling to me to see my London belongings unpacked among the filth at the farm. On the walls and ceilings patches of flaking paint and damp had changed shape but stayed the same, like ghosts or clouds or icebergs.

The whole farm, in fact, felt like an island, floating on its own through the countryside, and I was like Robinson Crusoe on it: I found myself, without knowing what strange weather had sent me there, completely cut off from where I came from (which was Crusoe's origin as well as mine – we were born in the same place, York). I did not, on the first day, walk through the empty barns, the pig ark, or the stables where my grandmother used to house seaside donkeys from Scarborough over the winter. I decided not to drive three miles into the village where I grew up. For one thing it looked like snow. For another, I knew that I would recognise people in the village and they probably wouldn't recognise me. Instead, I leafed through the Visitors' Book, which had been left when my uncle rented the house for 'holidays', after my grandparents died. (The Complaints Book, it should have been called: mostly about the laundry – dirty, holes, absent. A few, showing courage in adversity, produced some moderately witty abuse.) Short-term tenancy hadn't worked out, and it became necessary to sell up.

My uncle had installed an Internet connection for the Visitors, a mixed blessing, and each time I checked my emails or made an abortive attempt to type up my notes, or looked at the news online, my old village, which was only just hidden behind the hill, seemed to drift off to a greater distance. But in between the checking and the typing, when I walked around the house, it kept coming back to my mind, each memory in succession seeming the more dusty and antique.

Our house, which we moved out of when I was eleven, was a red-brick semi-detached ex-council house which Margaret Thatcher had sold us. My mother taught several subjects at the local school; my father drove north four days a week to what was then Teesside Polytechnic, where he taught and still teaches chemistry, though it merged to form the University of Teesside and Middlesbrough, and then became Middlesbrough University.

I was taken to school on a school bus – a Pullman bus that picked us up each morning, except on snow days, and was exactly like the ones in which strike-breaking miners, not far away, were taken across the picket, although we didn't have grilles on the windows to protect us from thrown eggs or stones. Each day the bus collected pupils from seven villages including mine, then deposited them at another village in front of the North Yorks County Council C of E Primary School, as was announced on the front of the modern concrete classroom, which had a wall of windows and stood next to the old Victorian schoolhouse whose windows were set high in the walls so that inmates could not see out. A portrait of the Queen hung inside – it must have been done in the 1950s, as she looked young, chocolate-box and regal. Underneath her were Blu-tacked posters of a carrot called Herbie who told us to eat vegetables and a squirrel called Tufty who advised us to stop, look and listen. We had assembly, gym and lunch, which we called dinner, in that hall. (Dinner was called tea.) At my grandparents' home the meals had different names.

At school everyone had school dinners: Monday – sausages, beans and chips; Tuesday – fish fingers, chips and beans; Wednesday – 'salad': salad cream, corned beef and cheese-and-onion crisps; Thursday – cottage pie; Friday – 'meat' (nondescript), chips and beans. You could have a half or a whole, but you had to eat everything on your plate. The whole school said grace before dinner, someone in year six sing-songing matter-of-factly at an efficient speed: 'Dear God. Thank you for the food we eat, thank you for the combine harvesters and wheat, thank you for the birds that sing, thank you Lord for every . . . thing. Amen.'

We also prayed in assembly – it was a Church of England world. There was Sunday school, which my parents used as a babysitter; at Christmas we did Christingle; in the autumn

Harvest Festival, although the offerings, which came from the village shops, were of Kia-Ora, Penguins, Yops and Yazoos and Heinz soup. And it was a County Council, Church of England world: my best friend, whose mother came from south London, and her grandparents, even further (so they said) from Jamaica, was the only non-Caucasian student at the school. She told me that she was related to the fictional characters in a sitcom set in a barber's shop in Peckham, which we both followed and analysed as if it was another world, and it was.

The bus picked us up again at the end of the day. There was a song we used to sing, going home, about different ways of killing Thatcher. The driver dropped us by the post office and I walked home past Mr Whisker's house. Mr Whisker, perhaps to satisfy his name, took in stray cats. His garden had a lawn the size of a double bed on which there were always half a dozen sprawled tabbies and tortoiseshells. Children, like historians, make weird, radical connections, most of which are phased out later in life. One of mine was the association of this garden of cats, whose heads turned like synchronously cranked machinery when you passed them, with the state of omniscience – a concept (along with omnipresence and omnipotence) that Miss Taylor was struggling to make us understand at the time.

After school my time was spent playing out. I used to call at my friend Kylie's house straight after tea. 'Is Kylie playing out?' I asked, squinting at Kylie's mum, then I'd run off if she was grounded. She was frequently grounded. She and I and the others made prank calls out of the village telephone box. We started fires at the bottom of the large garden at the old people's home. We rearranged the directions on the road signs at the crossroads (when a neighbour called some transport-related subset of the authorities the school was informed and we were all taken into the assembly hall: 'I feel very let down,' said Miss Taylor, 'that it's the girls who have been doing this'). We played bulldog in the graveyard. Once a group of us got a hiding from the farmer, Mr Whisker Junior – his father was the cat man – for trampling his barley. 'I know your dad,' he said to me.

At the time, the village, unlike my grandparents' house, seemed connected to the real world by radio, television, the twice-a-week Coastliner bus between York and Scarborough, and other people like the postman or the mobile-librarian. My grandparents' farm, in contrast, belonged to old age. But when I returned to Yorkshire, everything that I remembered about the village seemed ancient too: singing on the school bus, the portrait of the Queen, grace, corned beef, getting a hiding and playing out. Unlike some historians, I am not preoccupied with the question of whether that world was better or worse. But my memories felt out of sync – too close to be so far away, as it were, and too recent to exist in the parallel historical world which belonged to my grandfather.

The whole world, to Jimmy, was a history textbook, and when I was not at home or out around the village I was with him, in History, going as far back as I can remember. My first classroom was a pram with brown patterns on the lining in which I sat listening to his version of Aesop's story about the man and the lion. The man, who does not have a name in the fable, and the lion were, apparently, having an argument about who was the strongest, when they passed a stone memorial onto which a (human) sculptor had carved the image of a muscular warrior standing above a dead lion, his arrow pointing down. The man pointed to the sculpture: stone proof, he said, of man's superiority.

'"If a lion had made that sculpture," said the lion,' said my grandfather, '"it would depict a single lion resting a single tawny paw elegantly atop a whole heap of maimed, mauled and partially eaten human bodies."' I got the point.

He couldn't resist adding certain details to the story: the

lion's muscovado hide which, like sand, turned into discrete colours – black, brown, white and yellow – when you came up close. The picture of the dead lion did not show any blood, he said, and at first the man had thought it might be sleeping. The man was surprised to discover that he was slightly allergic to lions – he started to itch and sneeze when the living lion approached him, just like my grandfather and I did when we were bothered by my grandmother's dogs.

My grandfather was a historian because he loved these details, not just some details, but every detail and each for its own sake. In one of the early notebooks I found a quote to this effect: 'A feeling for and a joy in the particular in and by itself is necessary to the historian, as one takes joy in flowers without thinking to which of Linne's classes or of Oken's families they belong.' 'The historian's challenge,' he wrote, 'is to abandon himself to the facts.'

I had originally planned to spend a fortnight at the farm going through these notebooks and the other papers, and to see if there was anything worth publishing in the files. I was also to clean, and to throw out as much of the old rubbish as possible before the house went on the market in early spring. But it was harder than I had expected. Bits from other writings were run into the notes without proper attribution, so it was difficult at some points to tell who was the author of what. And I found it impossible to throw out the very first book I found in the desk – or in fact, on the desk, before I even opened it, which was a paperback selection from Herodotus' *Histories,* which must have been the last thing Jimmy was reading when he died. I knew I shouldn't keep it. The copy was mildewed and I had my own. But Herodotus was the first historian, and my grandfather's favourite, and as a child I heard how Herodotus had travelled on foot through ruins, palaces and deserts in the ancient world, holding conversations with the ordinary people he met and recording the stories they told him – even, said Jimmy, when those stories seemed fantastic. Herodotus hardly ever passed judgement on the histories he discovered. He accompanied his readers through the past, in different tempers, climates, and various states of physical comfort and discomfort.

Herodotus, my grandfather told me, is known as the father of history. I did not hear, until I studied history as an undergraduate, that he is also known as the father of lies. Like my grandfather, he created his own parallel historical world. It is often when he gives specific details about his sources that those sources are doubtful – he sketched the shape of an informant to fill the empty space out of which invented or falsely detailed stories came. My grandfather hadn't told me that.

1 Edward IV

i

The file marked '1471' began anachronistically in 1461, with some notes on the Battle of Towton and an article, cut from the *Echo*, about the pub we'd been to when we went to the village.

Getting to the newly reopened Rising Sun at Towton is a testing experience. Drivers coming out from York can either go down the A162 through Grimston, in which case flooded roads will accost them at this time of year, or they can carry on up the A64 until you hit the next junction and then have to double-back on themselves in order to arrive at their newly refurbished destination. Knowing the area well, we chose the latter route on our way there last week. The new manager of the Sun Eddie had been very friendly on the telephone despite the fact that he did not yet know that I was from the papers.

Towton is famous for the battle that happened in 1461, and our waiter told us that archaeologists had discovered the skeleton of a horse buried near the battlefield. He said that it was buried standing up – I wonder how they did that! Although this horse had legs, perhaps it is the same one as the ghost horse that is reported to float legless through the Rising Sun at night. We went at lunchtime so we cannot bear witness to these reports.

On arrival me and my lovely lady friend (who is also my wife Hannah) were received into the bar where we enjoyed a G & T served by a friendly buxom barmaid, but an ongoing game of pool in an adjacent room would have impaired our experience had we been compelled to eat in this room.

We went on into the 'dining room' where we ordered a bottle of house white which came very quickly and was nice and cold but a little too sweet for me. Hannah elected a goat's cheese tartlet while I was going to go for the classic of steak and chips. However, observing the menu, I noticed that Ed had cheekily put horse steak on the menu and, ever a bold eater, I took up the challenge. When they came nice and promptly but allowing time for all the food to be home-made, Hannah's tartlet was cheesy and delicious, the onions and goat's cheese inextricably linked, while my steak was indeed a 'rare' piece of horse done 'to a T'. Unfortunately Hannah was let down by the texture of her tartlet which she described as slightly slimy, but fortunately being greedy we managed to clear our plates and we did not have to see anything go to waste.

We went without pudding and overall the bill came to £45.24 which is not unreasonable considering. However, it is only now, reading the receipt for this article, that I realise we were charged for an extra portion of chips we did not have.

Dining at the Rising Sun was overall a very pleasant experience and I would definitely go back again. Their bold choice of putting horse on the menu worked well.

Despite the past history of Towton, it is a pleasant village where the staff were prompt and the prices reasonable. I just wouldn't order anything that comes with chips. If I had time I would go back to ask for a refund.

The article took me back to the Rising Sun before its refurbishment, when Jimmy and I visited it. I was about ten.

Our trip is still clear in my mind – clearer than many memories of more recent events. At the pub he ordered one fish and chips, one steak-and-kidney pie, one orange squash, one pint of John Smith's and one pre-lunch sherry which he allowed me to sip (it tasted like raisins and sheep dip). Jimmy offered a drink to the barmaid, handing over a twenty-pound note which he'd smoothed out like a ticket.

'Thank you, sir,' she said. 'I'll have the money if you don't object.'

He didn't. He asked her if she knew the direction of the battlefield. She didn't, but we found it on our way out, marked with crossed swords drawn in biro on a map in the porch, and we left and drove on up the B1217. A farmer was ploughing to our left, and a flock of seagulls rising and falling in his wake. We pulled up at a plain iron cross and descended the slope onto the battlefield, which was bounded by a small stream clogged with lopped trunks and logs from the coppiced stands of ash and alder at its edge. The Cock River had been reduced by gradual infill over the years, and even my grandfather could cross it easily with a single stride. He stood higher than the horizon at the other side; taller, to me, than the cooling towers at Pontefract and Castleford. He introduced me to those distant towns – Cas Vegas, Ponte Carlo – but then turned his back on them to begin the lecture, gesturing north towards the border, beyond which groups of Scotsmen were even now, I believed, joining the Lancastrians, promised land and money in return for service during the campaign. Although it was very cold for March it had not frozen: the rivers were full and fast-flowing and the ground which had been churned by hooves was heavy going. 'It is an irony of civil war,' said Jimmy, 'that it destroys the land it is fought over and upon: the land is both the means and the end; the soldiers too.'

The bloodiest battle ever fought on English soil began on Palm Sunday in March 1461, during a spring snowstorm. More men died that day than died during the first day of the Battle of the Somme, my grandfather said; the heralds reckoned twenty-eight thousand, which was a whole single per cent of the English population. His own father, he told me, losing his way for a moment, had been too young to fight at the Somme.

At the beginning of the battle, Lancastrian forces had held the advantage of higher ground. But the strong wind spat snow into their faces, and it lifted the Yorkist arrows across the plain while the shower of Lancastrian archery was buffeted back and fell short of the enemy line. Under the storm of arrows that attacked them, the Lancastrian front broke, and because they did not want to retreat they had to funnel down the slope and ford the River Cock, crossing into the battlefield proper – a long flat plain which was scarred, in the middle, by a shallow depression marking the boundary between the Lancastrian troops and those of the House of York.

The Yorkists were led by a teenager, Edward, who was at the front of his army fighting hand-to-hand, unlike his elder cousin Henry VI, who stayed at the rear of the Lancastrian force with his back to the conflict – perhaps it was here, the battle swinging behind him, that he was happened upon trying to convene a discussion about biblical doctrine among a small stand of oak trees. Henry was a lover of peace, but he was troubled, according to many accounts, by intermittent bouts of insanity: Shakespeare's simple king, finding himself at Towton, was at a loose end when his men poured down the slope to fight, and reduced the magnitude of the situation as he waited to hear the outcome – 'here on this molehill I will sit me down' – while below him the river ran swollen with snow and the spilt blood of his soldiers' appendices, which poured out of holes and over the whole field. As they said at that time, few of the men would be hale and whole again.

It was hard to see who was winning – the snow, blowing sideways, covered the soldiers like a net. The mud was churned so the horses sank and stuck. Thin hounds were greasing around the bodies on the ground. Lines of soldiers, pushing forward, rank after rank, dealt a succession of blows on the already dead human faces.

Then more Yorkist forces appeared at the top of the slope and the Lancastrians were driven back again – across the Cock beck where they were crushed, divided and driven over ditches into different fields, where they were found hiding among the trees and in the chapel in the village, and cut down, group by group, by Edward's soldiers, fighting with sword, poleaxe and spear, and running them ten miles to the gates of York.

After the battle Edward waited for his soldiers to return to him, then moved south the next morning. He commissioned a chapel to commemorate the fallen men, but the chapel was never built. The chroniclers and historians did not stay long either – they left with the troops and drew up lists of the fallen by subtracting them from the original number, instead of counting the dead.

When they had gone the local people came out to find members of their own families, to help the wounded, and to get what they could off the bodies. Strange, familiar shapes broke the surface of the beck: lopped trunks and legs of fallen and trampled men, and one of Henry's messengers who lay underwater, face up, a hole in the head, the body entirely submerged so that its jacket, pillowing full of air above the surface of the stream, created a false stepping stone.

Our visit to Towton was short. There was nothing to do on the field, except perhaps re-enact the battle and Jimmy did not approve of re-enactments.

In the aftermath, the chroniclers announced a 'universal death', but they blamed the outcome on the bad weather – the snow showed that God was on Edward's side, they wrote, although I would have thought that bad weather affected the winning side as much as their victims.

'One of the strange things,' said my grandfather, 'is that we can now retrieve details from the battlefield that were lost the day after it happened.' He explained how excavations using satellite images and radio-sensing technology have enabled historians to recreate a virtual map of the battle, and to date the blades, hammers and other battle rubble under the surface of the field. They have brought back details of the people who fought there, like those of a tall teenage boy who was found with several other bodies in a mass grave. The archaeologists thought this group were probably on the losing side and had probably been hunted down somewhere towards the end, probably trying to take sanctuary in the small chapel in the village. The boy had a broken left elbow and thirteen strikes from defending himself with a bent arm across his upper body. The only left-hander in the grave, the archaeologists recorded.

It was strange, my grandfather repeated, that we could, here at the end of the twentieth century, retrieve details from the fifteenth century that had been lost in the seventeenth century, when Daniel Defoe took his *Tour thro' the Whole Island of Great Britain*. At that time, said Defoe, almost all historic facts about the battle had been forgotten, and even the memory of its location was only sustained by tradition, and sometimes, the upturning of fragments of rubbish which guided the country people, and the country people guided their visitors, to the site of the battle. 'But we had only the story in speculation,' said Defoe, 'for there remains no marks, no monument, no remembrance of the action, only that the ploughmen say, that sometimes they plough up arrow-heads and spear-heads, and broken javelins, and helmets, and the like; for we could only give a short sigh to the memory of the dead, and move forward.'

The farmer in the next field was climbing down from his tractor cabin when we walked back up to the car, and my grandfather went over and spoke to him. Who, asked Jimmy, was the landowner?

'This is all me,' he said, 'but the battlefield's Heritage.' He didn't seem in any hurry to get back to his half-finished ploughing. It was a bit of a curse being so near the site, he said, because of the metal detectorists and the other treasure hunters. He had turned up arrowheads and other bits – but unlike most farmers round here, he wasn't hoping for treasure himself. 'Anything's buried can stay that way as far as I'm concerned.'

My grandfather asked if he knew about the horse that had recently been discovered by the archaeologists, buried standing near Saxton.

'How do you bury a horse standing up?' I asked.

'A crane,' said the farmer unhesitatingly, 'and you'd fill it up around him.'

We got in the car and at the motorway junction turned back towards York. On the way home Jimmy told me how Herodotus had committed to memory the names of three hundred heroic soldiers who died in the Greek wars. He also told me about the labyrinth on Lake Moeris, which was a gigantic memorial for fallen Egyptian soldiers. Of all the wonders Herodotus had ever seen, it was this labyrinth, he said, which beggared description. Herodotus described the labour and calculated the cost that must have been spent to build the elaborate memory. He enumerated the twelve roofed courtyards with six gates, the thousand and a half chambers with vestibules, the paths that zigzagged through the rooms and the stone walls covered with reliefs that the historian couldn't decipher. Herodotus, said my grandfather, didn't descend from these upper chambers to the underground tombs, because the Egyptians who showed him round wouldn't let him go down. You could only go down to the basement, they said, if you were a king or a sacred crocodile.

We drove past a series of bright red, white and yellow plastic signs advertising Burger King, Texaco, McDonald's at the services before Tadcaster. The towers of the Minster, covered in metal scaffolding, were in sight in the distance.

Herodotus' memorial was the beginning of history, said Jimmy. But it was also the beginning of the things that history lost – the unheroic soldiers who died anonymously. It is the historian's job, he said, to try to bring back the names of these lost soldiers, one by one, but also to remember that every attempt fails.

It fails, he went on, and not only because there are so many more soldiers than historians, but also because the present always comes before the past; the past is laid over the present and looked through, like a pane of glass. Other people, he said – by 'other people' he usually meant people who weren't professional historians – don't let things be what they are, they turn histories into parables.

We passed a Little Chef with a playground in which there was an orange elephant which had a slide for a trunk. Then we switched lanes and sped up past Tadcaster brewery, over a beck which had something man-made sticking up, though I couldn't work out what it was – maybe a shopping trolley, a baby buggy or a wheelchair.

'The best historians, in point of fact, are shallow people.' Writing from the inside, the historian loses himself in the mass of complicating details. Our job is to simplify things to cause and effect, cause and effect. 'The past should be cut off from the present,' he said, 'like an island.' The historian needs a perspective to assess the accounts. 'The historian should suspend his belief.' Perhaps that's what he thought Herodotus was doing when he made things up.

The first time I had heard about Towton was when I was a little younger, when my grandfather used to tell me stories from Thomas Malory's *Morte Darthur*. He didn't read much fiction. 'What is the point,' he would ask, 'in overpopulating virtual worlds with made-up characters, when real people are disappearing into oblivion all the time?' He had a vivid sense of all the faces and voices buried in unopened boxes in local archives – but, nonetheless, he knew whole tracts of the *Morte* by heart and could recite lists of fictional knights smiting one another in the battle scenes too. I heard the stories many times over when I stayed at the farm, or when we went out in the car, or when we went camping; but I had never actually read a copy until I found one on my first day back, on the top shelf above his bureau next to a *Just So Stories* and a *Pilgrim's Progress* which had also been awarded as school prizes, in 1926, at Montpellier Primary in Plymouth. The boards were buckled and there were yellow and grey moulds living on the pages.

Jimmy had told me the stories as if they were real histories: an apparently inexhaustible series of narratives in which a revolving cast of familiar characters – Galahad, Lancelot,

Guinevere – were always in flight from something or in pursuit of something else. But looking at the copy, I thought that it was more like the Bible. It was full of miracles, like Arthur pulling the sword out of the stone on Easter Day, and repeating the trick at Pentecost, Candlemas and on Twelfth Night. Outside the miracles, like in the Bible, there didn't seem to be much to life except begetting and being smitten down.

In the battle scenes the knights cut off legs, arms, feet, hands and heads – cut down, dropped dead. They fought with swords and spears on wet fields. The horses sank in the mud, the dogs ran around their hooves. The knights dealt blows on the heads of their enemies, then more blows.

My grandfather told me that the Battle of Towton may have been an 'inspiration', as he put it, behind these scenes in the storybook, though historians are uncertain about whether Malory was at Towton. And if he was, they don't know which side he was fighting for. Very little, in fact, is known about Thomas Malory's real life, but the few rumours we do have – of theft, banditry, prison break, factional defection, the abduction of a neighbour's wife – almost outdo the stories he wrote. It looks like he wrote the book in prison and he may have died there too. Historians don't know whether he was a Lancastrian or a Yorkist because different historical documents seem to show he switched camps: one chronicle of 1462 mentions a Thomas Malory, knight, in Edward's army during a campaign involving the besiegement of Lancastrian-held castles in the north-east, at Northumberland, Alnwick and Bamburgh; but in a different chronicle, Malory, or someone else with the same name, is named in the Lancastrian troops. The castles themselves were too strong to list or fall under siege but not so strong that they did not change hands, several times. Malory, too, must have gone from one side to another and back.

Or one or both of the chronicles could have been wrong. There are several different historical versions of the Battle of Towton, but they don't quite match each other so they cannot perfectly account for all the fallen soldiers. One, for instance, said that Antony Woodville was killed fighting with the Lancastrians, but we hear of him in other chronicles accompanying Edward York a decade later. It could have been his father or another man with the same name. Another account of the battle, now known as Hearne's Fragment, said that it took place at night, which seems impossible. The 1462 chronicler gave a list of soldiers who died at Towton in which he included many men who were still alive, and completely forgot to mention many of the dead. Some scholars think he made it all up.

'Suspend your belief,' my grandfather had told me, by which he meant that historians should ask the sources why they are telling what they tell. He taught me not to trust the sources but to hold them against one another, to isolate consistencies and inconsistencies, then work back to the truth.

Looking at it that way, though, the history turned inside out. The inconsistent chroniclers were wrong and Malory's romance was a true story. Its printer, William Caxton, wrote a preface in which he said that the *Morte* was not a collection of legends but a history of Arthur's reign – Caxton called it a 'great truth'. It was written like the chronicles, and scenes were set in real locations, like the Cornish convent to which Guinevere retired; but most importantly, Caxton was sure that King Arthur was a real historical king of England, not a figment of mythical imagination. 'In him that shold say or thinke that there was never suche a king callyd Arthur,' wrote Caxton, 'might wel aretted grete follie and blindenes.'

Also, Arthur was still alive. According to the legend the king had been buried hundreds of years earlier under a stone in Cornwall – or somewhere – but he was only sleeping, and would eventually wake up and return to rule. Caxton retold this story firmly and groundedly, as if this prediction for the future was just as dependable as anything that had ever happened in the past.

Reading Caxton's preface, I thought at first that the *Morte Darthur* sounded as reliable as the real history, and that Malory's invented inventories of knights, soldiers and kings were perhaps as real as the inconsistent lists of the dead which had been given by the chroniclers. But Caxton was misdirected – for one thing, he diverted the end, the final part, to the End, the purpose, thinking that the heading for the last section was the title of the 'wholl boke', which was why he called it the *Morte Darthur*, The Death of (the) Arthur. It was the copy of the *Morte* by my grandfather's desk that first seemed to show some kind of intentional arrangement, in Jimmy's files, behind what appeared at first to me as a kind of chaos.

Malory was inconsistent too. As the book went on his mistakes gathered. Sometimes a character came on the scene who had been killed in an earlier battle, because Malory couldn't always remember which of his creations were alive and which were dead, even though he kept drawing his readers back at the end of each battle, when the story should have advanced, to go back over the missing – he listed, with patience that can only seem loving, the genealogies as well as the names of the smitten-down characters, his own productions, after he had killed them off. Clarence, King Anguish of Ireland, King Carados of Scotland, Constantine that was Sir Carados' son of Cornwall, Sir Bohart le Cure Hardy that was King Arthur's son, Sir le Apres, Sir Fergus, Sir Driant, Sir Lambegus, Sir Clarrus of Cleremont, Sir Cloddrus, Sir Hectimere, Sir Edward of Carnarvon, Sir Dinas, Sir Priamus that was christened by

Sir Tristram the noble knight, and these three were brethren, Sir Hellaine le Blank.

I realised, leafing through the *Morte Darthur*, that Jimmy had told the stories as they came to mind, so that the version of the book which I held in my head was just a print of his memory of it, and the details, when I recollected them, were all in the wrong order in the real book.

A knight burst into court wearing the bloody rags of the jacket in which his father had been murdered – it was called La Cote Male Taile, which means The Badly Cut Coat.

Then Rience of Wales sent the king a letter in which he announced his intention to have Arthur's beard for his cloak made of the beards of eleven other, defeated kings. The book does not mention whether the cloak was small, or whether the beards were particularly luxuriant.

Then Galahad's hounds pursued a white hart through the forest to a castle keep and caught up with it and killed it. The owner of the hart came out of the castle and before the unfortunate dogs had time to realise he struck them all down all at once. Galahad defended their 'kynde', which means their nature, when he said, 'Why have ye slayne my howndys? For they did but theyr kynde.'

ii

It is usually hardest to throw out the first thing. Clearing
the house was much easier after I got rid of the school prize
books. I was able to go back to the study without looking
too sentimentally on it as my grandfather's old habitat. Standing
on the lower shelf, I threw all the books off the top shelf, one
by one, into a large box, then put Herodotus in too. Then I
put the box in the boot of the car. Back at the desk I began to
sort through the file, separating loose notes from things which
were relevant to the history.

Under the aerial photograph of Towton there was a photograph of my grandparents, probably taken in the late 1970s
or early 1980s. They were sitting in patterned armchairs in the
garden, his hand resting regally on hers. Liv was wearing a
green wax jacket and coral lipstick, and her yellow-coloured
hair curled around the silk scarf which was knotted under her
chin. Her mouth slumped at one corner where the cigarette
was absent. My grandfather, in contrast, was slight and
straight-backed, his nervy white face guarded with a clipped
and, at that time, still-dark beard. I propped the photo on the
mantelpiece.

Attached to the photo with a paper clip shaped like a snail-
shell was a black-and-white postcard reproduction of a painting
of a hunt, in which the lengthened bodies of the dogs and deer,

disappearing into a forest, gave the illusion of movement. I'd never seen it before, although I had heard, somewhere, about Uccello's other famous painting, the panorama of war on a reused canvas. In the middle of the battle, faintly but clearly, you can see the shape of the artist's wife's face, which had been painted over but came back through.

My grandfather addressed himself on the reverse of the postcard:

> Paolo Uccello 1397–1475, real name Paolo di Dono, called Uccello because he drew so many birds and displayed them about his rooms, that to visit him was to keep company in an aviary. Was obsessively preoccupied with the creation of depth in his pictures and would stay up all night attempting to find the vanishing-point while his contemporaries were still painting linear but flat narratives in the 'comic-strip' style. The Hunt is probably his last painting, painted in 1470, postcard purchased by myself at the Ashmolean Museum, Oxford, 12.12.64.

Unlike Uccello, who had put so much effort into creating a lifelike representation of the hunt, my grandfather was not interested in the reality of hunting. He was interested in hunting as a traditional pursuit, but it was my grandmother who hunted in real life, and she who looked after the farm too, with the help of two men, both of whom were called William. She kept rare breeds: Muscovy ducks, Teesdale sheep and British White cattle. Inside the house was a counter-collection of animals which testified to her love of hunting: a stuffed giant tortoise of uncertain age; a series of nineteenth-century pictures – *The MEET/ The CHASE / The KILL*! The landing was decorated with a pair of antelope horns, souvenirs from the Boer War; and the (amputated) hoof of a (deceased) horse, set in silver, stopped the front door.

The inside of the house, though, was really my grandfather's environment. Liv was always outside on the farm and he was always in, at his desk with his books and papers. I am not sure why they married – I have heard different accounts of the courtship – but it was convenient that he had unexpectedly inherited a farm that he could not run while she, who had grown up on a farm, had no land of her own.

Somehow they had a daughter and two sons (my father was the youngest) but they slept in separate single beds when I knew them. They never ate together, except when they had guests, though neither of them ate much anyway. They both drank. She liked to hunt and he never hunted. His one hobby, outside history, was an amateurish enthusiasm for rudimentary machines and contraptions. The two interests merged only in the traps and snares she set for rabbits and magpies, which he used to check on his daily walk. When I try to remember, I think I rarely saw them together.

Conflict was at the heart of his theory of history – this was Herodotus' idea, but my grandfather reconceived it. 'It is from the conflict of the universal with the particular,' wrote Jimmy, 'that the great catastrophes arise.' He wrote about revolution and war and had no illusion that the history of humans was a history of civilisation or progressive improvement. He was fond of using what he called the principle of waste paper to illustrate this, waste paper being toilet paper. Moving the latrine inside the house, he said, was a great backward step for Western civilisation, and yet it was only recently that we began to defecate on our own doorsteps, so to speak (Herodotus agreed that urinating inside, an Egyptian practice, was against nature). Jimmy used an outside latrine, and he hustled the rest of the family to follow his example. I would say he was preoccupied with the idea of inside and out. He mythologised himself, and all historians, as outsiders, looking in.

His keen sense of what belonged in and what should remain outside meant that my grandmother was exiled through the back door to pluck and gut a bird or a rabbit, and she had to sit on a stool in the wind and sometimes snow, with a bin liner rolled open at her ankles, into which she stuffed fistsful of feathers; often they blew out again in a trail across the stackyard. I was allowed to take a footstool and sit opposite, and when she snipped off the heads with scissors I could play with them, hovering the wrong heads over the bodies to create snipe-billed pigeons and duck-headed pheasants.

She pricked at the joints and membranes with a sharp knife so that they jumped apart. Then she took back the skin. The soft loopy junk inside was quite similar to human organs, she told me, but downsized. The birds and rabbits had blobs and flippers for stomachs and livers, and yellow beads in the intestines. They smelled sharp and I wasn't to touch. It seems to me now that these bodies are the more delicately manufactured for being made in miniature, like suitcases full of carefully folded baby clothes – not that they were delicately handled by my grandmother, who washed them briskly, after she'd killed them and gutted them, with Fairy Liquid in the butler's sink. For the lice, and the cigarette ash.

The lead shot made only tiny punctures in the carcasses which were, when skinned, pink, purple and yellow, and sometimes glowed with a phosphorescent membrane. Much later, I found an illustration to a volume of medieval fables which pictured the souls of human beings as the bodies of harried game – hares, rabbits, woodcock and quail – driven across the landscape by the Devil with a pitchfork. The body, it said underneath, is actually the opposite of the soul, and animals do not have souls themselves.

When my grandmother finished she put the corpses in an industrial-size deep-freeze in the barn with a rusty lid held down with a small rock. In the freezer once, there was a whole jointed doe, which had been road-killed at the hairpin bend on the way to the village. William and my grandmother brought her back in the Land Rover. There was an area at the top of the haunch which was covered with moving maggots so that from where I was standing, outside the vehicle, it flickered like it was being shown on a screen. Though the wood was full of deer, I had never seen one close before. I got a good look that time, though. You have to kill it to see it properly. We often saw the deer in the margins of the fields – one of the few species, my grandmother said, that was on the increase – but no one on our shoot had the licence to kill them.

On ice, everything looked like meat rather than dead animals – it was hard to imagine that the joints and steaks had ever been alive. Each cut of beef that returned from the abattoir corresponded to a part of the cow's body, but they came back wrapped in cellophane, like the silage bales on which the cattle fed. My grandmother sold a small amount of beef and the occasional brace of game to a butcher's shop in town which has since closed. She took cash for them, and as far as I know, the meat was her only source of independent income at that time.

She never named her animals other than for breeding and slaughtering purposes, but that was not to say she was not sentimental. The ancient greyhound who accompanied her everywhere was closer than any human relation. He was staid and dignified, an elder statesman, with coarse, long grey hairs sticking out of his silky black coat. He set the pace, following at her heels, and the other dogs followed behind him.

My grandfather hated the dogs and took a swift kick at them whenever he could. As much as possible, he kept them out of the house. The door into the porch at the back was a modern one with white wood framing twelve square panes of glass warped to look like the surface of water, and Liv's dog would sit outside, patiently, waiting for her to appear. When you passed the door you saw his blurred black shape, like something seen through water, and eyes magnified to two large uneven yellow patches. You could see him there from my grandfather's desk.

Jimmy and I were both allergic to dogs, and also to horses, cats and haystacks. We would probably have been allergic to foxes, if we could get close enough to find out. He and I never went fox-hunting, but sometimes my grandmother would make me beat when there was a shoot. Jimmy, who disliked it as much as me, was never made to beat. That was because he was an adult, they said, outrageously.

The pretty Italian forest in the Uccello picture was not much like our wood in January where, toggled into my duffel coat, given an old hazel stick, I was coerced into trudging along the bank of the beck half-heartedly hitting at the rotting logs and tree trunks. From the bottom of the gorge I could see the guns advance above us but I could not see the nearby beaters through the porridge of undergrowth, though I heard them crooning and stirring. I was self-conscious about making these weird animal noises, and resentful at not being paid as the other beaters were.

It was rare for a bird to come down near me. When they did, they came riffling through the air and the branches, like someone was throwing books out of the sky.

I was eleven when Liv decided it was time I had a gun. She took me off PE one afternoon, during the last week of term before Christmas, after sending a note for my form tutor: 'I'm taking my granddaughter shooting,' she wrote. 'I don't approve of netball' – she thought herself very witty, but I couldn't hand that in so I wrote an alternative saying I was going to the dentist, again.

The clay pigeon place was in a patch of new plantation woodland near Helmsley. When Liv turned off the road we drove up through the course, which was set in stands around a winding track, like mini-golf or an ornamental railway. The clubhouse was a faux log cabin with an Irish flag flying and a pair of guns crossed above the entrance. Through the open door you could see an unmanned reception desk, but the woman came out when we drove up. Two small boys, probably her sons, were taking turns to sit on a skateboard to roll down the slight slope. 'Stop that,' she said sharply, when the larger boy pushed the smaller off the side. She had a sharp red nose and was wearing a striped puffa jacket.

'Has she shot before?' she asked, looking at me.

'No, it's her first time,' my grandmother said, adding untruthfully, 'but she knows what she's doing.'

'Have you shot before?'

My grandmother replied, slightly stiffly, that she had.

'Well, you haven't booked in for an introduction.'

There followed an argument in which my grandmother

insisted I did not need an introduction, and the woman, who was already indignant about the unbooked extra, showed herself determined to save us from ourselves.

'We legally can't,' she said. 'And it's not me spending my afternoon cleaning brains off the floor.'

'Next time I'll lie,' said my grandmother.

'Well, next time won't be her first time, will it?'

She thawed out a bit as she gave me the safety introduction, to which I only half listened. I remember her telling me not to use the gun as a walking stick because it would stop up with mud and backfire. I remember that she put her arms around me to show how I was to brace it against my shoulder and plant my feet against the recoil. She had bad circulation and her bluish fingers which arranged my hands were cold and smooth. Follow the bird, the woman said, keeping your barrel tacked one point in front of where you want to hit it. She tried to have me wear one of the yellow children's helmets that were kept behind the reception desk, but Liv put her foot down. A compromise was reached and I was fitted with a pair of green earphones.

Then the woman sent the two of us off on the course. The track ran into little regular clearings in the pine trees. The first disc came wobbling so slowly across our horizon that it looked like it was being pulled along on a thread. The first time I didn't fire, then I missed the next two, then hit the next, which wasn't too bad, my grandmother said.

The decoys fired from the second stand came slightly more quickly, then they came progressively faster at each of the next few. They started to come from unexpected directions, then two came at once, from different sides, so you could shoot a right and a left if you got them before they crossed disorientatingly in the middle. I had hit quite a few by the time the first drops of rain fell, when we called it off. 'Not a bad shot,' my grandmother said again, when we were driving back down the track.

At the next shoot, in the holidays, I was given a gun and split off from the beaters. It was bitter weather, the wind making a whirring sound in the empty trees where the bank dropped. The guns walked across the fields in a loose line so I didn't have to talk to anyone. My feet made a hush-hush sound on the several-days-old snow. When a bird flew over our line, I stood in the correct position and looked up but I wasn't really watching the bird. I waited till the man closest to me fired, then timed a respectable moment, then pulled the trigger. I knew I was aiming into clean air. The shot was way off the mark. I imagine it would have been quite emasculating, had I been a man.

Liv used to hold the shoot lunches in the short barn. We usually needed the strip light on, even though the room had a plastic window.

My grandfather often came in for lunch, bringing his own chair. He greeted William, William and the vicar, who was a keen shot. It was an odd group: there were also two local landowners who came sometimes with friends, paying to shoot, and the beaters, who were my neighbours in the village, who were paid by John, the manager of a large farm nearby. John also paid for the pheasant chicks which were bred up in our woods. In the spring we came across them on our daily walk, as tame and stupid as the chickens, running around the clearing in which their blue plastic feeder was kept constantly full of feed.

Jimmy didn't touch the meat pies or the canteen of tomato soup but he would take a brandy and a can of stout. He didn't waste time shooting, and he'd decided it was ungentlemanly to ask how much had been killed – that wasn't the point of the sport. This was convenient because it meant he didn't have to make conversation and could concentrate, instead, on history. It was during one of those lunches when he told me, in a low and unnecessarily urgent voice, about hunting during the reign of Edward IV.

Edward took the throne after Towton and during peace he hunted regularly. One day, a few years after his coronation, he called the mayor and aldermen out of London to come to him for no reason other than to hunt and be merry. His guests, like the animals, came freely into Windsor Park, which was much bigger then than the park that survives today. It was fenced at the edges so that there was no escape for the deer, who entered the park through one-way deer-leaps and couldn't get out. The course of the hunt was predetermined.

Although the park was so large, the castle at Windsor was not, at that time, much more than a hunting lodge, and several tents were brought to accommodate Edward's ladies – several tents, because Edward was swift to seduce, and easily distracted. He overcame all women by money and promises, said one chronicler, and having conquered them, he dismissed them as simply and completely as he disassembled their temporary encampment in the woods.

At any rate, he dismissed many. But at least one of Edward's mistresses was kept for the length of his life. Mistress Shore's Christian name was Elizabeth but she took the name Jane – we do not know why. Historians have argued over the details of Jane Shore's early life, but it seems that she was a merchant's daughter who taught herself to look like a gentlewoman by mimicking the gestures of ladies she watched from the corner of her father's shop. According to Thomas More's chronicle, Jane Shore was the 'merriest harlot' in England. 'Proper she was and fair: nothing in her body that you would have changed (unless you would have wished her somewhat higher).'

More knew Jane Shore in her old age – he was at the court of Edward's grandson, Henry VIII. When he met the king's grandfather's mistress he searched in her face for the remains of good looks. Portraits are usually done at the height of power for men or beauty for women so it is unusual to find a picture like this, of the mistress in her old age. Mistress Shore, wrote More, 'delighted men not so much in her beauty as in her pleasant behaviour. For a proper wit had she and could both read well and write, merry in company, ready and quick to answer, neither mute nor full of babble.' Some people thought she was dead, others said she looked ugly and old, but More reincarnated her: 'Some that now see her,' he wrote, '– for yet she lives – deem her never to have been well visaged. [For] she is old, lean, withered, and dried up, nothing left but shrivelled skin and hard bone. And yet being even such, whosoever regards her visage might guess and imagine which parts, now filled, would make it a fair face.' There are no known surviving pictures of Jane Shore.

The deer was thought to be an especially long-lived animal. In one parable, Charles V, King of France in the fourteenth century, had hunted a stag wearing an ancient jewelled gold collar that was inscribed *Hoc me Caesar donavit,* which means 'Caesar gave this to me'. And at that time, there were several other stories about miraculous events which happened during a hunt. Jesus appeared to St Hubert and St Eustace between the tines on a stag's antlers. In Malory's *Morte Darthur,* a pursued white hart passed perfectly through a church window and did not break the glass. Just like this, wrote Malory, did the Virgin Mary conceive.

My grandfather told me all this from memory, while I had my soup and he drank his drink in the corner in the short barn. He'd sat himself right in front of the gas heater, obstructing its small panel of prickly flames, so everyone else was kept in the cold. He went on.

Perhaps the most famous example of the idea that courtship and conquest are like hunting and killing is Thomas Wyatt's poem about the most famous mistress of Henry VIII, Anne Boleyn, whose eventual marriage to the king brought about (via a circuitous route) Thomas More's execution. Wyatt compared hunting to trying to hold the wind in a net, and he wrote about Caesar giving his target a diamond collar, in 'Whoso List to Hunt' – to list means, in this instance, not to catalogue a group of things, but to wish or to desire.

'The hunt in medieval literature,' said my grandfather, 'was not always a metaphor for conquest – it could be a gratuitous excursion, or a metaphor for any other elusive, pointless diversion.' (He had plagiarised this point, though I didn't know it at the time, from another historian called John Cummins.)

Sometimes, he went on, especially in fiction, the hunt was simply a prelude to the story, or an elegant means of getting the characters lost.

On Edward's hunt, though, there was little chance that any of the hunters would lose themselves in the forest. Early in the morning a handful of front-riders set out to find where the animals were, then drove them to the pre-appointed path. Herds of females and juvenile males, rather than antlered stags, were chased all morning. They were directed by beaters, unarmed woodsmen, and fresh hounds which were set at points throughout the route so that lagging dogs did not slow the pace. Archers, hidden in their surroundings with sprays of branches and leaves, dispatched dozens of animals at the end.

The kill was broadcast on the hunters' horns, then the hounds were allowed for a short time to tear at the exposed flesh, in order to sharpen their taste for pursuit, before the carcasses were ritually dismembered. At the end of the day Edward sent venison freely into the city, as meat for the public consumption.

My grandfather paused at that point while William offered, and he accepted, a third brandy.

'I wonder if the deer tried to go backwards through the deer-leaps,' he mused. 'I wonder if things changed for them within the park. Did they have any sense that they were inside an enclosure? Did they think they were wild?' Was there any sense of difference, he wondered, when the animals jumped of their own accord into the park, and created for themselves an enclosure and an outside world?

They set off at dawn and ran all day towards their deaths. When they panicked and bolted away from the dogs they cannot have realised that the path they took had been mapped by the hunters before they set off. Perhaps some of them came to realise it at the end, when they must have seen that the arrows which hit them came from archers in disguise as trees.

The notes in my grandfather's file on 1471 reminded me about the shoot years earlier – in my memory, the one hunt lay within the other: Edward's tents were pitched in my grandfather's histories, which he told in the strip-lit barn. I could easily draw his notes on this subject back together, because I already knew the facts.

I had the same feeling when I read the next part of the history, but I had not heard that story before, at least not in the way it was written up. The most interesting part of the chronicle seemed to me to have to do with another event which happened in my own lifetime. My memory of that story is as follows.

My grandfather took me round York Minster on a January afternoon after school, perhaps a year after we went to Towton. There was still some pale sunlight but it was a windy day, and the space in front of the cathedral widens out of several narrower streets, so the winds meet there, surprisingly powerfully. I was pushed sideways when we came out of the shelter of Upper Petergate.

We went in at the south entrance. Inside, the light coming through the rose window landed a shape like an ammonite fossil on the stone floor. A girl in a cassock was standing behind the information stall by the First World War chapel – she tipped back her head to peer at us from under her too-long fringe. Her hair was the colour of a fox's fur. Her name badge said: VINCENT. When my grandfather went over I stayed by the door, feeling self-conscious, and watched two little choir-girls, hardly more than toddlers, coming up the steps. One was pale and thin; the other, smaller and rosier, was wearing tiny spectacles. They both had unruly curly hair and their gowns were excited by the wind – it looked like they were wearing living things. A teacher appeared out of nowhere to hurry them towards a dark entranceway to my left, from which, in the church quiet, I could hear the same bars of piano playing, then branching into various voices, then breaking off, coming down from a practice room above.

The girl at the desk was nodding. She dipped down and disappeared, then handed my grandfather an envelope and he came back, opening it. He was wearing his black suit and carried a walking stick under his arm. Under his other arm he had his black hat, pinned to which was the Richard III Society badge showing the king's portrait and the caption: 'I am not the monster I am made out to be!' My grandfather took a small key out of the envelope.

The door was on the other side of the altar screen on which there was a line of statues of kings of England. We paused for the history lesson: William, William, Henry, Steven, Henry, Richard, John, Henry, Edward, Edward, Edward, Richard, Henry, Henry, Henry. Behind us the nave looked huge. The chairs had been taken out for the month so that visitors could experience how it would have been in the first place, before seats were put in. Until recently the space at the centre of the cathedral was empty.

The door was hidden behind the main entrance to the chapter house. It opened onto a narrow, steep staircase leading to a room running above the L-shaped passage which connected the chapter house to the nave. The room was called the mason's loft. It was dark. It appeared, at first, to be nothing more than a scuffed floor in an attic. At one end of the room, which was unheated and very cold, was a fireplace. At the other I could see a sort of chair notched out of the thick wall. The chair looked like one of the deans' seats that were recessed in different places around the cathedral below, but in fact, said Jimmy, it was a toilet, working by way of a clever architectural arrangement which diverted the rain falling from the sky to the parapet so that it flowed down the gutter, through a junction of pipes into the cistern, and flushed detritus along a flying buttress out into the chapter-house yard.

As my eyes adjusted some shapes began to appear in the scuffs on the plaster-of-Paris floor: pointed arches and curves too perfect to be accidental. But the marks were closely interconnected and it was impossible to see the whole picture.

He explained how it worked. The stone mouldings, vaults, arches and windows were drawn on a 1:1 scale on the soft, slightly powdery surface; then templates were made up from the drawings. It would not have been possible to get such huge stones up the narrow stairs, so the templates must have been taken out to masons' huts, now gone, where stones were cut, carved and fitted together, before being separated again, then winched up.

The floor was soft so that the marks could be swept over by successive generations making new windows and stones. There are other drawing floors under this one, he said, which have been covered over with successive layers of plaster, like strata in the earth.

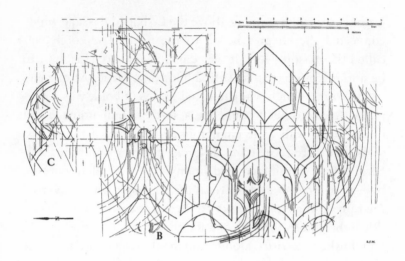

Both my grandparents were atheist, but in the early 1980s Jimmy volunteered for a short while at the Minster. He felt unmoored, he told me, immediately after his retirement – he had been a founder member of the history faculty and felt cut off outside the department: like a king without a kingdom, he said, characteristically immodestly. This was before the grandchildren were born.

It was Jimmy's job to conduct the quarterly public tours of the loft. Because of his background he was hardly ever made to stand, like the other vergers, at the corners of the nave to restrain tourists from using flash photography or climbing on the footings of the pillars. Instead he gave tours of the walkways and corridors which narrowed through the upper parts of the building. On open days, he also showed visitors around the masons' yard, where the large blocks of stone were cut and shaped with orange machines. He was, if he did say so himself, better than the masons at explaining how the bits and pieces that lay, during the preliminary phases, in loosely linked lines like vertebrae, with numbers and letters pencilled on their undersides, would, in time, be fitted exactly into some arch or corner in the building.

During his breaks he sat in the staffroom with the other vergers, who drank milky tea out of cups and rationed biscuits from a Fox's or a Lyons tin. They talked about their ailments, the other vergers and occasionally Maggie, who divided opinion. They were mostly very religious indeed.

When it was announced in the spring of 1984 that the new Bishop of Durham was to be ordained at the Minster, several of the vergers were unhappy about the choice. David Jenkins, they told my grandfather, already had a name.

In April, two months before his planned ordination, Jenkins appeared on a television programme called *Credo*. Jimmy only ever watched the news at six, so he didn't know about *Credo* until he heard about it from his colleagues at the Minster, who added their voices to the calls for the bishop to be dismissed before he had even been appointed. On *Credo*, Jenkins had discussed the possibility that the stories in the Bible were not literally true, but were a kind of common expression. Each story, said Professor Jenkins, was a way of articulating belief in something; the belief was sustained by the fact that people repeated the stories. Even Mary's immaculate conception was like an image or a metaphor, or 'a story told after the event to express and symbolise a faith'. 'I wouldn't put it past God to arrange a virgin birth if he wanted,' he said drolly, 'but I very much doubt if he would.'

Later on, the media picked up the story. The comments were repeated on the radio and in newspapers and on the television again for some time until the vergers complained that they could hardly move for hearing that the future bishop had compared the miracle of Jesus' empty tomb to a conjuring trick with bones, or assured the public that there was absolutely no certainty in the New Testament about anything of importance.

It was the idea – of God's resurrection – that was the important thing, said the future bishop, and he brings his wonders out of natural personal relationships.

After that statement there was a marked rise in the calls for his dismissal. BBC switchboards jammed. Newspaper editorials made demands. Protesters pitched up outside Lambeth Palace. Thatcher's Lord Chancellor, Douglas Hailsham, went public about his personal feelings on the matter. 'I much prefer the word of Matthew, Mark, Luke and John', he said, 'because they were there and David Jenkins wasn't.'

Lord Hailsham was wrong, my grandfather pointed out. The traducers, translators, scribes, secretaries and authors who put together his gospels weren't all taking things down on hand in the crowds at Galilee. History, said Jimmy, is quite different from what happened.

The date of Jenkins' ordination was brought forward by senior figures in the Church who wanted to get the controversy out of the way as soon as possible, and who felt that the appointment was especially significant. They moved the date to 6 July, the day St Thomas More was executed.

On the morning of the ordination there was a huge crowd outside the Minster. Staff had to use the side entrance, where protesters and reporters were not admitted. From inside, my grandfather saw a grey car arrive, then Jenkins was bundled through the door in the middle of a group of canons.

The cathedral filled up. Stewards at the doors kept out those who did not have tickets. Some of those who did have tickets couldn't get in, and even Jimmy, ushering people to their seats, ended up at the back behind a pillar.

He saw the bishop's purple hat come in, moving on the

surface of the crowd like a shark's fin. The arch matched the shape of the windows, pointing up.

When the procession approached the altar it disappeared, first behind the sticking-out flower arrangement, then behind the thick stone pillar which was right up in front of Jimmy's face. A crucifix was secured to the upper part and below that a painting of St Anne – Anne, my grandfather told me, was the grandmother of God, Mary's mother. The small late-medieval picture which got in the way of his view showed her with Mary and Jesus in a bluish landscape. Anne is the patroness of housewives, women in birth and grandmothers.

When the service was under way a disturbance agitated the middle of the crowd. It was clear that a vicar, who was standing below the lectern, was protesting, but much of the sound of what he was shouting was lost in the huge space. My grandfather craned his neck to see the little black figure escorted backwards up the aisle by two policemen, the legs ineffectually scrambling. The policemen took the man through the first set of doors into the glass porch at the back of the cathedral. Then the man got a good sharp elbow in, and while they were opening the great wooden doors he made a dash back. Both sets of doors opened at once and an immense gust of wind huffed into the nave. The stand of flowers rustled, but stayed upright on its silver pedestal. It did not lift off any hats.

The picture of St Anne was firmly strapped to the cathedral, much more solidly fastened than the flowers or the hats, with a strip of metal right round the pillar. But, said my grandfather, with the wind it somehow came out of its fittings and it seemed to rise several feet in the air before sliding back down the front of the pillar and landing on the floor. The rest of the ceremony went without a hitch.

•　　•　　•

Jimmy was back in the cathedral six days after the ordination, when he witnessed a second extraordinary event which made the first look like an omen. At night a bolt of lightning struck the south transept of the cathedral and set fire to the building. The great rose window began to melt, scorch and explode in parts, and flames were already being drawn up the tower at the centre of the Minster when the firefighters were finally able to put out the blaze. The ceiling collapsed.

In a way, said my grandfather, it was the salvation of the building which did the worst damage. The burning roof gave way under thousands of gallons of water and it was water, not smoke, which ruined the song sheets and drowned the music books in the choir library.

In fact, he told me, it was the second time that lightning had struck in that place. Lightning striking twice was proverbially unlikely, but not impossible. The first time was in 1463. The fire in the Minster in 1463, he said, was taken by contemporary chroniclers as a sign that more bad weather was coming, just as the sudden death, some years earlier, of the lions in the Tower of London had been taken as a warning from God. The historians' predictions came true, he said – the civil war went on.

Things weren't much different among the vergers in the 1980s, who talked about heresy, miracles and retribution over the noise of the hairdryers they were using to dry the hymn books. They quoted appropriate passages at one another: 'He makes lightning for the rain, he brings the wind out of his treasuries.'

While repairs to the cathedral were being carried out, fragments of the rose window were collected and reassembled in an exploded circle in the crypt. The cleaning phase of the restoration work was to be carried out in public. The rose window, which had been set high on the wall of the south transept, could be seen from a much better perspective – much closer – than it had ever been seen before, or, at least, it could be seen by visitors at closer quarters than it had been seen by anyone since it was traced and set by medieval masons and glaziers in the twelfth century.

That afternoon in the masons' loft, my grandfather told me to my surprise that I was one of the visitors who had seen the broken window. He had taken me in my pushchair to the crypt. But I was newborn in 1984 and I did not remember it any more than I remembered the cathedral's original completion in 1472.

iv

The *Historie of the Arrivall of Edward 4* started in 1471 when an exiled twenty-eight-year-old man called Edward, formerly King Edward IV, landed back on English soil. Returning, in fact, rather than arriving. The chronicler followed him on the journey back through his country for a final attempt on London and the throne. The period spanned by the history happened to fall during Holy Week.

The *Arrivall* was written by an anonymous historian who did not give his family name or any details about his personal character. Anything we know about him is only known from the way he told the story, in which he stood in the background in every scene. He was one of the people watching in the crowds that gathered wherever Edward went; he was also among the soldiers going on foot behind the former king, and with the townspeople who followed Edward's horse when he paraded through the streets at the centre of a procession. The chronicle does not make clear whether its author actually fought in the battles, or whether he stayed back in the empty tents at the Yorkist camp, watching and recording from behind the lines.

There are two known existing versions of the *Arrivall* and they are in different languages. The first, a sixteenth-century copy made during the reign of Edward's great-granddaughter,

Elizabeth I, is in English. The second, which is bound in brown calfskin, is in French. This copy has ornaments in the margin, and pictures, but the text has been abridged.

The two copies of the history are similar in many ways – they share some epithets and syntactic constructions, and they list identical names, dates and numbers, such as the titles and quantities of men killed in some of the battles which are recorded in the history. But both versions are what palaeographers would call bastard texts: splinters or bad copies of the urtext, which is an imagined original perfect history which is no longer in existence. The scribes who translated from the originals were, like the historian himself, anonymous, and you can only tell that they were there at all because of the mistakes they made. My grandfather taught me how to follow, across several centuries, the movements of one man's pupils as they descended the page of his copy-text. Eyeskip, which caused him to miss passages; homeoteleuton, which caused him to repeat the endings; the switching of homonyms or the addition of clumsily written expanded clauses and commentaries. These little hiccups, my grandfather taught me, are the small errors which make the writer visible. We can only see him in what he ran together or left out.

It looked like my grandfather had taken information from other chronicles and quotations from other modern historians, as well as from the *Arrivall*, in writing his history of Edward's return journey. But he didn't properly attribute all the other sources so it was almost impossible, going back through the notes, to work out who was the author of what. It was, in fact, easier to get back to the circumstances under which the parent copy of *The Historie of the Arrivall of Edward 4* was composed, because the author explained himself in the preface. A few days after the history finished, at the end of May 1471, when one of the two kings was dead, the historian sat down to begin to write his own history. When he had completed it he carried it himself back to Burgundy, which was where it had begun.

In 1470, after ruling for nine years, Edward was dethroned by a Lancastrian army fighting under his former ally Richard Neville, Earl of Warwick, who had switched sides from York to Lancaster. Historians have called him Warwick the Kingmaker.

When Edward fled from England, his boat went off course. He meant to head straight towards Burgundy where his younger sister Margaret lived at the court of her husband, Duke Charles the Good. But God, or the weather, intervened and a huge gale blew up and diverted the boat.

Two years earlier, in 1468, a Norfolk gentleman called John Paston and his brother, also called John, came to Burgundy in Margaret's wedding party. John the elder wrote home to his mother, also called Margaret, about the court which he described as the most extravagant in the world, as had other visitors before him. 'We are all in good heal here,' he wrote to his mother. 'I think there were never Englishmen had so good cheer out of England that ever I heard of.'

At the court there were pageants, musicians, a library and clothes the like of which Paston had never seen. The courtiers, he said, were as richly dressed as cloth of gold and silk and silver- and goldsmiths' work might make for them, 'for such gear and gold and pearl and stones, they of the duke's court, neither gentleman nor gentlewoman, they want none, for without that they have it by wishes, by my troth, I never heard of such plenty as here is'.

Paston heard about the wedding feast of Charles's parents, at which wild men were brought into the great hall on the backs of roast suckling pigs, and a live sheep, dyed blue with gilded horns, came out of a pie.

Margaret married Charles at 5 a.m., just after dawn, in the church at Damme, three miles from Bruges. Then the wedding party rode into the city, where they were received as worshipfully as all the world could devise. The town was decorated with signs and coats of arms on banners and stonework, and mock toucans which played in mock trees in the streets. The canals were lit with torches; the bridges furnished with flowers; the streets hung with tapestries. Wine spurted from sculpted arches. But the centrepiece of the spectacle was Margaret herself, riding in a gold carriage with white horses. On her blonde head she wore a coronet which was decorated with pearls and white roses for the House of York, red, white and green enamelled letters spelling her name, and interlocking initials 'C' and 'M'. Masques and dramas which represented the new couple were performed at points along her progress, and polyphonic compositions were played by musicians across the city. The new princess was popular straight away because she hung out of the window to wave to the crowds, not minding that it was cold and raining.

John Paston went through Bruges in the duchess's train, watching sections of the pageants that were 'played in her way' – they had been planned along the prearranged route through the city so that the most exciting parts happened as Margaret passed by. Paston, coming a little way behind, always got to the play a moment after the miracle, or when the lady had just been saved, or after the Devil was vanquished. (The *tableaux vivants* stayed the same.)

He passed through the town square where there was a dwarf leading a giant in chains through the empty jousting arena. The gate to the arena was guarded by a golden tree made out of a wooden board, and on the other side there was a real pine tree which had had its bark and branches gilded and its needles left green.

When the crowd thickened the procession slowed down, and Paston fell further to the back. He saw the very ends of the plays. Then he saw the actors dancing, bowing and packing up. He got stuck behind one of the decorated stages as it was wheeled off towards the city gate – a man dressed as St John in a coat of coarse skins sat dangling his legs off the side, between one demon with a painted face and another who had pushed his mask to the back of his head so that he could drink.

Paston was among the last to arrive at the great hall, where the wedding gifts were on show on the walls and tables – a unicorn's horn made into a sword and some saints' relics in jewel boxes.

In between courses they watched scenes from the life of Hercules. Hercules fought monsters, giants and Amazons. A real ship sailed through the hall on wheels hidden behind boards painted with waves. A battle was fought, and rows of Burgundy's most accurate archers fired hundreds of arrows which showered back down from the ceiling as if it were raining inside. The battle inside the room was surprisingly lifelike. Historians are not quite sure how it was brought off – perhaps the arrowheads were blunted.

The celebrations went on the next day and the day after. Charles's brother, Anthony the Bastard, was unsurpassed in the jousts.

'And as for the duke's court,' John Paston wrote to his mother five days later on 8 July, 'I never heard of none like to it save King Arthur's court.'

When Edward's boat went off course in 1470 he was forced to make early landfall at Texel, near Alkmaar in Flanders where

Louis de Gruythuse was the local governor. Louis rode out to meet Edward. The two men already knew one another – Louis was a merchant and nobleman who had acted diplomatically in England a few years earlier – but it wasn't until Edward's stay in Burgundy that the two became close.

Edward had a number of intense male relationships. A decade earlier, according to one chronicle, he had 'made much' of Edmund, Duke of Beaufort – so much, in fact, that the young duke slept each night in the unmarried king's bed. 'It is certainly tempting,' conceded one historian, quoted anonymously, 'to believe that Edward was indeed prepared to cast convention utterly to the winds. But what we probably have here, in fact, is Edward in chivalric rather than sexual mode.'

Another scholar of the period had remarked on the fortuitousness of the fates' conspiracy to throw Edward and Louis together twice, first in London at Edward's court, and then in Bruges during his exile. 'What is striking about this kind of so-called "cultural" connection is that it was to a large degree fortuitous,' said Dr M. Vale, noting that the link with Gruythuse would not have been made if Edward had not been forced ashore by winds at Texel.

But whether the cause of the storm was fate, luck, God or meaningless atmospheric variation, the historical facts remain the same. For much of his stay Edward chose to lodge at Gruythuse's town house in Bruges rather than at court with his sister and brother-in-law.

He visited Margaret, though, often with Louis. She took them to the library – Louis' personal library was second only to Charles's – where they looked at painted maps and books of miracula containing pictures of the unicorn and the leviathan.

They saw an allegorical entertainment in which an unnamed character was taken by another character called Memory to see the World of the Dead. Among the tombs in the World of the Dead were tombs of characters from the Bible alongside tombs of characters from the Greek myths alongside tombs of Burgundian shopkeepers who had been active in local politics and commerce until they had, recently, died.

The third time Edward and Louis visited the court, Margaret received them at the royal menagerie, where they saw real lions. Then they went to the thesaurum, where they saw a unicorn's horn and another monster's foot.

Towards the end of Edward's stay, he watched his brother-in-law taking part in a masque. Charles vanquished a series of foes in a variety of costumes and disguises. A green stone, taken from his thesaurum, was brought in as a theatrical prop. The stone prophesied his victory over the French, which prophecy promptly came true, at least in the masque.

Edward sat with the audience, which was made up mostly of courtiers, but also of some invited aldermen and towns-people – they applauded their leader enthusiastically.

When the army was ready Edward led them out of Bruges in a public progress, according to the American academic Cora Scofield, who wrote in her 1924 biography, *Edward IV*: 'With that readiness to give pleasure which was one of his most endearing qualities, [Edward] walked as far as Damme, instead of going by boat as he had planned, in order that the friendly people of Bruges might have the excitement of a procession.' Miss Scofield, working at one of the desks at the Guildhall in London, imagined the burghers of Bruges plashing along in the puddles of the recently cleared storm, with pipes and drums, home-made flags and fortified wine, behind the young Englishman on his horse.

When they got to Damme they waited for a while, but

the wind was too high so they went home again before the fleet set out. It was nearly a week before it was safe to sail. Edward's boat was called *Anthony*; the history doesn't say why.

The fleet headed directly towards the Norfolk coast. But, again, Edward was deflected. Like Noah, he sent two scouts from the boat to find out the lay of the land, and, like Noah, he received a negative report from the scouts. The people at Cromer did not support him.

At that point Edward might have gone back to Burgundy. Other usurped kings have lived out their lives at foreign courts. He could have stayed in exile in Bruges watching miracles in pageants, visiting the lions and taking part in jousts of peace, which was jousting with blunt weapons. Instead he told his fleet to set out to sea again, then headed north, and when the wind got up he gave the order to turn back towards England, where his mother was still living, in sanctuary, with several members of his household and his pregnant wife.

Great storms, winds and tempests, as the chronicler described it, finally put them onshore on the east coast of Yorkshire at Ravenser. Dropping anchor at the height of the storm in the early hours of the morning, Edward and his crew waded up a silty beach on a shapeshifting spit of sand and shingle that is known today as Spurn Point – shapeshifting, because the sand is held together by reeds, shunted into different forms projecting from the mainland at variant angles, so that the land at which Edward came ashore was not the same ground which can be visited now at that precise geopositional point.

The history says that the crew camped the night at a 'power village' near Ravenser while the gale blew itself out. Ravenser, which is also called Ravensper, Ravensporne or Ravenspurne, is a village which no longer exists. The erosion of that part of the coast has caused over thirty villages to fall into the North Sea, although their ruins are still sometimes uncovered by the low spring tides. A few place names recall the drowned settlements: Old Aldborough has disappeared, but Aldborough is still there; the same happened with Withernsea and Old Withernsea. Hornsea exists but Hornsea Burton and Hornsea Beck have gone. Other names, including Monkwike, Colden Parva, Cleton, Hyde and Sand-le-Mere, have been completely submerged.

During the dark it was impossible to tell what had happened to the other ships from the fleet, which had scattered in the high wind. But the next day cleared to unexpected sunshine, revealing along the beach the dreck of the storm. Cushions of kelp and bladderwrack were stretched out to dry on the sand which was still dotted from the rain, and from up and down the coast Edward's company came towards him and converged at Ravenser.

When the troops exchanged accounts, it was found that a single boat had been lost, and it was a ship full of horses. The sailors described the sea as an animal: the muscles of water pounded the resisting muscles of the animals and won, and the boat sank. The history does not mention what happened to the horses, but it is likely that over time the bones of each creature collapsed into the skeletal frames of the others, and that a jumble of interlocking ribs and vertebrae, ulnae and patellae still rakes the North Sea bed.

Some of the troops were Burgundians, Easterlings and Danes, borrowed and hired from allies and neighbours of the former king. The boatloads of foreign soldiers didn't go unnoticed at Old Withernsea, Cleton and Sand-le-Mere. Whether because they thought it was their duty as subjects of

Henry VI, or just because they were sick of war, a force assembled from the local villages and it was clear that Edward would have to fight or negotiate if he wanted to get past. He chose to negotiate. He gave the crowd an abridged version of his plans: he had not come for the crown, he said, but to reclaim the duchy of York, which had – he reminded them – been in his family for generations until it was stripped from his father Richard in December 1459.

The crowd parted for Edward and he walked easily back to his tent. Then he sent for his advisers.

The quickest way to get to London, they knew, was to re-embark and cross the Humber mouth. But anyone who saw an army getting back on their boats and going out again on the water would think that they were returning to Burgundy. Edward was reluctant to perform his own defeat, even if it was only an illusion, so the army set out on foot. The history does not say what happened to their boats. They 'held the right way' to the city of York, north, away from the destination. They hoped that by backtracking the army would be better able to achieve its ends.

They came to Beverley, then Kyngstowne upon Hull. Hull closed its gates to the army, although the chronicler says that the citizens were only following orders from rebels, whom he calls pests and stirrers, who had threatened the ordinary people. When they had passed the two towns they saw an army coming towards them.

The army had been assembled by 'a prist' and a local gentleman, John Westerdale and Martin de la Mer or, as the chronicle calls him, Martyn of the See. Edward rode out in front of his own troops, and repeated the claim to his father's duchy. He did not, according to the *Arrivall*, 'discover' or 'recall' his claim on the throne, which turned on a single clause written at Westminster in 1460 and was, as the chronicle says, 'unto this day never repelled ne revoked'. Westerdale's army disbanded. Edward's army went on.

At each stage of the journey a few messengers and horses were sent on excursus to see how the land lay. The countryside looked empty, but the riders returned every time with news that people were assembling throughout Yorkshire, invisible and quiet, gathering always just beyond the horizon or out of sight in a nearby valley. The movement of the troops was haunted throughout their route by these presences which collected at the edge of Edward's sightline. But none of the groups made manifest war, as the history puts it, and the army moved forward.

On 18 March 1471 they came into the vale of York where, in the distance, the large western towers of the Minster could be seen, covered in wooden scaffolding – the building was nearly complete. 'Trewthe is,' says the chronicle, that when Edward was three miles from the city, a single rider came from within the walls towards him. The rider was Thomas Conyers, Recorder of York, who spoke to Edward for a while, and then turned and returned. News filtered through the troops that the recorder had issued a warning about York, which had been a place of Lancastrian pilgrimage since 1468. Conyers advised Edward to retreat, predicting he would not pass the city walls, and if he did, that no one would survive. Conyers blocked the gates.

York had not, historically, been Yorkist. In 1468, the year that his sister departed for Burgundy, Edward ordered the chapter of York Minster to remove a statue of Henry VI from their quire screen where it was being honoured by faithful Lancastrians. The statue was the last in a line of eleven statues of kings ranged along the screen which divided the church in two: William, William, Henry, Steven, Henry, Richard, John, Henry, Edward, Edward, Edward, Richard, Henry, Henry,

Henry. The church obeyed his order, but Henry's followers only came back after its removal and paid their respects instead to the wooden hollow recessed into the screen, the space where the statue had been.

When Conyers rode back to the city, two other gentlemen rode out. These gentlemen, Robert Clifford and Richard Burgh, told Edward that he had a good chance of being welcomed, whatsoever their recorder had said. They rode back to York, but when they disappeared into the distance, Conyers appeared again. He had retreated and returned home, then turned round, rode out to meet them again, and again, on this second excursion, he warned Edward that the people did not want him in York, and Conyers could not open the gates or allow him to pass the walls.

At this point Edward had gone so far in his journey that 'in no wyse he might goo backe with that he had begone'; no good would come of it. He resolved with himself constantly to 'purswe that he had begon', though it were to him uncertain. He continued to go forward.

'And so, sometyme comfortyd and sometyme discomfortyd,' Edward arrived at the city gates. Everyone hushed while the commanders conferred. Then Clifford, Burgh, Edward and a small party – perhaps ten, perhaps fifteen other men – broke away from the rest. The portcullis lifted, but not the whole way up, so that they could pass in. They disappeared. Everyone, for some reason, was whispering.

Inside the gates Edward conferred first with the city elders. Then he stood on the steps of the city walls to talk to the crowd – promising, for a third time, that he had come to reclaim his dukedom. He won them over and his troops were quartered overnight.

On the morning of 19 March 1471 the masons and carpenters in the Minster rose early as usual. They went to work at dawn, like hunters, or soldiers on the move. From a God's-eye view in the western towers, which were finally nearly complete, the workmen saw their former king slip into the cathedral and give thanks at the altar. Then he passed below them again, and the sound of slippers slapping on the flagstones receded. He did not look up.

Edward left York through Micklegate Bar, which took him back again to the death of his father, Richard, a decade earlier. Richard of York's men had been trapped like fish in a net, according to one chronicle, and routed at Wakefield Castle. As a warning to his supporters the Lancastrians took Richard's head to York and impaled it on Micklegate Bar on an iron spike wearing a mocking paper crown.

When they got out of York the troops passed Towton field.

Then they continued unexpectedly quickly through the surrounding country, most of which was owned by the Earl of Northumberland, who was one of the most powerful magnates in England, and a Lancastrian. They had expected that Northumberland's large personal army would attack, but the hills were empty. Nothing appeared between the horizon and the sky.

According to the chronicle, nothing was the best thing the earl could do. Because the earl sat still, says the chronicler, all men sat still. By doing nothing, the earl was just as responsible for Edward's passage as if he had actively helped him. You are either with us, or against us. 'Wherefore the Kynge may say as Julius Cesar sayde, he that is nat agaynst me is with me.'

So Edward went on freely. There was hardly any communication between one place and another. Each town and village was isolated in its own small world. Successive groups of people in each new settlement were convinced, by Edward's persuading them, that all those who had gone before them were sympathetic towards the Yorkists. The people thought that Edward's passage was in itself a kind of 'declaration and evidence' that 'in all other countries were none but his good lovars' – so every new place that the army passed through was converted to Edward's cause without noticing their conversion.

V

My grandfather once explained to me how the historian Thomas Carlyle defined the present as a 'conflux of eternities'. Each passing moment, according to Carlyle, was a point at which every single thing which has ever happened in the past converges on every single thing that will ever happen in the future. Causes and effects are so long, tangled and complicated that we will never know the pure origin of anything, he said. Every moment is the convergence of all moments. 'Actual events,' said Carlyle, 'are nowise so simply related to each other as parent and offspring are, and every single event is the offspring not of one, but of all other events.'

My grandfather had reservations. Some moments, he pointed out, were more important than others. 'While some seconds *just go by*,' he wrote, in an essay in response to Carlyle – 'On *On History*' – 'unmoored from cause or consequence, other moments press the past onto the future, changing what went before them as well as that which comes after.'

It was about halfway through the history when the army got to Daventry in Northamptonshire, which is now probably past its heyday. In the 1920s the BBC broadcast from the town, and it is also famous as the site of the first successful tests on a device modelled on the position-finding systems of bats and dolphins – radar. But that came a long time after Edward's arrival.

Edward rode into Daventry three weeks after landing at Ravenser. The troops were tired from walking the long way to London. They had still not fought a battle.

Edward was in trouble. He had landed as a would-be king, then reduced his claim to duke. Now the chronicler describes him as a kind of nomad – a displaced wanderer, shunted from place to place, unwelcome among his own people. 'Infortwne and adversitie had fallen hym full often, and specially upon the sea.' The army arrived at Daventry on the eve of Palm Sunday.

Edward went straight to the parish church with a small group of men. It was bare and shut up for Lent. There were squares of black cloth hanging over the pictures; the icons had their doors closed; the half-burned candles were all out.

The men knelt for several long minutes before the altar. There was heavy rain on the roof. Then Edward led their prayers. First he prayed to God, then to St George, then to Jesus, then Mary, then back another generation to St Anne, who was the patron of the small parish church – it was her portrait under the black cloth.

The next day, Palm Sunday, a long line of local people joined a procession which wound through the streets of the town, carrying crosses made out of stalks of straw. They went around the marketplace and towards the church, which was a little way out of Daventry, attached to a Cluniac priory; Edward was the centrepiece, riding on a grey horse at the midpoint of the trail of people which went both before him and after him, but all of them moving inevitably towards a priory and a church which no longer exist – they were, at that time, south-east of the town, near the current A45 bypass.

The rain started up again before they got to the church.

With so many troops the local people had to stand at the back and in the aisles, but Edward sat down on a pew in the middle of the church, allowing the local gentry to take up their seats at the front. In the morning light the interior of Anne's chapel looked even more bare than it had the day before. The veil over the cross was slightly dusty. The congregation sang three repetitions of the anthem Ave.

In front of Edward there was a thick pillar, and attached to the pillar was a covered crucifix. Below the crucifix on the stone pillar in front of the king, said the chronicler, was a 'lytle ymage' of St Anne. Though he never wrote about himself, the chronicler must have been standing behind Edward at the back of the church because he described the image – it was small, made of painted alabaster and at that time covered with four firmly shut boards. The chronicler remembered again that the icons were to remain closed for another week. The icon, he said, was fixed firmly with a band that went right round the pillar, in the manner of a compass. Edward knelt beneath the cross.

After the third repetition of the anthem the men sat and the church went quiet. Edward's head dropped forward like he was putting it on a block and all the other heads, greasy without their hats and hoods, slumped too. There was a moment of silent prayer, then it was interrupted by a cracking sound.

The heads picked up individually, but the chronicler, who hadn't lowered his head or closed his eyes, saw the cause of the crack before anyone else. One of the boards covering the icon strapped onto the pillar had split. There was another snap.

The door of the icon lolled slightly ajar. There was another crack, and another board gave, and the door swung open, then the other board went, and the other door swung open too. The people in the front rows, who could not see the other side of the pillar, leaned back to look. One boy got up and then they all got up and pressed around close to see what the chronicler, standing at the back of the church, could already see. On the second surface the colours were more intense. St Anne sat in the middle of a pure blue background holding in her hand a miniature, pink-veiled Virgin Mary who held in turn in her tiny clasp a homunculus: a miniature, miniature representation of Jesus.

St Anne displayed herself openly to the church, and to none so widely as to Edward, who had been kneeling right in front of her, and knelt back down before the stone pillar. A moment later the boards drew back and clasped together again as if they were sucked in by an undetectable breath.

After the service Edward gave thanks and continued to move towards London with some behind-riders, spears and archers travelling in his wake to protect him from enemies who might attack the 'backhalfe'. On 9 April Edward sent 'comfortable messagis' to his wife Elizabeth who was still in refuge at Westminster Priory. Elizabeth had given birth, during Edward's absence, to their first son, also called Edward.

vi

Archbishop George Neville, Bishop of York, was the Earl of Warwick's youngest brother. Bishop Neville had risen through the Church during Edward's reign. At the feast celebrating his episcopal enthronement were served, among many other things, 4,000 pigeons, 104 peacocks, 100 dozen quails, 400 swans and 400 herons, 113 oxen, 6 wild bulls, 12 porpoises and seals, 1,000 sheep, 304 calves, 400 plovers, 204 bitterns, 200 pheasants, 500 partridges, 400 woodcocks, 100 curlews, 500 stags, bucks and roes, 4,000 cold and 1,500 hot venison pies, 4,000 dishes of jelly, 4,000 baked tarts and 2,000 hot custards with a proportionate quantity of bread, sugared delicacies and cakes, and 300 tuns of ale and 100 tuns of wine. (The history doesn't describe the kitchens.) Neville was a rich man.

It is clear that Neville had done well under Edward's rule. On the other hand, his elder brother was now leading the Lancastrians. The archbishop, like the country, was divided. At any rate, he was a churchman so he did not need to actually fight. He went to Henry's side when Warwick called his men together.

Londoners came out of their houses to watch the Lancastrian court, such as it was, process round St Paul's, through Cheap, through Cornhill and back to Walbrook. At the front rode a man with his eyes on the ground, bearing a pole with two mangy foxtails attached. Then came a few gentlemen, then Henry Lancaster, the former King Henry VI, who had been helped onto an old horse. Somebody had got hold of an old blue velvet robe which they hung over his slumping body. A company of servants straggled behind on foot.

The crowds were quiet until the horses had passed by. Then they said that Henry's gown was so shabby because he had 'no more to change with'. It was, one man said, like a *tableau vivant*. The king looked like an old actor playing the part of the king. His person was, after all, right 'litel and feble' and supported on either side by two men, the bodies of their horses pressing together, pressing the riders' legs. To Henry's left was an old nobleman called Lord Zouche. On his other arm, at his right hand, was Bishop Neville.

None of the chronicles explain who devised the plan to get Edward's troops into London. When he arrived, the day after Henry's sorry procession, he found the city gates closed against him. Perhaps someone had read it in a history – my grandfather once told me Herodotus' story about Phanes, who was caught by his enemy Amasis and held captive by two huge guards. According to Herodotus, Phanes had no hope of escape until it occurred to him that there was a simple way to get out: get his guards drunk. He did, and slipped off. In the end it was just as easy, if not easier, for Edward to enter London: he came right through the doors and gates which had been closed against him. The chroniclers didn't set down whose idea it was, or how they got in touch, but the Archbishop of York who had, only a few hours earlier, supported Henry through the streets, arranged for the common men who were guarding the gates to be sent off to eat at the usual hour, and then he had the gates unlatched. For the second time that week the doors swung unexpectedly easily open for Edward, and he and his men came into London while the guards were at home having their tea.

I n London, Edward saw his son and heir for the first time. Then he took his army north to meet Warwick.

Troops from both sides arrived at Barnet on the evening of 13 April 1471, which was Easter Eve. Advancing in the dark, Edward set up camp below an escarpment on which Warwick's troops had settled. The lines lay closer than either side could see, and when Warwick emptied his ammunition into the night, the fire from cannon and handgun swept over the heads of Edward's army, falling on fallow land to the rear, so that during the night, the single tactic required of the Yorkist army was quietude.

As Easter Day broke a thick fog descended, and neither side could see the strange alignment by which Edward's army had come in 'somewhat asiden-hand', rather than 'even in front' of Warwick – the lines overlapped to the left, but from inside the mist neither side could see how things lay. The left hand of either front found itself advancing and advancing without meeting an opposing force; the arms were forced to reorientate; the ends curled back in on themselves and this caused the whole formation to rotate, propelled by an invisible momentum, like the hands of a clock. Edward and Warwick were at the fulcrum, on foot and fighting hand-to-hand. At the western end the Earl of Oxford headed a Lancastrian force which outnumbered and very quickly routed Edward's flank. His decisive defeat was not reproduced at the other end of the battlefield, but, fighting blind, the Yorkists thought they had lost and broke south through the village of Barnet and all the way to London, where they called defeat. In London, this premature announcement of the outcome was taken seriously, and envoys dispatched to the Continent wrongly heralded Edward's loss.

Oxford's victory could have been the end of the battle but for the fact that his men, giddy with winning, were distracted and went looting. They were marshalled together again and told that the battle was not over, and blundering back into the foggy field, another strange confusion came about. The troops could not see how the battle lines had swivelled, and they did not realise that the devices of streaming stars they wore appeared, through the fog, uncannily similar to the rising sun that was worn by the supporters of the House of York.

Trampling into the rear of the line, the Lancastrian force pleated, attacked itself, and now it was Oxford's men who fled the scene calling treason and defeat. This was the second end of the battle. But then the line ravelled even further back, to the very end, where Warwick's middle brother, the Earl of Montague, was commanding his force. According to some of the sources, Montague had switched allegiance mid-battle, and was discovered wearing Edward's colours. According to other recorders, the confusion of the counter-attack had muddled one of Oxford's men, who could not tell who the enemy was. Either way, an axe went into Montague's head.

Warwick saw his brother killed and he saw Oxford's men retreat, and he determined for himself that the battle was now ended. The kingmaker was caught in the forest, shucked of his armour, and executed before Edward, who wanted him alive, arrived.

· · ·

John Paston fought at the battle, and afterwards he wrote home to his mother, Margaret, in Norfolk. His brother John had been injured by an arrow in his arm. I do not know why Margaret called both her sons John – perhaps her husband, whose name was John, was a megalomaniac. Perhaps she liked the name, or perhaps she thought that only one of her sons would survive.

It was the older son John who wrote the letter from Margaret's marriage ceremony, but he was wounded at Barnet and John the younger wrote home to his mother after the battle, saying that he trusted that his brother would 'be all hole within right short time'. A few weeks later the wounded man also wrote to his mother. He needed money to pay for his food, drink and leechcraft, but the wound had healed. 'I am whole of my sickness,' he wrote, 'and trust to be clean whole of all my hurts within a sevennight.'

These quotations from the Paston letters were copied out into the notes in the file. I noticed that the two men, both called John Paston, who had both been fighting at Barnet on the losing side, spelled the word 'whole' differently. When I looked at the word in the dictionary, I realised that there were several spellings used interchangeably at that time: hoole hol hoill hal hale hool whoale hoale wholl and quholl, and perhaps more. The *Arrivall* described Edward's army as a hool felaweship, a hol host of individuals.

But these words could also mean 'hole' – a word which was used, by Malory as well as by the Pastons, to describe a wound. Like the historian's twofold definition of the net, as a contraption for catching fish, or a lattice of holes tied together with string, this word, hole or whole, could refer to something completed, or to something missing.

Most modern historians think that Barnet was a soldiers' battle. Tactics and command did not determine the victory so much as did the foggy weather, which brought about a series of unlikely mix-ups. After Easter, Edward returned to London and took back the crown, and new histories, including the *Arrivall*, were written up.

Traffic converges in the City of London at the intersection where it is streamed off, between Martin-Le-Grand and Edward Street, to Cheapside or the Holborn Viaduct. My grandfather and I were not the only ones having our lunch in the ruined church – city workers sat on other benches around the former nave, swallowing sandwiches, some tinkering with hand-held communication devices which seemed hi-tech then, but would probably look rudimentary now.

It was October half-term; I was in my last year at primary school. The rocks from the ruined church lay in collapsed formations, like the stones in the Minster stone-yard – but these were remains, not plans for future work. A line of pillars had turned into stalagmites held together with creeper, behind which we could see the dome of St Paul's two streets away. Traffic flowed steadily between, streamed in different directions by the one-way system. The beginning and the end of the queue were out of sight.

Jimmy was in London to look at some manuscripts in the Guildhall library, a couple of minutes' walk away, and he brought me with him to see the Tower of London, first thing in the morning, and now St Paul's.

At the Tower we had gone into the chantry chapel in which

Henry VI was said to have been executed in 1471, which was annexed to the octagonal chamber in the Wakefield Tower. A green-and-gold wooden latticed screen divided the chapel from the main room, which also contained a replica of Edward IV's multicoloured throne. According to the chronicle, Henry Lancaster died there, 'of pure displeasure', soon after Edward's victory. The envoy's words, like the latticed screen, gave a perspective on Henry's small sacred space, but, again like the screen, they obstructed the view too. It seems more likely that Henry was executed on Edward's orders – perhaps by Edward's brother Richard, the future Richard III, though my grandfather would have argued that Richard was sorely slandered by this unfounded rumour.

According to the information, the oratory wall was restored in the 1920s, after which the windows were left empty – holes giving onto the river. The invigilator didn't know what had happened to the original fittings, but he told us that the window had been rebuilt with fragments of old stained glass, some of which dated back to the time when Henry occupied the Tower. He explained how the strata of pictures piled on top of one another gave rise to the word 'storey' standing for each layer of the building: from the Latin, *historia,* narrative, to the medieval *storye,* each level of a building can be told by a strip of windows, each strip giving a series of pictures, each series of pictures telling a story which has been broken up into a row of apparently isolated observation points.

The reassembled window did not tell any such story – the comic strips had been taken apart. It was a jumble of intensely coloured fragments from other illustrative windows – mostly finials, scutcheons and patterns from ornamental borders which had been cut and resituated in the centre. I could see one beanstalk, one white rose, the muzzles of unknown animals, one demon's jaw, a clipping from an angel's or a bird's wing, swatches of beard and several anonymous hands in the irregular latticed framework. I could not see any whole pictures. I said it was pretty, and my grandfather raised his eyebrows.

Later on that day, when we sat down in the ruins of Greyfriars Church, he told me the history of its destruction. In 1666 the original church burned in the Great Fire, after which it was rebuilt to a design by Christopher Wren. Wren's church was destroyed in the Blitz by a firebomb on 29 December 1940. After that the City decided not to rebuild it again. A relentlessly alive municipal flower bed was maintained in the former nave. White, red and pink late-flowering roses were still opening there that October.

The historian Cora Scofield would have passed Wren's church when it was still standing, on her way to and from the Guildhall, where she carried out much of her research. At the beginning of her two-volume biography of Edward she printed a few lines of acknowledgement to the anonymous librarians and archivists who had helped her find her materials. She thanked the young men who worked behind the desks at the Guildhall, who used to go down to the stacks to locate her manuscripts. For some of the Guildhall librarians, wrote Scofield, her word of acknowledgement 'comes too late' – it was 1923 – and her thanks would be laid, she fancifully thought, like flowers, 'upon their soldier graves'. She didn't list any of their names.

'If we went back further,' my grandfather went on, 'Edward York passed by when he got back into London.' The returning king went first to the cathedral to thank God and the saints for his victory. Warwick and his brother Montague passed us in two wooden coffins – their bodies, wearing loincloths, were openly displayed in the cathedral for two days, partly out of respect for their nobility, and partly to let the public see that they were truly dead.

'And then we would have to go only a little further,' Jimmy went on, 'to see the stone laid in the church, somewhere here above our heads, that was a memorial to Sir Thomas Malory, who had died on 14 March of that year, on the night that Edward landed at Spurn Head.'

When Malory was buried at Greyfriars Church, Jimmy told me, his *Morte* had not yet gone to the press. William Caxton was busy with other business in 1471 – he was living in

Burgundy at that time, and had been, since the previous year, struggling to complete a translation of a history book called *The Recuyell of the Histories of Troy* from French into English. Caxton found that translating the book was harder than he'd thought it would be when he set out. The task caused him to remember his own 'unperfectness' not only in French, which was his second language, but in his own tongue too.

He slowly completed five quires and had made it, painstakingly, through half of the sixth when he decided to abandon the translation. But then he made the mistake of mentioning the project to his patron and countrywoman, Edward's sister Margaret, Duchess of Burgundy.

Margaret asked to see the papers, and having read the document (and corrected some of its rough Kentish English), the duchess ordered her subject to 'continue and make an end of the residue then not translated'. It was, said Caxton, a 'dreadful commandment'. He did not want to continue with the excruciating work, but dared 'in no wise disobey'.

He made it to the end in 1471, in a year which he described in his prologue to the *Histories* as 'the time of the troublous world', not in any single place but everywhere: 'universally'.

This history was different from all the other histories that had gone before it because Caxton decided to print it on his printing press. It was the first book to be printed in English – it was, wrote Caxton, not written with feathers and ink, like 'other bookis' were, with only a few copies passed from hand to hand through a sequence of readers. This book, he reflected, could be printed for many readers, or all readers – to the end that every man may have it at the same time.

I took out our sandwiches and removed the lids from the cups of tea, but my grandfather was still going back in time – past Scofield, Wren, past Edward's own journey back to the throne he was on before, past Malory's dead body and Edward's arrival, then past Caxton's translation, back to Edward's victory at Towton at which, he said, our own ancestors had fought. 'Our great-great-great –' he dropped his voice to indicate that the series went on '– grandfathers were at the battle.' I asked which side we were on. He told me that members of the family had fought on both sides, and I asked how he knew.

'The mathematics of the population statistics,' he explained slowly, 'mean that we are the direct descendants of many, if not most, if not all of the troops at Towton.' Such a high proportion of the able-bodied population fought and died there that we are probably descended from any who have living descendants. They are all our ancestors, he said, and we are all – he waved around at the office workers and the buses – related to the victims of the battle, and to the people who killed them. Then he paused again while he blew the steam off his tea. 'Probably,' he finished carefully.

ix

The story of the miracle in Daventry parish church must have been a hoax, I thought, or else the historian made it up. There may be atmospheric explanations for the phenomenon. I read somewhere that prehistoric cave paintings in France, which had been sealed off from the outside world for tens of thousands of years, were ruined only a few seasons after their discovery by moulds breeding on the walls of the cave, the moulds having been caused by tourists' breath. Perhaps, I thought, damp weather in the spring of 1471 affected the icon, and a sudden influx of extra breath with the unusually large congregation caused the wood, when the repetition of the anthem was sung, to buckle and split.

The author of the *Arrivall* chose to read it differently, as a sign that God approved of Edward's claim to the crown – which was itself a path traced backwards, through the branches of the family tree, to former kings. And at the same time he saw the miracle, which he himself had created, as a prediction of Edward's own 'good adventure' in the future; his prediction was correct. Edward won the next battle at Barnet.

It seemed more reasonable to me to think that it was not miraculous intervention which caused victory in the battle, but victory in the battle which caused the historians to go back in time and create, or recreate, the morning of the miracle. The only thing that was odd about reading the *Arrivall* was the fact that the history took me back to the stories which my grandfather told me from his own life, which I had almost forgotten, so that when I read the history I felt like I already knew what was going to happen. The past came out in a known pattern, like I had had a premonition of it, or as if it was already my own memory.

That day in London was, as far as I can remember, the only time I ever asked why he hadn't written his own family history. The historian who thinks he is writing from the inside is a fraud, he had said. 'It is preposterous to try to get speculatively into other people's thoughts, dreams or sexual lives.' He told me the story about the huntsman who was turned into a deer and hunted down by his own hounds, as punishment for curiosity. 'To make the historian the subject of his own history is to turn the hunter into his own quarry.'

'But why don't you write your own history?' I was a child, and therefore persistent.

'You sound like an old neighbour of mine,' he replied. 'Mrs Philip.'

After finishing the history I cleared some more old books and some broken implements from the barns, and stacked some of them up, for a bonfire, on the waste ground at the bottom of the garden where we had held the dog's funeral.

I drove the rest to the tip, which was a few miles in the opposite direction to the village, on a kind of mini industrial estate outside the nearby town. There were three large brown skips around a concrete court, and several smaller recycling bins for clothing, bottles, plastics and paper. At the entrance there was a cairn of broken electrical goods which was not officially signposted, beside the kiosk in which the tip man sat – or should have sat, but it was empty. I tried to lift the car barrier but it kept plopping down again, and it was cold and already getting dark, so I decided to come back another time.

Instead I went to the library in town and looked through their newspaper archive – articles from the 1980s weren't online. The librarian was particularly unhelpful, but eventually I found copies of the *Chronicle* and the *Echo* from the relevant dates, and sat on a dwarf chair in the children's corner to read them. There were several 1984 news reports on the fire in the Minster after David Jenkins' ordination, but what had caused the fire was inconclusive – it could have been arson, or a chemical treatment recently applied to the roof beams. As I expected, there was nothing about anything unusual in the ceremony itself, apart from the two protesters who had been thrown out. There was nothing about a picture of St Anne or a gust of divine wind in these news reports or in any other contemporary sources.

Jimmy had grown up in Plymouth, and that was where he and I and Liv went on our summer holidays. My grandparents took responsibility for me, and my parents took responsibility for the livestock, and everyone had a rest. Liv drove the whole six-hour journey from the north-east to the south-west of England, sitting in silence up front with my grandfather. I went in the back with the dogs.

We stayed by the sea on the Cornish side of the river mouth, in a rented holiday hut which had cold water but no hot, and lamps but no electricity – it was like going back in time. I slept in a bunk bed, alternating top and bottom to practise sharing.

From the window the bay looked small, with a stout headland on the Plymouth side opposite a longer slender arm reaching far out of sight at sea, over which the sun set. Every day my grandfather and I used to walk up to the derelict medieval chapel on the headland. My grandmother stayed with piles of overdue paperwork from the farm. She tried to catch up while she was away, but she was always running behind.

From the headland, on a clear day, the lighthouse could be seen standing next to the burnt stump of its old footings. At least five lighthouses have been ruined on that spot.

My grandfather, inevitably, told me several stories about

several generations of lighthouses (I don't know if they can all be true) one day on the headland when the rain suddenly intensified and we – he – decided to wait it out in the chapel, which did not have any windows or doors in the frames, so that when you looked at it from the cliffs you could see clean through to the horizon.

Inside there were some illegible yellow graffiti and a Celtic cross, its engravings fading. While we waited for the squall to pass my grandfather told me how one of the old lighthouses had been moved, brick by brick, and reassembled, landlocked on Plymouth Hoe, where visitors climb it for the view. Another had been demolished by the great storm of 1703 – which Daniel Defoe memorialised in his first book, *The Storm* – after the engineer who designed it had publicly, dramatically announced his wish to be alone with only the lamp and beacon inside his own construction during the greatest tempest in history, a wish which was granted when he and his tower were washed away.

The rain was beginning to ease off by the time my grandfather told me the last story. By then the clouds had come down and hidden the lighthouse from our view. In the late eighteenth century, he said, the lighthouse caught fire. The lighthouse keeper, who was an old man in his eighties, gaped open-mouthed from the bottom of the stairwell up to the blaze at the top, which returned down a stream of melting lead pouring like a waterfall into his open mouth. Miraculously the keeper was rescued from the burning building, but he died a few days later in bed in Plymouth.

The doctor who performed the autopsy discovered a large nugget of lead which had set into a perfect cast of the light-house keeper's stomach, which he kept and sent to the Royal Society. 'I think it can still be seen in a museum,' said Jimmy, 'but I forget where.'

The authenticity of the doctor's block of lead was called into question by the gentlemen of the Society, who were sceptical that a man in his eighties could survive several days with a molten, heavy and highly poisonous ballast. The doctor took offence, but he was a man of science. If something is called into doubt, the experiment must be repeated.

He melted lead and funnelled it into the mouths of dogs and down the gullets of his own chickens. Then he watched them die, and was pleased, or perhaps merely vindicated, to see that they died slowly. He sent these findings to the Society, saying that his account had been verified by the long time it took the animals to die.

The lighthouse is mechanised now but still standing in the bay which was otherwise usually empty, even in August. Ferries and fishing boats kept out at sea and rarely if ever strayed close to the beach, and it was only the occasional diver's boat which came within the headland, keeping clear of the light-house, and heading straight towards the only other objects in the bay: two buoys, one pink, one red, which marked the wrecks.

It was in the summer of 1914, Jimmy explained, that a group of submarines went out on a routine exercise from Devonport. While they were in the bay it became clear that the A7 was in difficulty. She did not rise again after she had dropped. Occasionally a molehill of bubbles appeared at the surface where she had gone down. The other submarines made quickly back to Plymouth to get help, found help, came straight back out again in what seemed like good time.

When they rounded the headland they saw several miles of flat water and realised their omission. They crossed the bay again and again. They traced a net of trails across it, but they didn't find the chain of bubbles to follow, like bread in a fairy tale, back down to the submarine. They came back with tugs to drag the bay.

On the fifth day they finally located the A7, but it was too difficult to dredge and raise her, and too late to save any lives – the air had run out days before.

A relief fund for the widows appeared in *The Times*. Strangers sent substantial cheques. The whole city, slightly melodramatically, took to mourning.

'When my father came into Plymouth station,' Jimmy couldn't help adding, 'in September 1914, he was surprised to see so many people waiting on the platform were wearing black.'

He had already told me a little about his father, who was, like Jimmy, called Thomas Thompson. Jimmy was named after him. I liked these family stories more than the stories about old lighthouses. 'Where was he going? What was his name?' I asked.

'He was arriving, from South Wales. He had signed up as a cadet in the navy.'

'On the train?' I wanted to keep him talking, but my questions were not inspired.

'It took three trains.'

'Then what did he do?'

'His name was Thomas, he married my mother in 1916 and was killed in the same year; then I was born,' he said shortly. 'You know all these things.'

'How do *you* know, about the people on the platform?'

I was no match for him. He ignored me, and returned to subjects dearer to his own heart. 'Other people,' he sighed, 'forget things as soon as they happen. Turn the page and the last story completely disappears from your mind.' The pink buoy marks the A7. The lighter, reddish buoy marks a synthetic wreck that has been put in to distract recreational divers from the temptations of the designated war grave – Service at Sea: cuttlefish, sprat, wrasse and flounder in the mud; nudibranchs, whelks, limpets and mussels on the bodywork, kelp and sagartia, jewel anemones, plumose anemones, various hard corals and the soft corals called dead man's fingers. (Nearby there is a third wreck, HMS *Scylla*, dating from the second war.)

Occasionally a school of dolphins or the odd basking shark would come into the bay, and in the late afternoon my grandparents and I used to look out for their fins. Scanning the water with binoculars, I remember catching sight of the frogmen in motorboats pulling up at the buoy, then somersaulting off the sides of the dinghy in black suits with large webbed feet and cans of air strapped on their backs.

Jimmy had no family left in Plymouth, but he had Mrs Philip, who had grown up on the same street as him. Mrs Philip, like Jimmy, had lost her father to the war at sea in 1916. I was about six, the first time he took me to visit. Mrs Philip was even older than my grandfather, and had, incredibly, been his baby-sitter. She called him 'boy', and she called herself Mrs Philip, not because that was her surname but because that was the name of her husband, who was long dead. She lived in Flat 28 on the seventh floor of a tower block at the western end of Plymouth Hoe, along the end of the park, the promenade and the white facades of the seafront houses.

When we came out of the stairwell, the front door of the flat opened right into Mrs Philip's front room, which had large windows looking out over the dockyards, then the bay. They were double-glazed so you couldn't hear the sea though you could see it all around you. Mrs Philip usually lived with her granddaughter, Holly, who was old enough to be my mother. Holly was so fat she couldn't get about, so she lived on her grandmother's sofa. She made me think of the evil octopus witch in *The Little Mermaid*. Her limbs were only partly apparent under the blanket in the half-light behind the drawn curtains. Her grandmother, whose strong old-fashioned scent I can still smell, remains more clearly defined. I can remember the plants she grew in shoeboxes on the kitchen floor, and the mixture of doubt, delight and guilt I felt, when, conducting one of my early research projects, I snooped in the bathroom cupboard and discovered that her luxuriant set grey hair was, in fact, a wig.

Before we arrived there, Holly had been sitting before the television and her grandmother in the window, behind the curtains, with a pair of expensive binoculars. She had never been abroad or even to London, but she had seen almost a century of boats pass in and out of the bay by the time she died. She knew the names of all the Brittany Ferries and the pleasure boats, and noted the registrations of the fishing boats and battleships in an A4 notepad. Holly, making a rare interjection, prophesied that these records would in the future be worth a fortune, when someone needed them for catching criminals.

I was given lemon squash and a saucer of pink and orange biscuits called Party Rings. There were also two toy tin battleships and an enamel bowl full of water. Mrs Philip was long-sighted, her flat was gloomy, and I was very quiet – I think she may have thought I was a boy.

Nonetheless I set about my business, tuning in and out of the conversation as I silently crashed and sank the tin boats again and again. The bowl took the part of the sea. One of my battleships was submarine A7 going out on a routine drilling exercise. I let go of it and it dropped an inch or so to the bottom of the bowl. The second boat circled the perimeter, howling, trying to find where its twin had gone down.

They were getting on with their own version – Mrs Philip

and her photograph albums. Mrs Philip's father, and my grand-father's father, had been, as she put it, 'comrades', and she had a photograph of them together, my great-grandfather looking uncannily like my grandfather except for the fact that he was tall and Jimmy was not tall. My great-grandfather had a thin, serious face and wore a peaked hat that said VIVID.

Mrs Philip herself featured in the picture of the great-grandparental wedding. The couple are standing on a public street against the wall of a church. The bride is very small; her mouth is the only part of her face that can be seen under the shadow of her large dark hat, smiling hard. A large group of small children stand around them looking in different direc-tions. One little girl is holding the bride's bunch of pale flowers. Another girl has a walking stick and a kind of scaffolding, blurred but visible, on her legs – that was Mrs Philip. She had had polio, and it had left her permanently slightly lame so that she always walked leaning into one leg, like she was on a keeling ship. The braces had left her with an odd unladylike stance, with her feet planted apart and her toes facing outwards, like the Colossus.

The albums went on.

The photographs from the interwar years had been merrily captioned. 'Bathing lovelies!' it said under a square shot of three grim-faced women in black swimmers, sitting on deck-chairs on Torquay beach. 'Fancy a dip, Pedro?' was presumably addressed to the inquisitive dog.

There were a great number of photographs of dogs, but there were not many pictures of Jimmy. It was not our family album, so all the pictures showed him out in public. Still, there were enough for me to see, looking back, that he was brought up as a little princeling. His mother had to go out to work, at an industrial launderette run by a Chinese couple on Mutley Plain, so he was passed around from household to household on a street on which there weren't many fat, golden-headed, fatherless male babies. In the earliest, he is an enormous infant in a pram with three solemn little girls standing beside him. In another, a decade later, he is already taller than his mother, holding a shoe at some kind of fete. It was a man's lace-up brogue. Neither he nor Mrs Philip could remember the significance of the shoe; it was a source of some merriment.

The girls on the street had taught him how to read before he went to school. He did well at the eleven-plus and at grammar school, and his history teacher put him up for the Oxford entrance exam the year after he left. 'I've never had a proper job,' he said, maybe with pride, maybe with shame. 'I've never done a day's work in my life.'

After the war he was invited back to Oxford to help out with teaching all the extra undergraduates, and he published his first monograph on diplomatic correspondence in late-medieval Europe.

I don't believe Mrs Philip had read this, or any other of his publications, but she knew he was a historian.

'Why don't you write our history, boy?' she asked, more than once, when they went over the pictures – but he didn't see the crossover, or perhaps he was just a snob, because he never bothered explaining to her what he had explained to me.

xi

At the end of our visit we walked down the hill past the rebuilt lighthouse. We went up, once or twice, for the view over the sound, though I was always more interested in the graffiti on the stairwell. 'Nicola + Jane = slags'. 'Tom is a camel'.

The lido on the seafront was full of salt water. It had been popular between the wars, but wasn't busy when we were there.

After the swim we walked back towards town, passing the war memorial. The cenotaph for the Second World War was a semicircular surround, with a pillar memorialising the first war in front of it. A copper Neptune on half a horse came galloping out of the wall a little way off. To our right, between the memorial and the sea, was another memorial, to Francis Drake. I heard the story about how Drake finished his game of bowls before thrashing the Armada – an act which led, ultimately, to the foundation of the Plymouth Hoe Bowling Club, a flat-roofed bungalow with several pensioners sunning themselves on the deck out front.

We looked for the names of people Jimmy had known – these names meant nothing to me. We could not find his father's name. Perhaps it was because there were so many, listed under their positions (Ordinary Seamen, Clerks and Assistant Clerks, Boy Telegraphists, Engine Room Artificers). Perhaps it was because the memorial was awaiting restoration – some of its copper panels had been robbed, in the late 1980s, for scrap metal, and weren't restored for several years. I was told this reprovingly, as if I had organised the theft, because it wouldn't have been anyone of his generation.

I asked how his father had died, and he said he was lost at sea in 1916, when he was still a teenage naval cadet. And he started to tell me about the Battle of Jutland, which took place in the North Sea on the evening of 31 May 1916, but he didn't know much about it, and could only go back over the official version of events.

Everything had been very quiet until six in the evening when the battle began on several fronts at once. Radio operators could get nothing out of their contacts except the repeated statement: 'We are engaging with the enemy.'

There are few coordinates on which to plot a map of the action, but it seems that many crews from the different navies converged very near one another, but that smoke from the guns and engines of so many battleships, as well as incoming sea mist, blew between them and obscured the lines of sight. Both sides sustained heavy losses and both claimed victory, at first.

At this point Jimmy became a little confused and seemed to lose his way, stopping and starting as he told me about a meeting between Admiral Jellicoe, commander of the fleet, and Herbert, Lord Kitchener, Secretary of War, who couldn't decide if they'd won or not.

Afterwards we met my grandmother in the cafe at the top of Dingles department store in the city centre, which she was fond of and Jimmy hated. It was a place for old people. It looked out over the city and had a central island with tea, rock cakes and saffron buns, round which a carousel of pensioners revolved. After completing their orbit the customers queued, then took off one by one from the cashier towards an empty table. Teapots, saucers and spoons trembled on the trays until the table was reached and the load could at last be laid down.

Liv was in a foul mood after doing the paperwork all day, and missing her animals. She would take her time having her tea. Only occasionally, when it was very hot, would she hurry through, anxious to get back to her greyhounds who may have been suffering in the heat of the day. She left them attached on extendable leads to a post outside the hut.

When we got back the dogs were lying down in the sun but awake. They slipped apart from one another, and stood and stretched, when Liv went over to water them. I followed.

'Do you love the dogs more, or me more?'

She thought about it. 'You don't love something more or less. You either love it totally or you don't – like being pregnant.' She bent and poured warm water out of a bottle into the dogs' plastic bowl. Their eager heads got in the way and they snapped their jaws to drink greedily. 'It is easier to love the dogs,' she said.

I took this in.

'Do you think they love you back?'

She didn't reply, but turned and started to walk away. Then she turned back, making a 'shh' noise, and the dogs left the water and ran towards her until their leads ran out, then, held back, their heads rolled back and they flattened their ears and fixed their eyes on her face and grinned, and did a kind of dance at her feet.

There was dust everywhere. The room needed cleaning, but the Hoover had disappeared. I knew there was one, somewhere; an anthropomorphised piece of equipment named Henry by its manufacturers, with a cutesy face drawn around the suction tube/nose. Not a good brand. I remember its casters (legs?) were broken so my grandmother and I had to lug it along the old track that had never needed to be tarmacked down to the church, which Liv used to clean on Saturday mornings.

When we arrived we opened all the windows that could be opened, to let in the air and out the insects. The church filled with whispery breezes. Once, as we approached, we saw a pale shape ghosting inside the building, like the dot of white in the eye of a portrait, and when we went in we found a white pigeon batting against the glass, dropping strings of white shit down the wall and over the memorial stone ovals. I used to spell out the words on those memorials while Liv did the arrangements and vigorously hoovered the aisle. When I was older I read a hymn book or a mouldy Authorised Version, sitting in the ditches between pews. It felt strange, like sleeping upside down in my bed, which I was only allowed to do if there had been bad dreams.

Liv cleaned with enthusiasm. She scrubbed the stone flags

like she wanted to scrub out her husband's surname which was written on them. She filled bin liners with 'old rubbish', and left pieces of church furniture, only slightly broken, with the bin bags at the gates. She stood holding the Hoover like a ghostbuster, as if the idea was to suck the breeze out of the church, but she dropped cigarette ash when she went, and lozenges of mud from the treads in her boots. The dogs, trailing faithfully after her, brought in more mud and dropped hair, and ultimately her labour was in vain.

I can't remember my grandmother ever cleaning her own home – the Hoover was only used at church – and I don't know why she volunteered as a cleaner. Perhaps it was out of an unspoken sense of community, but I suspect it was more likely some weird kind of stand against Jimmy's position at the Minster.

The church was Saxon, and medieval murals had been discovered under a Victorian screen when the church was restored between the wars. As the Listed Buildings man said, the building was of considerably greater historical interest than anything in its parish. It was unusually low, made of thick stone, with a single stout buttress at its western end, and at the east three wide lancet windows – it looked more like a barn or chapel than a proper church. It was just beginning to fall down when I was a child. Someone, possibly Liv, had tacked green plastic sacks across the cracked clear-glass windows in the vestry, so that the fading legend 'Molamins Sheep Hi-Energy Feed' could be read, upside down, over the opening. The roof was coming in. The church was home to a large population of bats.

It was because she was cleaning the church that Liv got involved in the bat dispute. During the early years of the twenty-first century, during the last years of their lives, both my grandparents got involved in this row, and took things out of the vicar's hands. It was at that time that alcathoe's bat, a new species of tiny bat, was identified in Yorkshire.

When the chiropterologist was sent down by DEFRA to identify the species of bats in our church, the vicar, who was a quiet man and oversaw the running of several local churches, was happy to let his parishioners take care of the affair. My grandmother and I walked down from the farm, and when we got there, to our surprise, my grandfather's car was already parked next to the bat woman's van outside the church gates.

Bat woman – that was what she called herself – lived on a community farm near Wensleydale. She was small and bespectacled with short dark hair cut like a helmet – two longer strands poked down the side of her face, where sideburns could have grown, had she been a man. Her pinstriped man's overcoat was decorated with pin badges shaped like bats in different poses and sizes. Unnecessary to say, the bat woman did not really understand my grandfather's attitude towards the small tenants sleeping and shitting in the only local item of historical interest.

First we walked round the outside of the church. Bat woman pointed to the eaves and to the yew trees by the wall as possible locations for bat accommodation, proposing that the parish install bat boxes and heating systems to help the bats through harsh winters, during which their heart rates dropped almost to a full stop. Jimmy's response was tart: the bats, he suggested, could consider developing their own systems of central heating, gas and electric, if they were particularly keen on these facilities.

'Oh no,' she said, undiminished. The rabbit, for instance, she said, which was now so common hereabouts, had adapted successfully with human help – when they were first introduced to England farmers used to dig their burrows for them.

She beamed and recited the Act (1982, as amended) again,

like a mantra or prayer: No human interference with any structure or place which any wild bat uses for shelter or protection.

She would have to go back to the van for the equipment. It was impossible, even for a specialist, to differentiate the alcathoe bat's squeak with the naked ear. The tiny bats had flown over on their tiny wings from mainland Europe. It defied belief, she said – each individual bat was the size of a thumbprint. She held up her own thumb and looked at it as if she were seeing, for the first time, the genetic lines, one inside another, layered incontrovertibly on the pad.

'Bats are our only mammalian relatives,' she said reverently, 'capable of true and sustained flight.'

Under dissection, she told us, bats' wings have the same internal scaffolding as our hands – bats are mammals. They developed off the same evolutionary line as humans. 'Probably from fish!'

The presence of an alcathoe population was confirmed. My grandfather maintained that the bat woman, in league with his dastardly wife, had released one of the little buggers from her pocket. But it was immaterial in the end, as the roof reached a tipping point in the autumn, and had to be repaired or else the rest of the building would have gone very fast and the bats would have had nowhere to hibernate in the winter. By that time, the episode with the bats had already put ideas in my grandmother's head.

ii Peter the Great

i

I didn't open the next file until the next morning. There was frost on the grass when I woke up and I sat inside with a coat on to go through the documents, but I had to take off my gloves to unfold the first piece of paper. It turned out to be a poster with diagrams of Rube Goldberg machines which were never actually made. My grandfather loved this kind of pre-industrial contraption – he had eighteenth-century engravings of orreries on the wall of his study, and on the shelves books on early lighthouses, histories of the engine, the loom, 'Man Down the Mine'.

Old age did not get in the way of Jimmy's enthusiasm. Unlike most men of his generation, he was unfazed by modern technology. In his last years he used his weekly allowance of free Internet at the public library teaching himself, with online tutorials, to master Excel, PowerPoint and Skype.

On the poster each picture showed a concatenation of causes-and-effects leading to a simple, sometimes completely pointless action like, say, tipping over a milk jug, via a series of junctions. Each junction had a different mechanism, so one arrangement might have a pulled string swinging a pendulum into a drum which dislodged a socket dropping a load on a balanced scale which tipped, and, by lifting a bar, started a ball rolling.

I think that Jimmy thought of himself as a bit of a Heath Robinson – he endlessly doodled primitive switches and hinges in the margins of his notes, although it was William who worked on our farm who executed his commissions for various simple mechanisms, mostly extensions to light pulls, or devices for lifting pallets, logs or hay bales, which William didn't use. Jimmy also set traps for vermin. My grandmother acted as if she found her husband's exercises mildly amusing and tried to stop him wasting the time of 'the men', as she called the farm workers, perhaps pointedly.

In the second file there was more rubbish among the historical notes than there had been in the first file, and it was more disorganised, and the handwriting had deteriorated. It may have been put together later than the first file.

When I had finished I dumped the Rube Goldberg poster and the rest of the rubbish in another load in the stackyard. Then I put on another jumper, another pair of socks, and my grandmother's boots and went for a walk, to clear my head.

I walked west of the house into the beet field, which looked like it had not been harvested that year. The roots had got to the surface of the earth and were scattered around like ancient teeth. They weren't rotting – it was too cold – but some of them seemed to have collapsed in on themselves. When the sugar-beet factory was still open it used to fill the air with a sweet milky smell on the days when the chimney was smoking. Once, when we were stuck behind a trailer piled high with beet and going at about seven miles an hour all the way to York, my grandfather told me the history of how the Yorkshire landscape was planted up with beet in the nineteenth century, to replace the West and East Indian sugar cane which had, until then, supplied what he called the national sweet tooth. It was a long ride.

I didn't come across anyone else while I walked, though I could see smoke above the village roofs. The recent snow had mostly melted from the garden, but there were still patches in the furrows and at the margins of the field, where the dark earth was written in lines out of the white snow and the white beet. Standing on the gate and looking out, the same colours were echoed in the white markings on the high hill – chalk scars, Jimmy had told me, from intensive agriculture during the two wars.

Sheep had got into the next field and eaten the kale right down to a series of ribs sticking out of the ground – for once, the sheep escaping was a good thing, in that it prevented the leaves rotting on the stalks. Hippocrates advised against growing cabbages near human habitation, because of the stink (unwholesome, agreed the horticulturalist John Evelyn in *Fumifugium*, Evelyn's discourse on air pollution). The final field running to the beck was turnips. Like the beet they lay about the field like broken lamps. They used to be fed to the pigs, when we had pigs.

Then I walked down the beck to where it met the river, then along the river down in the low fields. Last year's floods had taken away part of the bank.

I walked past the pig ark on my way back to the house. It was still quite new – we had got rid of the old brick piggery after my grandmother died. When she started to lose her memory she chalked bossy reminders about the order of ceremonies for pig feeding on the back of the green door. 'Have you done the water?' she asked herself. 'Check the hose is off.' The last instruction she wrote on the outside wall: 'Close the door.'

When I got back I realised I had locked the keys in the porch. I went right round the building, trying each window. The furniture, under dust sheets, looked in the gloom like icebergs floating through the cold house. I expected at least one window to be open, and I even climbed the trellis onto the roof of the porch to try the sash window at the end of the landing, but they were all tightly secured.

I do not remember the house ever being locked when my grandmother was alive. The doors were usually ajar or banging in the currents of air which ran between open windows in different rooms. The back door was always open; it was not until after she died that Jimmy installed the automatic lock. Opening and closing the house was one of their many small conflicts: she walked through the house opening every door and window, and he went behind her closing them again – he felt the cold – but this was one battle she often won. Even in winter I remember him sitting at an open window, wearing a black coat, writing on a board over a blanket on his knees. Snowflakes drifted in, kamikaze, making tiny bombs of smoke on the bar fire at his feet.

I decided to smash a window, climb into the farm and call the glazier in to repair it. I fetched a sledgehammer, but when I stood in front of the window and caught sight of my swing in the reflection, I found I didn't have the stomach for it so I called directory enquiries, then called a locksmith, who said he could come round in the afternoon. I sat in the car to keep warm while I waited, and wrote up my own notes on the contents of the file on the tsar.

ii

Peter the Great's Great Embassy never, officially, visited England, but the second file in my grandfather's desk contained a history of that visit. Peter spent much of the winter of 1697–8 in London, but he was travelling incognito, as my grandfather explained in the biographical notes that came at the beginning.

Peter the Great was the first tsar to leave Russia during peacetime. He wasn't known as Peter the Great then, of course, but he wasn't known as Peter Alexeyevich either.

The embassy travelled through Livonia, Courland, Brandenburg and the United Dutch Republic before arriving in England, which was the farthest west point of the journey. The empire was left in charge of two very old advisers and one younger nobleman who had a pathological fear of dirt, which he tried to control by avoiding physical contact with other people, furniture, door handles and food. The tsar, meanwhile, took on a fictional alias so that he wouldn't have to make contact with too many eminent people along the way. He travelled incognito, sometimes dressed as a carpenter, calling himself Peter Mikhailovich. Many of his ambassadors wore similar disguises, and historians have debated whether they were more successful as apprentice labourers or in their official diplomatic transactions.

More than 250 people travelled with the embassy including these ambassadors, courtiers and engineers, naval officers, cooks, servants, translators, trumpeters, dwarves and fools, and musicians whom Peter accompanied on his personal drum.

Peter was generous, unconstrained, enthusiastic and erratic. He took meals at unusual hours. He was not keen on ceremony. He liked fireworks, navigation and engineering and he was good at practical tasks. His revenges were harsh.

He was tall and thin, and suffered from a stutter and a nervous twitch which affected the left side of his face and body, particularly his left arm which jerked uncontrollably when he was nervous or excited. He had warts on the right-hand side of his face. His hands were rough and his palms calloused. He was proud of these rough patches because they had been made by physical work over a long time. He showed them off, inviting the people he met to touch them, as if they gave proof of something.

The biographical notes were attached to a colour photocopy of a 1650 'prospect' of Riga, which was then in Livonia and is now the capital of Latvia. The picture was very detailed. Each small window and every stake in the fence were drawn with a fine pencil, but for some reason the colouring looked pallid to me, and the hillside on which the city was built seemed almost transparent. The whole town was completely empty, except for two tiny figures standing outside the walls in the fields by the river. By magnifying a corner I could make out the high-brimmed hat and the stick that the left-hand man used to walk. The other figure was outlined less definitely, but he looked to me like a younger man, or maybe even a girl, whose head was slightly tilted like he or she was listening to the older man. They looked like ants on hind legs.

My grandfather had numbered the slipways down which the boats were taken to the water, so there was a large 6 pencilled between the two. The picture is unsigned; the anonymous artist must have been watching from the other side of the river.

The picture reminded me of the time my grandfather first told me about Peter in Riga, though I didn't hear about his Great Embassy to London then. I was at sixth-form college, and had come back to the farm to help my grandmother plant flood defences. Her low fields, which had a lake in the middle, were bounded on two sides by the river and along the back by a steep bank. One year out of three or so – whenever there was a long freeze – meltwater came down off the Wolds and flooded the flats at the beginning of spring, as it still does. Each spring it took a little more of the riverbank with it, so the low fields were gradually shrinking.

My grandmother and I and a small team of volunteers were making a plantation along the short bank. After a lengthy application process Liv had been awarded a grant from Natural England to cover the purchase of a thousand saplings. She was to match the money and buy another thousand for the creation of Natural Flood Defences – the idea was that the roots would hold the earth together when the water rose. Natural England was a new body operating a new set of conservation schemes that came out of the Countryside Stewardship activities piloted by farmers including my grandmother in the 1990s.

That week, a representative from Natural England was due to arrive to inspect the plantation, their cheque having been cashed by my grandmother a few months earlier. Unfortunately, she had as yet failed to buy the saplings or plant up the bank.

In the hurry, some volunteers from the village, mostly retired, came to help get the young trees in. We worked in pairs, one digging a small hole, the other holding the sapling upright while the first filled up the earth around the roots and heeled it in. Then we wrapped the tree guards round. Some guards were staked but we didn't have enough stakes for each one.

It was February and the recent rain had left the sky clean and the river high and brisk, and my boots sank slightly into the damp earth. There was one small bright patch of blue in the cloud cover.

When we came to the end of the second row we started to run out of trees and I went back to fetch more from the car, which was parked uncomfortably on the causeway in the middle of the lake – we thought of it as a single lake, although the large body of water to our left was completely cut off from the smaller one to our right. My grandfather was in the front seat, reading. It was his policy to avoid all her projects, and where possible to disturb or interrupt them.

'Do you think ice is wet or dry?' he asked when he caught me in the rear-view mirror, as I hauled the white pannier out of the boot. Individually labelled saplings poked whip-like out of the sack: alder, guelder rose, oak, ash, blackthorn, willow.

'Wet ice is water of course,' he reflected, 'and dry ice is not frozen water, it is solid carbon dioxide.'

The trees were heavier than they looked. I put them down for a moment and sat in the driver's seat with the door open. In the mirror I could see grey heads clambering slowly along the bank. My grandfather, following my gaze, commented unkindly: 'Zombie invasion.' My grandmother was pacing among them with tea and Hobnobs, and imperiously pointing out directions with the silver-tipped stick she used to discipline her dogs.

'Dryness, of course,' Jimmy went on, 'is the condition of history.'

He had already told me how the first histories came out of the driest climates in the world. Damp consumes historical documents, and it was the driest of all things – fire – which created the first archive. Fire annihilated the earliest large human settlements in Mesopotamia, now Iraq, when it burnt through the city towers, bastions and blocks of ziggurats which, taken together, formed settlements that historians have called 'civilised'. But the first writings of these first cities were done on clay tablets which set in the heat like stones. The fire which destroyed the first civilisation formed the first lasting archive. And the second archive was the ark, which populated the planet by saving every non-swimming thing from total submersion – by keeping things dry.

The ice archive, like most archives, holds things out of the water. Jimmy proposed, while we were sitting in the car, that ice could be said to have a kind of memory, though probably not a conscious one. It holds the contents of the notebooks of Arctic explorers and the splinters from trees in Norway which were used to build their sledges, the temperature of the water that Noah may or may not have sailed on, whole woolly mammoths, frozen fish, the age of the Arctic continent. 'And other things,' he said vaguely. It does not, however, hold salt – Arctic and Antarctic ice alike expel salt and dirt when they freeze, he told me. They freeze so slowly that the large crystals from seawater are pushed out, along with other detritus, while the water congeals, so that the frozen matter is, at least in its initial state, pure freshwater.

This seemed strange to me, because I have always thought of icebergs as pillars of salt, ever since I heard the story of Lot's wife at primary school, and tried to picture her transformation into that peculiar image, which was God's mysterious punishment, Mrs Taylor said, for looking backwards.

'Many of the best historians, of course, have dry skin.' He was looking at his own hands.

I must have inherited my eczema from my grandfather. My father and his siblings do not have it – perhaps it skips a generation, like twins. I got eczema when I was nine months old so I do not remember life in a body without it – my skin has always come off leaving a trail of dust behind me wherever I go, though it has been worse than it is now. When I was very small and staying at my grandparents' house they sometimes wrapped my hands and feet in bandages to stop me scratching while I slept. This was something Jimmy's mother had done for him when he was my age. He called me The Mummy, while shrouding me, and told histories about the Egyptians taken from Herodotus: how the pharaohs were buried in the midst of their whole households; cats were buried like Gods; and bears (which were rare in Egypt) had to be buried as soon as their bodies were discovered, on the spot where they lay.

After I started school the eczema got a bit better, but Leanna wouldn't hold my hand when we were told to be partners in the crocodile on a trip to the Viking Centre. She said I was scaly, like a fish. I went crying to my grandfather later on, but he only looked at his own hands again, like Lady Macbeth, and said that Leanna was an astute child. Eczematous skin was indeed more similar to a fish's scales than normal skin. He told me to stop whining: as afflictions go, he said, having unusually wrinkled hands is not terrible, nor is the fact that the salt stings when you swim in the sea.

In the car mirror I could see my grandmother put her things down to plant a couple more trees, working alone and more quickly than the others. She straightened up to retie her silk headscarf but her fingers lost it flapping around her head. Her face was wrapped in blue silk which blew up above it like a prayer banner. William was standing nearby, and she rested one arm lightly on his shoulder, leaning at arm's length, and the other hand fumbled with the blindfold.

Listening to my grandfather's history was more interesting than planting trees, and easier, but I knew I ought to go back to work.

'It is no good, trying to hold back the water,' Jimmy intoned, staring out over the heads of the ducks, coots and geese on the lake, to the river beyond.

'What are you talking about?' I said.

'Your grandmother's policies are ridiculous,' he said. He listed, in a gloomy, trance-like way, the damage his wife had done and was still doing to his farm. She fatted up her animals, and let his buildings collapse under decades of her dirt and grease. The delft tiles had come off the splashback, the original furniture was broken, the flint and stone on the floor had cracked. In the garden the vegetable patch was a rotting mat of ancient plants which had bolted years earlier and fallen in on themselves. A branch had broken off the ash and damaged the holly hedge which ran around the lawn, and the lawn had disappeared under mud. In the barns all the implements were falling apart. The heads came off the rakes and hoes. The axles on the wheelbarrows had rusted up so badly that they would not go.

I had not seen my grandfather in the garden even once, never mind actually gardening.

'It will only get worse,' he self-pityingly concluded. I think he was referring to the announcement my grandmother had made on Bonfire Night.

I found it difficult to listen, not because I didn't believe what he was saying about my gran's slovenly housekeeping, but because I couldn't remember the farm ever having been different. As far as I could see, Liv and Jimmy were both to blame for the state it was in. Both of them did nothing. It was like the old stories in which warring gods bring chaos on the earth – neither of them, on principle, repaired the roofs on the buildings, or shut up the pullets at dark, or saw to the garden. Everything returned to its natural state.

I got out.

It was the melting of the ice that prevented Peter Mikhailovich from crossing the River Dvina at the town of Riga in the month of March in the year 1697. Peter Mikhailovich, as he wanted to be known, was waiting out the spring thaw.

Riga was the first city Peter came to after leaving Russia, but in 1697 there was no bridge over the Dvina, and boats could not get between the icebergs until they shrank.

Approaching overland, the city was cut off between the river and the clouds spread thinly over the ziggurat-shaped eaves and red-tiled roofs. In the pale glare the slope on which the town was built was like a transparent panel. White stone, bleached wood and windows gave through to the sky behind: the windows were unshuttered but had glass panes, each room was bare and had on the other side another window which looked out as if it were floating on the water. No backyards, no neighbouring walls; the only view was empty sky.

There were wild bears in the forests of Livonia at that time. Coming to the edge of the forests, there were scores of starving, emaciated peasants walking the frozen countryside, looking for food and firewood. That year the famine killed thousands – contemporary historians called it a 'universal' famine. Coming in from the countryside, immediately before the city walls the meadows ran to the water. There were landing jetties on the river. The thaw had just begun. Large bergs and crocks of ice were concluding their careers in the fast-moving yellowy river.

Riga was a Swedish colony, well defended against invaders, wild animals and starving peasants. Moats, walls and walkways rose up out of the river, patrolled by foreign sentries, cutting off the city from the outside world.

The Swedish governor, Erik Dahlbergh, only heard that Peter was approaching Riga when he was already nearly there. Dahlbergh dispatched a cavalry with trumpeters to welcome him, but the horses crossed paths, several miles east of Riga, with the small group of forerunners including Peter, who arrived early, unexpected by the governor. Post out of Russia was censored to protect the incognito, so the letter that came through from the governor of Pskov, which was the last town on the Russian side of the border, did not mention that the emperor himself was hidden in his own party, in disguise as an ordinary young man.

The embassy was received half-heartedly at a modest dinner. A small expense of salted meat was drawn cautiously from the winter stock.

The thaw came very slowly that year, which was bad for the famine-struck peasants and also for Peter Mikhailovich, who did not much want to stay in Livonia. It was as easy as you might expect for a heavy-drinking Russian, standing six feet eight inches tall with warts on his face and a nervous twitch, to go about unnoticed. There was little that Dahlbergh could do to stop the Rigans staring. Every time Peter Mikhailovich went out, as a sign of respect, a seven-gun salute was fired – this did not help the incognito. He spent much of his time in Dahlbergh's house, looking at the governor's collection of diagrams, perspective drawings, architectural blueprints, maps and plans. He saw cherrywood models of the new fortresses at Gothenburg and Riga, and several instruments of war made in miniature out of the same material. The weather prevented him from doing much else, during daylight.

One evening, several days after the Russians arrived, a Swedish sentry was patrolling an area of the ramparts when he caught sight, out of the side of his eye, of a long shadow. At first the sentry wondered if he had caught the silhouette of a buttress, and blinked. When he came closer he saw that the shape was hairy, like a bear – he wondered if it was a bear woken by hunger from hibernation. But the figure the sentry saw as he approached was not a bear. It appeared to be an unusually tall man wrapped in bearskin, writing or drawing in a book. A piece of tape was in the crook of his arm. He held it up with one eye closed, the other squinting, as if he were measuring something. Then he wrote something down.

The guard called for the bear-man's attention, but the man did not turn out of profile and his arm jerked, brushing the shout aside. The guard challenged again and the man shouted back, an alien sound which ricocheted and disappeared. A foreign language. Finally the guard raised his musket and the man turned properly, his hands in the air. 'Peter Mikhailovich,' he repeated. The tape, the pencil and the book were confiscated. The guard's cold fingers stumbled through the pages as he tried to keep the trigger of his musket still looped under his thumb.

Pictures of Riga's defences, numbers, labels and pages of notes in an unrecognisable cipher or alphabet. The defences were drawn, listed, numbered and keyed. The guard arrested the man and took him in to his superiors.

His superiors, to his surprise, released the hostage with his book, his tape and his pencil, the foreigner still expostulating incomprehensibly at the sentry.

The next day Dahlbergh received a group of ambassadors, who complained about the arrest of one of their party. They parted and the young man himself stepped boldly through the crowd, like he was coming out of a forest, to harangue the governor. Peter Mikhailovich said he was not angry because he expected special treatment as a representative of the tsar (though the tsar was mighty indeed). He was angry because Dahlbergh and his sentries were very rude hosts. All guests, he said, should be treated as honoured guests. Every member of the embassy, however apparently inconsiderable, should be treated as well as the tsar himself. Even so inconsiderable a personage as himself – he was a mere carpenter, he added, by the way.

The ambassadors had to stay in Riga for several days after that because the breaking ice was still heavy, and the river remained completely impassable.

Jimmy's notes were badly written, and it wasn't clear how much was hearsay. He did not properly explain the framework, so it was easy to forget that Peter Mikhailovich, as he called him, was really the tsar, and it was difficult to tell whether Jimmy was repeating what the Russian ambassadors had said, or expressing his own opinion, when he wrote that every dwarf, every cook, every fool and every carpenter in the embassy represented the tsar himself.

As my grandfather described it, the account of Peter's Great Embassy survived almost wholly in anecdotes. The fact that the tsar was travelling under a made-up identity meant that official accounts of the trip couldn't keep up with word of mouth. Anecdotes, which are secret stories or unpublished histories, had come into English very recently, in 1676, when the poet Andrew Marvell first delivered the term in his publication *Mr Smirke* – before that time, my grandfather proposed, history held back no secrets. It was only after the anecdote had come into being that peasants, diplomats, princes, soldiers and shopkeepers could all tell throwaway stories about what they witnessed when Peter came by. These amateur historians go unnamed in the documents, so the origins of the stories are obscured, and sometimes it seems like every account could come from the same individual whose experiences had been passed on and on and on – Chinese whispers, Jimmy called it, politically incorrectly – and not set down until several substitutions had been made in favour of the truth, and the reality was replaced by a memory of something else, like the story of the mimic who was asked to impersonate himself, and found he had forgotten his own voice. The best of the historian is incorporated, too, in other people's experiences. To write about the historian is to write about someone who was, through a combination of research and imagination, thinking himself into the body of the Tsar of Russia which was, in turn, in a cheap uniform, in disguise as a carpenter.

The memory of Riga must have grown in Peter's mind. It must have seemed worse when he looked back because the tsar called Riga 'the accursed city' when he returned, thirteen years later, with a battery of cannon on wheels. Peter claimed the first salvo of the first assault for himself and it was very sweet, he wrote that night in a letter to a friend, to vent Russian cannonballs at the palisades and bastions, and to rain bullets on every man in the whole town. 'Thus,' wrote Peter, 'has the Lord God enabled us to see the beginning of our revenge.'

But what was he revenging? Jimmy wondered. He took revenge on the place, rather than the person, who had offended him. In point of fact, Peter was taking revenge, like a petulant Canute, by destroying an environment he could not control – it was the cold weather that slow spring which had kept him in Riga while the ice was melting. There is no point, concluded the historian, in attempting to hold back the might of the water.

The frozen river did, eventually, melt in the spring of 1697. Peter crossed and moved west through the Duchy of Courland, where the Russians amazed the locals with their capacity to drink wine and roar. The Courlanders said they were baptised bears.

Peter arrived at Konigsberg, now called Kaliningrad, at night by boat with a small group of men. Most members of the embassy were still miles behind.

His group halted here. He could not carry on into Poland because Jan Sobieski, the Polish king, had just died, and the succession was uncertain – it was and still is difficult for a head of state to visit a state without a head. So Peter was held up at Konigsberg and Frederick didn't receive him until the morning.

Frederick was the elector, but he wanted to title himself Frederick, First King of Prussia. The tsar's endorsement would have helped him style himself so. And so he emerged, in the morning, accompanied by a great number of attendants and in full regalia, ermine and sceptre, a design of crowns on his satinate robe. He was a ruddy man with a broad nose and a sensible set mouth, looking out from under a wig which looked like a young sheep. A moustache shaped like a whale's tail covered his philtrum. Peter, dressed as a sailor (inappropriately – not only because he was not a sailor, but also because he was miles from the coast), and eating his breakfast, looked up.

'Your Royal Highness,' he said, throwing back his chair. He kissed the elector's hand, bowing deeply. He sent greetings from Tsar Peter, whose humble servant was in awe in the presence of so exalted a personage. Really, said carpenter Peter, he could hardly believe Frederick himself was not an emperor. Perhaps the tsar, back in Moscow, would hear of Frederick's great majesty, and offer support to his claim to kingship. Peter himself, though a humble carpenter, certainly hoped so, and was only sad he could not do more himself.

The Muscovite ambassadors, who were standing along the back wall, looked on, bearded and scowling.

• • •

The next evening, after hunting all day, Peter and Frederick watched a bear fight. One of the bears was an old female with no teeth and grey strips of skin visible on her back. The other was younger and smaller but male, and livelier. Peter insisted on betting and chose the older bear.

Chains connected his bear to a post, the other to a railing that ran round the edge of the ring. When they were released the bears moved towards one another and hugged. Tipping their heads back and baring their gums, it looked like they were about to bite or kiss. They moved lightly around the canopied ring like they were dancing. Peter's bear lost, though hardly any blood was visible when she fell down.

Later, Peter's musicians entertained the court and Mikhailovich, wearing a red coat with rows of gold buttons, accompanied them on his own drum. He was overexcited at the end of the evening, his left arm spasming in applause.

A few days later the caravan of the Great Embassy finally arrived, after travelling overland across Europe with tents, trunks full of sable and brocade, the pelts of wolves and bears, salmon, smoked fish, honey and vodka. Frederick greeted them and made several formal enquiries as to the good health of the tsar. He had his satin cloak on again, and his wig, and his ermine. The diplomats solemnly replied that they had left the tsar in Moscow in good health, and Frederick, to everyone's surprise, let out a high-pitched squeal and started to giggle. The bearded Russian ambassadors looked down disdainfully. This was a man who wanted to be a king. Peter Mikhailovich, watching from the palace windows, gave himself another round of applause.

After the embassy arrived Peter Mikhailovich went on again, moving west until he got to Koppenbrugge, where his way was blocked by the large household of Frederick's wife Sophia, who was passing through with her mother, also called Sophia.

When the women sailed into the low-ceilinged room at the inn, Peter covered his face with his hands. The women were large and elegant, with elaborate hair and strangely structured dresses. 'I don't know what to say,' he said, in French.

At dinner Peter was uncomfortable with the unfamiliar silverware and with the linen – he preferred a ewer and basin to wash his hands – while at the same time having to navigate conversation with these women who seemed to know more than most men.

Sophia started a conversation about Descartes, who had written of a man sitting on his own in a small, cold room, thinking about thinking. This sounded like a boring kind of book to Peter. Slowly, though, the ladies' practised conversation (he sat between them) put Peter at ease. After dinner he tried to excuse himself from dancing. No gloves, he said. But again the women persuaded him. He flinched with surprise when his arms came into contact with the younger Sophia's whalebone exoskeleton, and shouted something in Russian which made his ambassadors laugh. Sophia drilled him in the steps of the Polish dance, then signalled for the music to start and the two fronts, male and female, began to move around the room.

At first each pair of partners seemed to recede in the universal movement. Faces disappeared in the machinery of limbs which operated complicatedly. Peter was not a very good dancer. His steps began to syncopate, dragging a beat behind the pattern. He forgot to jump after turning Sophia, and they both stood still for a moment or two, waiting for the room to catch up. Rows of arms extended at once, legs turned out and were retracted; waists pivoted within the crooks of arms, and skirts, driven by speedily pedalling feet, swung from one space to another.

The next time he jumped forward too quickly, forcing the next person to stand aside so that the apparatus could return to its previous position. Peter did not seem to realise that he was standing in the inner circle with all the women. He was applauding everything again, and stamping his feet in time. Sophia tried to steer him back onto the outer circuit but he turned like clockwork, like all the ladies, still on the inside, while she tried to make him turn her at the same time. Their arms, which were locked together, were lifted higher than the other dancers' arms. The Prussian courtiers said that it looked like they were fighting.

The musicians, trying not to snigger, brought the music to an early end, but the Russians did not realise because they didn't know the dance. When the music stopped, Peter dashed up to the musicians to congratulate them, then shouted for another song. He bent down and misplaced a large over-affectionate kiss on the little Princess Dorothea's face, then tried to rumple her hair – the wig keeled sideways. The only disappointment, he said, was that he couldn't drum and dance at the same time.

iv

On the day Peter arrived at Zaandam, after travelling overland through various mid-European electorates, there was a story going round the Three Swans. Gerrit Kist, they said, had fallen out of his boat.

Gerrit Kist was a local blacksmith who had worked at a royal forge in Moscow before returning home to live in a small wooden house by the river. On Sundays in winter Gerrit used to rise early, leaving his wife Mahlah in bed. He went out on the river before the town woke up and sat in the dark with bait, line and traps to reflect on his soul before church. The eels he caught slipped about below him. He was a melancholy man, according to the storyteller.

That morning a shout interrupted the quiet and Gerrit turned without much interest, expecting a couple of drunk traders on their way back from a big night out in Amsterdam, or a larger boat clearing its route. The figure that made its way towards him was, apparently, a tall epileptic Russian standing upright in a little fishing smack and shouting 'Gerrit, Gerrit Kist!' Gerrit Kist stood in his boat, removed his hat, and fell backwards into the icy river, where his catch of eels detangled themselves from a metallic knot into separate silver threads, and shot back into the Zaanland mud.

Later that day, according to the history, a carpenter named Peter Mikhailovich enrolled at one of the shipyards, then took a room in a wooden house near Kist's. The bed was so short that Peter slept curled like an unborn child, or with his feet dangling off the end like a drunk. Napoleon, when he saw this cabin, which has been preserved as a memorial to the tsar's stay, was supposed to have said, 'For the great, nothing is too small!' (My grandfather noted that Napoleon himself was, in point of fact, a fairly average height.)

Peter planned to stay through spring to next winter. He had come to Zaandam for the boats. With more than fifty private shipyards located around its rivers and dykes, it was the greatest shipbuilding town in Holland, which was the greatest shipbuilding power in the world. He had his ambassadors take jobs as apprentices in the shipyards, and instructed them to dress in loose workers' uniforms – local linen, red jackets and white canvas trousers. Unlike his noblemen, though, he didn't think of these clothes as a disguise. In fact, he said, the carpenter's uniform suited him better than his real outfits, the imperial robes, the emperor's old clothes. When he visited the families of Dutch shipbuilders and engineers whom he had hired to work at Archangel and Moscow, he proudly claimed kinship with the workmen. 'I, too, am a carpenter.' He showed the families the calluses on his hands.

Problems with the incognito began with an incident involving some plums, some mud, a group of Zaandam schoolboys and His Imperial Majesty's hat, which culminated in Peter barricading himself in a local pub called the Otter, and shouting for help. Within a few days most people in Zaandam knew that Carpenter Peter was a tsar in disguise, and the council had to issue a proclamation which stated that it was the duty of each citizen to uphold the fiction. Gerrit Kist himself denied that his new friend was an emperor until his wife Mahlah, who was a bit of a Mrs Noah, according to her neighbours, slapped him in public and told him to own up.

By day Peter helped to assemble the large merchant vessels in the shipyard, but before dawn, after lunch and on Sundays he took his little fishing boat out on the river, sometimes with his new friend Gerrit. The boat gave Peter freedom to discover the country, which was arranged around a network of man-made waterways. He lived relatively anonymously until the day he was out in his boat and a small flotilla appeared on the flat water, out of the blue.

Fishermen were charging pennies to take families to see the emperor. They steered their rowing boats towards Peter's craft. Six feet and eight inches of him were already the property of history, and the nameless Dutch townspeople wanted to see what history felt like. Zaandam doubled the guards on its bridges but the trippers proliferated at a greater rate and pushed them aside. The boats were unbalanced without their catches of eels when the passengers hung over the sides to get closer – red cheeks and yellow teeth skiffed towards Peter, who zigzagged upriver away from this toy navy, doubled back into its midst and then put defeatedly to shore, where another crowd was gathering. It was a miracle that nobody was drowned in the crush.

He jumped from the boat to the bank without mooring properly, then pushed through the grasping crowd waving his arms like a windmill, and accidentally clouted one man over the head. Congratulations, Marsje, the man's friends joked, you've been knighted.

Peter stayed on at Zaandam because of the shipyards. He heard that the Zaandamers had invented engines which moved whole new ships over the dyke between the shipyard and the river, on which they could sail off.

The town councillors were discreetly informed that one of the Russians in the shipyard was interested in this phenomenon. When they consulted the building schedules, however, they saw that no ships were due to be moved, so it was agreed that a special show would have to be arranged.

Moving the boat overland was to be turned into a public spectacle, my grandfather told me, just as it was in Werner Herzog's film *Fitzcarraldo*, in 1982 – 'before you were born', he said – which showed a 320-tonne boat dragged overland through the Amazon rainforest. *Fitzcarraldo* was a fictional feature, but the boat was real and it was really manoeuvred by the cast and crew over a hill between two forks of a tributary of the Amazon – an act which Herzog described as 'useless'. In the end, the director said, there had been no point in moving the boat without the use of special effects, other than that it was 'more real'. The film was based on a true story in which an explorer had moved a 32-tonne boat across a similar distance, so the boat which Herzog moved for his work of fiction weighed ten times more than the boat which had been moved in real life. (Jimmy had not actually seen the film.)

In Zaandam, workmen were sent down to the dyke. Stands were set up, and a small box was constructed in a place with an excellent view, in imitation of the royal boxes at the English playhouse. Railings were set up along the dyke for the common spectators. It was arranged among the shipmasters for one great ship to be assembled hurriedly so that it could be moved over the dyke, and sail off down the river. Then by night it would move backwards over the dyke and return to the shipyard, where it would be dismantled again, and in due course reassembled as it should have been, over time.

The night before the event was cold but clear. It was not known whether the boat would be ready in time – it was still being put together with wooden pegs in the hours before dawn; the workers were working by torchlight, and their torches were reflected in the water. They hoped it would hold. Peter was still sleeping – he was an early riser, and would wake at dawn, in good time for his appointment. But the townspeople were already awake, preparing themselves.

Bonfire Night was the only public holiday celebrated with any neighbourly enthusiasm in our village. The children went door to door with a wheelbarrow collecting junk and scrap wood for the bonfire, and a collecting box for the meat, which was supplied direct from the bacon factory which was where most of the inhabitants of the village who were not unemployed were employed.

I remember burning, in different years, effigies of Guy Fawkes, the Chancellor of the Exchequer, a local councillor whose contribution to a recent parking debate had been unpopular, and a red devil which signified Manchester United as well as Beelzebub, Father of all Lies. The year *Jurassic Park* was released, the weird local vet made a mangled-looking Tyrannosaurus Rex out of his children's soft toys. I was nine that year, and old enough, in my opinion, to look after myself. But my parents were going out in the evening, and my grandmother came round and picked me up in the afternoon. I was not asked if this was what I wanted. She hadn't come in the car, we were to spend the afternoon walking round the village, telling people to shut up their pets.

None of my neighbours seemed to mind her playing Lady of the Manor. They were pleased, in fact, to have the opportunity to talk about the behaviour of their disturbed pets: how the cat kept butting her head on the window, or the guinea pig ran up and down in its hutch making a sort of bubbling sound.

We were more than halfway round the village when we got to the top of The Ferns, which is where the retirement bungalows were. BEWARE OF THE DOG on one gatepost summoned us up coral-coloured paving stones on the garden path, past the bare rose bushes in bare earth. We rang the doorbell and nothing happened. We waited.

'Hello?' my grandmother called through the letter box.

'It's not working,' came back immediately – the voice was surprisingly nearby, through a window to our left. The glass was thick and striped so you couldn't see through it, and the glass door in front of us had the same pattern on its two large panes.

We heard a sloshing sound, like someone throwing a bucket of water. Then the light went on in front of us and an old lady's vague outline appeared beyond the glass on the door.

'What is it?' Her voice was clear and mistrustful. 'I've got a massive dog here,' she said, 'and he's very dangerous. He'll bite your legs off at the, on the knee.'

My grandmother explained that she was here about the bonfire. 'From the community support network,' she added, in a moment of inspiration.

'Right.' The woman sounded doubtful. 'I'll put him out, my dog, but he'll just be there in the yard, and I haven't any money in here.'

Through the glass we could hear and see her shape cross the room and open an internal door, then she said loudly, 'Go on out, you,' then she closed it again. She didn't attempt to make any barking or growling sounds.

Then she came up and opened the front door, only a foot or so at first, putting only her head round it. She had on a shower cap and her thin arms came out of a short-sleeved wrap – she had just got out of the bath. Behind her, you could see the wet footsteps going in a lonely circle round the kitchen floor.

'He's very big and he bites. You should see his teeth when he's eating raw meat. Liver. He's just out there and I'd let him in at any minute.'

My grandmother explained that we were here, in fact, to tell her to keep any pets inside, as the fireworks would be starting in an hour or so.

'Well.' There was a long pause. She looked at a loss. 'I suppose you want something for the guy. You're a bit old for it, I'd say, but you've got this lad with you. Turn round then while I get the purse out.'

'Lass,' I said.

We turned. For good measure I covered my eyes. When we were allowed to turn back she pressed 10p into my hand, then held on to my wrist.

'Who's picking me up for it then? They come round ferrying me about when they're after my vote or my soul, but who's taking me to the bonfire?'

I looked at my grandmother. She was looking at the woman.

'We're only here about the dog,' she said. 'Please do make sure he is safe. It can be so disturbing for them, they have no idea what's going on.' As we were walking back down the path she called back without turning, 'I don't know about arrangements for lifts and so on.'

That evening my grandfather and I attempted a historical re-enactment. As a general rule, he disapproved of re-enacting historical events. He didn't set much store by the experience of history, and turned down invitations to take part in Viking Weekend in York, during which the city was annually stormed by eccentric holidaying Norwegians dressed in hessian tunics, who played out battles on the 'Eye of York' – a patch of grass between the Castle Museum and the magistrates' court – then commemorated their invasion with cheap own-brand lager in the Sam Smith's pub by the River Ouse, into which the most enthusiastic commemorators occasionally fell.

He didn't think that first-hand experience was very helpful for a historian. He never wrote about the Second World War, which was the only event of historical significance through which he had lived – the latest of his histories ended in the 1920s when he was a little boy and too young to remember anything of importance himself. He thought it was the responsibility of historians to remember distant events, which were, as he put it, the parents of recent atrocities. 'It is only by looking back,' he said, 'that we can connect ourselves to that which has gone.'

In keeping with these principles, he didn't go to the bonfire, it being, so to speak, a re-enactment of Guy Fawkes' execution. That year, however, when at last I arrived home with my gran, after ensuring that each local gerbil was safe, he called me into his study and announced our next project: 'We're going to make some seventeenth-century fireworks.' In front of him on the desk was an old book, bound into an anthology, by a man called John White. The book was open at the title page, which said '1651' and it was dedicated to all 'lovers of artificial conclusions'. The book gave recipes for making the fireworks that Peter the Great would have had, he said.

Later, when the sky got dark, Liv strode off down the drive without a backward look. I watched her green shoulders and her swinging stick. Will was at the bottom by the gate, waiting for her to walk into the village. I wanted to go down with them. I had seen the stash of fireworks for the bonfire, proper supermarket ones made in China with names like Brilliant Lobster and White Astonish.

My grandfather read instructions out of his book. 'How to cast money away and find it in another man's mouth,' he said. 'How to make dainty sport with a cat.' Then there were recipes for grenades and flame-tipped indoor arrows, and after that were the recipes for a variety of recreative fireworks: rockets, fizgigs and wheels.

'"A dragon issuing out of a castle which will swim through the water and approach a horseman with a trident riding towards him." That might be a bit complicated. Aha. "If you will have a blewe fire . . ."'

The dog was at the door, whining. It was a loud sound more like clanking rusty chains than an animal. Jimmy whispered directions to himself. We were supposed to mix gunpowder with various poisonous compounds and roll the mixture into balls the size of 'wall-nutts'. Suddenly, he spoke up.

'Live yogurt might work. Have a look in the fridge. Do we have any yogurt?'

'No', I said, looking. 'Can I have a Pepsi?'

'No. You'll be up all night.' He walked out of the room, thinking, and in the hallway he opened the back door and pushed the dog outside. 'Bloody pest,' he murmured, almost affectionately. Then bending back over the book, he read aloud again.

'It is most laborious and very dangerous, but apparently if you follow White's instructions even a child can do it.' He straightened his back and looked at me. 'We'd better go and see what your grandmother has in the barn.'

The dog ran off round the barn and out of sight, and we went in.

In the far corner of the barn there stood a crowd of rusting cans of different sizes, each of which had a small yellow triangle reading Haz-Chem – which isn't a foreign language, as I then thought, but an abbreviation for Hazardous Chemical.

Back in the study we spooned out powders and rolled them into tissue sausages, then tamped them down, according to White's instructions, and choked them. 'It were a dainty sight,' he wrote, 'to see how pleasantly the sparks spread themselves in the ayre, and come down like streams of gold, much like the falling of snowe.'

While we worked, Jimmy told me about Herodotus, writing before fireworks were invented, describing the confusion of the Scythians when they saw snow for the first time. 'Whoever has observed heavy snow,' Herodotus wrote, 'will know what I mean when I say that the snow resembles feathers.' Herodotus thought that the Scythians must have been describing the snow when they described what looked to them like birds being plucked in the sky.

'Peter the Great also loved a firework display.' Fireworks were, apparently, Peter's third favourite thing, after navigation and carpentry.

vi

Peter woke up. He allowed his body to drop out of the short bed and rose, as he did each morning, aching on his side and in his lower back, where his bones had been cramped and taken the weight through the night. He went to the shutter on the window, bleary, yawning – and found hundreds of alert faces focused on it, outside, staring in. The street was blocked by an increasing congregation, who caught sight of his face, which was framed in the cabin's single small square window 'as if on a postage stamp', said Jimmy anachronistically.

While Peter prepared to go out and see the moving boat, the Zaandamers were on their way to a different performance in the same place. They wanted to see Tsar Peter in disguise as Carpenter Peter more than they wanted to see the great boat lumbering over the dyke like the leviathan on land. Already, so many men and women had crowded along the bank that the small polite rail constructed on the council's orders was completely forgotten underfoot. Every free space was covered with turned faces and waiting eyes. Maids and children hung out of windows. On the parapets of the pitched roofs whole households had gathered to wait patiently, while the sun rose, for Peter to come out.

But time passed, and Peter stayed inside. The people in the

front row were swallowed back into the crowd. New bodies came forward to replace them.

Whether it was ready or not, and the Zaandam shipmasters never let on, the ship did not move from shipyard that day. It stayed in a dry dock, and was taken apart again over the next week then put back together, properly, by the ship's carpenters later. The carpenters must have grumbled only very quietly and among themselves at the pointless week's work, as no complaints are reported in the histories.

Peter's small wooden boat was brought to the river instead. The tsar fought his way through the dense crowd to the nearest landing stage where he embarked and set off, heading west.

With each stage of Peter's journey he put more distance between himself and his own country, until he had gone so far round the surface of the earth that he began to approach the eastern tip of his huge empire, the Kamchatka peninsula, which, my grandfather told me, separates the seas of Bering and Okhotsk, and is said to be inhabited by a giant bear called the 'God Bear'.

In 2005, Werner Herzog released the film *Grizzly Man*, which also told the story of a bear that was seen as a 'saviour'. *Grizzly Man* showed footage which Timothy Treadwell filmed on his hand-held camera after he gave up human society to live in a National Park in Canada, with bears. He gave them names – Charlotte and Fern, Vivi and Mr Brown. In the end he was eaten alive by one, as was his girlfriend Amie Huguenard. Herzog said that Treadwell was 'fighting against the civilisation that cast Thoreau out of Walden', referring to the book, *Life in the Woods,* in which Henry David Thoreau sits alone in the countryside, performing various boring household chores and complaining about his neighbours.

One sequence, in the middle of *Grizzly Man*, showed

Treadwell speaking lovingly to a female bear as if she could return his feelings. In a voice-over, Herzog gave his own thoughts on the shot. 'What haunted me was that in all the faces of all the bears that Treadwell ever filmed I discovered no kinship, no understanding, no mercy. I saw only the over-whelming indifference of nature,' he said. 'To me, there is no such thing as a secret world of the bears and this blank stare speaks only of a half-bored interest in food. But for Timothy Treadwell, this bear was a friend, a saviour.'

Herzog often appears in his own productions, speaking invariably with a heavy foreign accent that has always seemed to me to be slightly hammy – as if the director wants his audiences to notice that every word he speaks is spoken in translation. His real voice, like the thoughts of the bears, is finally inaccessible. I have usually found this exaggeratedly lugubrious Germanic voice sort of funny, as if his treatment of the serious subject matter is set to topple any second into a slightly tasteless joke, with no punchline.

According to one story about the God Bear of Kamchatka, my grandfather told me, the name was given because it is the largest species of bear, but according to another story the bear itself was an incarnation of God. 'And if God chose to live in flesh on earth,' reasoned Jimmy, 'why would he choose to be a carpenter instead of a bear?'

Peter reappeared west of Zaandam, in Amsterdam, but the two English gentlemen who tried to locate him there couldn't find him.

The gentlemen, who had been brought to Amsterdam by their merchant interests, presented themselves at the gates of the East India dockyard with a letter of introduction from the Marquess of Carmarthen. The gatekeeper pretended to read the letter, but he couldn't decipher it because it was in Latin or English or something. He decided, because of the way the men were dressed, that he would call over the foreman.

The foreman said he would take the visitors round the shipyard, but it would not be possible to identify Peter Mikhailovich. The fictional alias was upheld within these walls, he said, even though every man in the dockyard knew who the tall Russian really was.

The dockyard workers, he explained, knew the tall Russian's identity because all work stopped when he arrived. The whole atmosphere of the shipyard, which was walled off from the outside world, changed when the new man came in. Assembly froze, the ships that were in the process of being built stopped; the ships that were due to be cleaned and mended remained dirty and broken, and when activity was resumed new instructions were given and things took shape differently.

The burgomaster gave orders to lay the keel of a frigate for the new apprentice to see, but the workmen were told not to build it in the usual way, in a dock. In the dock, the foreman explained, it was difficult to see where each part fitted. Instead the new frigate was to be artificially deconstructed and laid out flatpack-style, with each constituent loosely linked on the ground so that Peter could have an overview of the full plan and design, and see how the wooden parts would fit together.

Carpenter Peter was diligent. In three weeks he had made himself a complete taxonomy of the boat kit, learned the Dutch names of every timber, and drawn each joint into his book.

One of the English gentlemen (whose names my grandfather could not remember) described the busy environment: groups of men were pulling, shifting, cutting, painting and hammering at the skeletons of wooden boats which were rising, like Noah's boat, out of keys and planks of wood. And like Noah's boat, said my grandfather, all manner of things found on the planet were to be loaded and issued from their bellies. Amsterdam was the merchant capital of the world.

The eyewitness did not mention the fact that there were older boats being repaired in the dockyard too, but the historian Robert Massie, in his biography of Peter, described the process by which, in shallow tidal water, the older boats were rolled to their sides and scraped, using various flat-edged implements, of barnacles, kelp, algae and minute crustaceans; rotten planks were stripped and removed; and fresh tar was melted into the seams.

A small group of workers who were taking their breaks had seated themselves along the quay to watch three men trying to haul a mast onto the hull of a frigate. The English gentlemen and the foreman paused casually beside them. Two of the men were particularly short and one was very tall, which gave a slightly comic air to the process by which they tried to hump a huge pole over the sides of the half-finished boat. They hadn't pushed it far enough when the tall man jumped on deck and attempted to tip the balance, so his colleagues lost control and the mast fell heavily over the side like an overweighted scale and rolled along the deck. The tall man jumped, but his left foot was caught before he could pull it out and he screamed in pain. Some of the men on the quay cheered.

'That is broken,' said the foreman. 'Carpenter Peter, why don't you help your colleagues?'

A man on the dockside, whom the onlookers had not noticed before, was sitting on the stump of a log. He put down the hatchet with which he had been shaping a piece of wood, left his breakfast – bread and beer – and obediently went to help the group, climbing awkwardly on deck and taking the timber beneath his shoulders. Carpenter Peter, the gentlemen now saw, was in reality even taller than the tall man who had broken his foot. Slowly, Peter and the two short men, coordinating their sidesteps, turned in a counter-clockwise direction to reorientate the mast. Up it went. Carpenter Peter, sweating, nodded to his colleagues and returned to his stump where he ate his bread quickly and watched the other people go about their work.

It was Nicolas Witsen, the burgomaster of Amsterdam, who had found the solution to Peter's problem. Witsen arranged to lodge the embassy inside the walled East India dockyards, where the ambassadors could study ships out of sight of the public. Unlike poor Erik Dahlbergh, Witsen had done his research, and he knew how to please Peter. He knew that Peter's favourite substance was gunpowder. He knew that Peter liked fireworks and navigation. He purchased a large quantity of fireworks and threw a huge banquet in the embassy's honour. The guest of honour arrived late after stopping en route to measure a bridge – one of the light, flat bridges which, spanning the canals, hold together the streets, even nowadays, in Amsterdam and St Petersburg. Everyone was waiting when he arrived. Their food had got cold.

After the banquet there was a firework display, and after the firework display a mock sea battle was staged on the canal, 'between the Booms of Amsterdam and the Pampus'. Small boats fired real gunpowder at one another while Peter walked freely among the crowds who knew that the Tsar of Muscovy was hiding right in front of them, dressed as a common dock-yard worker. The crowds pressing on the banks pushed too hard, or perhaps the boats misfired. According to some sources twelve people drowned that night; according to others it was only ten.

vii

Our fireworks were nothing like the ones that John White described – they didn't take off properly, which was lucky, because my grandfather was just lighting them when the dog came trotting out of the wet brown ferns and up to my feet. It was too late to take him in, so I held him and he hung off the loose collar like it was a snare, lifting his front feet off the ground as he pushed forward with his hind legs. He was straining out with each outward breath, but didn't break into an audible whine. I didn't know what he would do when the fireworks went off.

Luckily, they didn't take but exploded quietly, with a powdery sound, on the ground, making small balls of light like planets in the sky – one white, one green, one purple. Each expanded, then shrank. The dog hardly seemed to notice them, and afterwards I took him inside. Jimmy, disappointed, lost interest and disappeared into his study. I interpreted this as a sign that I could at last go down to the bonfire, where everyone else, including my grandmother, had been for hours.

The last of the fireworks were going off when I went down through the fields, and it was only then that I understood what John White meant – the way the sparks fell and were put out in the night looked like snow falling on the sea. By the time I arrived, people were starting to leave. I had missed the burning figure, the bonfire had risen high and was beginning to sink. The broken armchair near the top had sat heavily lower and lower and given up its shape.

My friends had already been taken home by their mums. Their dads were still stood unsteadily by the barbeque, black shining bits of meat on it. As usual, there was too much meat now, at the end, and it had not been ready early enough. Two pensioners in slippers, nighties and coats sat on a hay bale, dangerously close to the flames in their nylon gear.

I found my grandmother on the other side of the fire, standing with William, another farmer, and the bat woman from the church. All four held one hand in a trouser pocket, the other round a plastic cup. They had their heads bent forward and Liv was speaking, but broke off when I approached.

'Stop scratching,' she said. 'Have you been playing with the dogs?'

I sneezed and rubbed my nose with a sleeve covered in dog hair. 'What are you talking about?' I asked.

'My low fields,' she said, and the farmer, for some reason, grunted with laughter. 'Come on,' she said, and then, appalling news: 'We're off home.'

Going back up the lane was much darker, after our eyes had got used to the fire. The track had grass in the middle between deep muddy tractor ruts. My grandmother didn't seem sure which to take as her path, and veered from one side to another. I stayed on the verge close in to the hedge, which went up to the top of my head. Liv could look out over it across her fields. She stopped to catch her breath. 'Things are going to change around here,' she said out across her landscape.

In the next field she put her foot into a puddle, pitched forward and went down. 'Fuck,' she said loudly. One leg was out to one side, her stick out to the other. In the middle, her leg was kneeling. She pushed off it and rose back up, and we walked on in silence. 'Excuse me,' she said stiffly, after a while. 'I'm all right.'

The bright kitchen light made her eyes look small and her face pale. The door opened, and Jimmy came in in his pyjamas. She leaned on the table with her knuckles, and directed herself towards him.

'Farming practices are about to change,' she said rapidly and loudly. 'I've been hearing from the bat woman about DEFRA. There's going to be a new body for protecting living things, the environment, living things.'

She was looking at my grandfather. Then she noticeably slowed and lowered her voice, as if she was explaining something to a foreigner or a child.

'This farm is to pilot a Countryside Stewardship Scheme. DEFRA are looking for pilots, and the bat woman works for DEFRA, and they'll give us money to do nothing, in various ways, but we can't farm any more, we have to stop repairing things and let them go to ruin. William will stop ploughing and leave margins at the edge of the fields; we'll throw wild-flower seed about and create some "meadows". We declare nesting sites under the old eaves, but only if we leave them in disrepair. They send you packets of the seed. It's an arm's-length body –'

'What's an arm's-length body?' I asked.

'A midget,' Jimmy put in quickly.

'It's an independent body set up at arm's length from a government department,' she said.

'A midget's body,' he said, 'may typically be as long as a man's arm.'

'She's already been recruiting. The church is signed up, and the bats are protected in the roof now. The graveyard is designated an area – a designated area – of environmental interest, which means you're not allowed to mow the graves or bring in cut flowers any more. Some of the older graves might go, they'll stack them up on the side, to make room for the orchids, and they have other protected things there – living things, not the dead. Field mice.'

It was as if neither of them could hear the other.

'While a midget is merely *conspicuously smaller* than the norm, the dwarf, of course, is a man of his own proportions.'

'Or a woman!' I added.

'We're applying to have the woodland designated Ancient,' she said. 'It's the future.'

'The cretin, I have heard, is one with an abnormally small head.'

They looked at each other for what seemed like a long time. Neither of them said anything. She went out of the kitchen with the stateliness of someone who is straining to be dignified, and slammed the door.

He added, 'Cretin, from Christian, to remind ourselves that the handicapped are related to all other humans.' Then he got up from the table and walked out, slamming the door again. When they were gone I helped myself to two pints of Pepsi and then took off to bed.

viii

Jimmy said nothing about that conversation the next
morning when he drove me to school. He said we might
have been a bit too cautious with the gunpowder in our
fireworks.

'Fireworks, of course, were not the only use for gunpowder.'
He began to tell me about Peter's trip to Delft.

During his days off from the dockyards, Peter Mikhailovich
used to take trips on his own boat through the countryside
around Amsterdam which was still in a kind of recovery.
Twenty-five years earlier, King William had cut the dykes to
flood his own country, letting the sea creep across the fields
and low farms. My grandfather explained that Holland was,
at that time, under threat from the French king, Louis XIV,
and that William had no hesitation in submerging his own
earth to cut off the enemy's advancing army. Behind the
waterline he had created, his army, which was less than half
the size of the French force, could defend itself.

When Peter visited, Delft was also in recovery, or perhaps
in irredeemable decline. 'Over the course of the seventeenth
century Delft drew inward,' wrote the historian Peter Sutton.
The town had been at the forefront of what historians call the
Dutch Golden Age, but there had been a tragedy in October
1654, when a warehouse stocked with barrels of gunpowder

exploded on the wharf, killing over a hundred and injuring thousands of workers and bystanders. They called it the Delft Thunderclap, which gives a false impression that it was an act of God or the weather.

When Peter approached Delft one Sunday afternoon in 1697 a thin mist began to blow over the water. It grew thicker, hiding the tulip fields, then the horses drawing the barges along the canals, and finally the canal itself. The quiet was ringing in his ears, like the silence after a gunshot, and he didn't realise he had arrived until a woman suddenly appeared from above, tipping a bucket over the quay so that the water ran down between the cobbles into the canal.

When the sun burned through the clouds more women came out of their houses. It must have been a day for spring-cleaning: several were mopping their doorsteps and the streets outside. Others hung white clean washing, like declarations of surrender, on lines over their yards. None of them spoke. Inside the houses copper pans gleamed and even the delft tiles, which you could just make out, shone with a clean glaze. Looking through a window Peter saw another woman pouring soapy water from a jug into a clay bowl. It was the cleanest town he'd ever seen.

That day, driving me to school, Jimmy described a painting of Delft during the clean-up operation after the Thunderclap: blasted trees and buildings, crows overhead, rain clouds or smoke over the city, and people scavenging or rebuilding. In his desk, years later, I found the postcard of this painting in a small packet inside a paper bag inside the file on Peter the Great.

In the same packet I found the Far Side cartoon which depicts a group of cows standing on their hind legs. When a car comes, one cow calls 'car', and they descend to all fours. When the humans have driven past, the cattle return to their hind legs.

The card was blank. I threw it out.

The final townscape in the envelope was probably the most famous – a large greetings card of Jan Vermeer's *View of Delft*: gold-edged clouds pulling over glassy water in the port. The clock in the picture shows 7. The buildings spread out across a single strip leaving little room for foreground or background so that the farthest rooftops, illuminated, draw the eye just as much as the nearby belt of sand. Jimmy had written on the card in barely legible writing. I had to use a magnifying glass to read it.

They say Vermeer worked with a camera obscura or light box which drew the view of the town in through a minute aperture made with a pinprick, and projected a stream of light to the easel or perhaps the wall; figures moved across the canvas; the tide ebbed; a gull, flying too close to the engine, caused a total eclipse.

It is thought that the artist worked from the second floor of an inn which no longer exists. What is most apparent, to stand here, now, at the site of that inn this morning, is that the stretch of water between the painter and the town is much wider than Vermeer pretended it was.

Postcard purchased at the Mauritshuis yesterday and written today 04 April 87, 7am. T.J. Thompson. Delft.

I used the magnifying glass to look at the front of the card – the roofs and walls were done in panels of yellow, red and ochre, and the city appeared to be almost completely empty, though in the foreground, standing on the belt of land running to the water, there were two small dark figures with their backs to the painter. I could hardly make them out, but with the magnifying glass it looked like they were talking to one another.

Jimmy didn't tell me about Vermeer when he talked about Peter's visit to Delft. He told me about Vermeer's neighbour, the microscopist Antoni van Leeuwenhoek. Some historians believe that Leeuwenhoek was the long-haired, narrow-eyed sitter for two Vermeer paintings, *The Geographer* and *The Astronomer*. When Peter was in Delft he met Leeuwenhoek.

Leeuwenhoek took his name, which means lion's hook, because he lived at the hook or corner of the Lion's Gate in Delft. His father's surname was Thoniszoon; I do not know why he chose to change it – both names are peculiar. Philips Thoniszoon was a basket-maker and Antoni, training as a draper, made his first microscopes to inspect the warp and weft. The microscopes he developed were exceptionally powerful and found their counterpart in Leeuwenhoek's outstanding eyesight – the detail in which he saw things would be unsurpassed for two centuries.

Leeuwenhoek, my grandfather told me, is most famous for the things he discovered with his microscopes, which were the subject of most of the odd and unselfconscious letters he wrote to a group of strangers in England. In these surviving letters Leeuwenhoek described his conversations, his little illnesses and his daily activities, in short biographical episodes, each of which leads to a hypothesis about the way the physical world worked, often at a minute level. The correspondence, which continued over many years and ran to several volumes, was conserved by the recipients at the Royal Society in London, the Society translating his letters into English and filing copies in their archives which remain there today.

If he specialised in anything, it was waste: in the tiny arena exposed by his microscope he discovered the first bacteria and animal spermatozoa. In the archives at the Royal Society there is a letter in which he describes examining the dirt on his own person, catalogued under the following title: 'Further observations of saliva, Leeuwenhoek's method for cleaning his teeth and the discovery of bacteria in tartar; examination of spittle from people of different ages and sex; observations of nasal hairs and blackheads (comedones); concerning the structure of the epidermis and comparing scabs with fish scales; discussion of pores and calluses.'

Leeuwenhoek was sociable and personable, and he showed his microscopic findings to the 'exalted personages' who came to see him: kings, tsars, philosophers, gentlemen, artists and even ladies, although the ladies sometimes ended up more disgusted than delighted by the tiny creatures they saw teeming in the food they ate or the grotesque prickled and cratered surfaces of hair and skin. Leeuwenhoek did not see anything grotesque about the miniature worlds he discovered in crumbs of cheese, insects' legs and dots of mould. It was in the nature of these miniature worlds that he could only ever look at a tiny fragment in any single moment: one day a nail clipping, one day a single hair. He looked at the dirt between his own teeth, at stuff taken from the mouths of two ladies (perhaps his wife and daughter) and at the same material extracted from the gums of an old tramp. He found so many living things there, even in the mouths of the ladies, that he wondered how his nice visitors would react if they knew that they were hosting so many thousands or millions or trillions of animal parasites. 'What if in future one should tell people that there are living more animals in the unclean matter on the teeth in one's mouth than there are men in the whole Kingdom?'

Leeuwenhoek emphasised that he was not unusually dirty. He cleaned his own teeth rigorously, every morning (he even specified the method). Nonetheless, he said, 'there are not living in our United Netherlands so many people as I carry living animals in my mouth this very day'.

Leeuwenhoek imagined his body as the watery habitat for the creatures he called 'little eels', himself as a whole country, like the famous frontispiece to Hobbes's *Leviathan* in which the state is one large body made up of many other smaller living bodies. According to Hobbes's theory, the Leviathan of the commonwealth only works when all these bodies, which Hobbes called actors, act in connection with one another. Leeuwenhoek's version is more literal, and includes human and non-human actors which can sustain or destroy one another.

When Peter visited Delft he invited Antoni van Leeuwenhoek on board his boat, and the two men spent two hours there together looking through the 'eel viewer', as Leeuwenhoek called his microscope, which had a minute lens like frozen condensation. He made Peter a present of one of these tiny devices, through which they looked at the animated 'eels' – bacteria and protozoa. When Peter Mikhailovich showed Heer Leeuwenhoek the hard skin on his hands, the draper showed the carpenter his own calluses, and told him how he had looked at shavings of skin through his microscope, and explained a theory about the sweat of their labour – Leeuwenhoek believed that it acted as a glue, bonding the surface of the skin into rough patches. He explained that skin looked like the scales of a fish, close up.

Peter did not stop at Delft, and nor did my grandfather. We were early for school – the school bus I usually took had not yet arrived, so I waited with Jimmy in the car, and he told me about Peter's next trip, to the university town of Leiden.

The booksellers of Leiden were famous, but there wasn't much time to browse the booksellers' collections, so Peter bought a selection of navigation tracts in different languages, and several prints of maps, including a map of Guinea which was stretched along the latitude with rhumb lines converging on two wind roses; east and west.

Because the map-makers did not know what the landscape looked like inside Africa, they had filled the space in the interior with a kind of garden of grass tufts with alligators, elephants, baboons and lions crossing the savannah. In the foreground, Negro cherubs with red wings lugged an ivory tusk through the shallows of the Ethiopian Ocean.

Peter's new map had been sponsored by Nicolaes Tulp, a seventeenth-century physician from the Netherlands who made money from mercantile interests in Africa and is famous, now, for Rembrandt van Rijn's group portrait, *The Anatomy Lesson of Dr Nicolaes Tulp*. Rembrandt shows a crowd of medical students, their faces painted with white light, gathered around the half-cut corpse of an executed criminal. Tulp means tulip: in the corner of Peter's map there was a badge showing a red tulip like closed lips. Next to the badge, in the foreground of the map, a small navy of Dutch merchant vessels was depicted being blown towards the coast of Africa.

The bookseller accompanied Peter to another house, several streets away, where his paper was made. Work stopped for the afternoon while the boys showed Peter how everything worked: linen rags and recycled paper were mashed in a large stone basin which looked like it was full of soapy water. The paper was made from a thin compacted layer of this recycled linen and paper pulp which was sifted on a wire grille, before being peeled off for use when it was completely dry.

In the back room, Peter made his own woodcut. He turned and bent over the work. Nobody could see what he was carving into the surface. His concentration was perfect. When he turned back round he blinked, as if surprised to find other people waiting in the same room. They put the plate face down on the paper, and rolled it through the press. They turned back the paper, and hung it up to dry, a picture of a little Christian called Peter stamping on the head of an Infidel Turk.

After he visited the bookseller Peter saw real tulips in the glasshouses in the botanical garden for which Leiden was famous – they were large and purple and dropping their petals. At that time there was a kind of Dutch national fever, which was described, by the English horticulturalist John Evelyn, as a sickness suffered only by florists or meaner gardeners who found themselves transported at the casual discovery of a new 'little spot, double leaf, streak or dash extraordinary' in a tulip, and subsequently pushed their prices up and up and up – Evelyn called it tulipa-mania, but the name didn't catch on.

In another hothouse, grotesque crimson, pink and yellow roses were also losing their petals to reveal their hearts. The hothouse air was not heavy with sunlight and rich perfume, it smelled like green water, sappy and dank.

Peter commissioned the chief gardener to make him a *hortus siccus* – a dried garden, which was a book containing samples of as many plants as the maker could find or buy. Each cutting, flower, seed or sample was dessicated so that it would always look like it had looked when it was living, though it was dead. The dry samples were pressed so that they could be preserved in two dimensions, glued into the pages of the book. Peter bought more than six hundred samples, or so.

In the file on Peter the Great, I found more notes on Peter's stay – it got late and Peter slept the night on his boat, and stayed on in Leiden the next day. In the morning, in the dark before dawn, he and his entourage visited the surgeon and anatomist Frederik Ruysch.

When Ruysch had invited Peter Mikhailovich to make an appointment at his famous anatomy theatre, Peter had thanked him. How about an appointment at 5 a.m.? Peter had suggested.

It was cold and dark inside and out. The doctor's face was lit by a single candle which picked out the surfaces of his forehead, cheeks and chin. He lifted the sheet on the operating table to reveal the body of an executed criminal. He cut and peeled back the skin on the corpse.

Peter wrote down the names of the cords and tendons, veins and muscles which bunched and dispersed through the body, providing links like roads or canals from part to part. But some of his diplomats, who disapproved of the doctor's dark methods, muttered at the back, and Peter, hearing them, called them forward. He ordered them to bend down, so they could see the corpse close up. Then he ordered each of his disobedient subjects to take a tendon of human meat between his teeth and bite through it.

After the dissection Ruysch lit more candles to light a whole company of articulated bodies and parts of bodies. In glass jars on the shelves there were sliced penises, cross sections of babies' heads, fetuses and deformed births, and limbs suspended in alcohol dressed in lace and silk. Other organs were displayed by exposing the internal parts of real corpses so that inside became out, and outside in. In the half-light, the candelabra made the room look like a great feast or dance. The forms of unborn babies were decked with preserved flowers and bedded on cockleshells, like cornucopiae. Little boys and girls were dressed as dancing nymphs, hesitating between one step and the next.

The children didn't show any visible signs of sickness or degradation, or of the deprived lives of criminal poverty out of which they had come. Adult figures reclined around the room too; their cheeks had been tinted with colour to affect life. Peter Mikhailovich said it was like heaven. Ruysch lifted the linen sheet off the corpse of a pretty little blonde girl and Peter kissed her. Two decades later, in 1717, Tsar Peter purchased Ruysch's whole collection and had it shipped to St Petersburg, where many of the bodies are still on display today.

I don't remember being told about Frederik Ruysch by Jimmy. I think his stories about Peter's visit had ended in the botanical garden, and I had never heard of Ruysch until I read the post-humous notes. When I did, I felt slightly sick from the wax and toxic embalming fluids which Ruysch injected into the dried-out bodies, turning them into whatever shapes he wanted, swagging them on set stages and decorating them with peaches or sickly wax roses. It seemed a grim way to make a living, I thought, and the medical benefits were dubious.

I had never heard about Peter's stay in London from 1697, and I did not know, until I found the account at the end of the file, that Jimmy had ever written on it. It didn't surprise me though – he considered himself qualified to publish on anything, from Alexander the Great to the Great War. 'The present, when backed by the past, is a thousand times deeper than the present when it presses so close that you can feel nothing else.' The layers bring depth, like looking down into deep water.

That sense of depth did not seem to be in conflict with his conviction that historians were shallow people. Writers of fiction, he said, might strive to achieve some profound statement by inventing their unlikely dramas. But it is the historian's job to remember things on the simplest, shallow terms.

He told me about the accidents and disasters which happened while *Fitzcarraldo* was being shot – many members of the cast and crew came to think that the film was cursed.

Several people were injured, some seriously, in the attempt to move the giant boat from one part of the Amazon jungle to another. Werner Herzog himself has spoken about how the experience of growing up in Germany in the aftermath of the Second World War has affected the nature of the films he chooses to write and direct, but a group of activists went further, blaming all the accidents that happened on the set of *Fitzcarraldo* on the history of Herzog's nation – they showed the local people pictures of Auschwitz, as a warning. This is what Germans do, said the European activists to the Amazonians. That was the 1980s – Herzog, who was born in September 1942, was two when the war ended in Germany.

Herzog always maintained that he hadn't exploited the people he hired to work on *Fitzcarraldo*, nor did he damage the jungle in any lasting way: it is now difficult to tell where exactly it was filmed, as the trees felled from the river-bank to move the boat have been replanted and grown back. With hindsight, Herzog blamed the accidents and disasters that happened during the making of *Fitzcarraldo* on nature itself.

X

The paths of Peter Mikhailovich from Russia and William, King of England, converged when Peter came into London in disguise on a tide of rubbish, changing ships to board a waste-disposal barge at the mouth of the Thames so that he could slip into the city unseen. He came up the river on a windy morning, swinging like his pet monkey on the rigging, and from that vantage point he invited the leader of his welcome party, who was one of King William's naval admirals, to join him – the portly sexagenarian admiral declined – before climbing down and changing out of his sailor's kit into a long wig and a brown leather coat with two rows of silver buttons.

Peter's stay in London was well documented in spite, or because, of the fact that the embassy never officially visited England, but it's difficult to separate the real history from the anecdotes going round, which were recorded in most of the sources: gazettes, pamphlets, letters and private diaries, like the chronicle kept by Narcissus Luttrell, a London lawyer, whose journal of 1697 my grandfather drew on in his own historical notes. Many of these amateur historians dealt in hearsay and gossip – at times, in fact, it seems that they preferred exaggerated or wholly fabricated stories over the simple truth. The name Narcissus, Jimmy noted, was not as unusual then as it is now, although it would seem to imply vanity, and a failure to discriminate between reality and illusion. In fact, Luttrell must have been named after Narcissus Mapowder, his wealthy maternal grandfather, who was from Devon.

The two heads of state met at Peter's accommodation on Norfolk Street, but the visit started badly when Peter's pet monkey sprang out of a dark corner and made the king jump. One monarch, one emperor in disguise, two ambassadors and several house servants crowded the small room, and the air was made even more uncomfortably close by the piles of furs, greasy candles melting to puddles and smoky fires lit throughout the house, all of which created an atmosphere that was not good for William who was, like my grandfather and myself, asthmatic.

Peter proposed a toast to their respective healths but it was eleven in the morning so he had to take his glass of canary alone – William didn't drink during the day (the historians emphasise that he was a sensible man). Eventually the king couldn't stand it any longer and asked for the window to be opened. Peter, who was used to Russian housekeeping, and not familiar with the British mania for fresh air, was puzzled, but he went over to the window himself and pushed open the latticed pane. The small king followed and stood by the window in bright daylight which lit his pallid, gently sweating face. He laboured little draughts of air down his contracted windpipe. Peter's ambassadors looked on with an expression of contempt. This was the man who ruled this country. A wall of heat from the room hit a pile of snow on the window ledge and water dribbled down onto the carpets. The winter freeze had begun.

The river froze over completely that winter of 1697, although everyone said that this frost was not as bad as the frost of 1683, which is still the coldest on record in London. I remembered, looking through the notes, a story from that winter my grandfather had told me in which an English nobleman named Orlando fell in love with a Russian princess, Sasha, while skating on the Thames. It was so cold, Jimmy had told me, that birds fell out of the air like stones and people froze dead while crossing the road. It was not uncommon to come across whole crowds standing as still as the Chinese terracotta army. The landscape was like a Bruegel winter landscape; 'the fields were full of shepherds, ploughmen, teams of horses, and little bird-scaring boys all struck stark in the act of the moment, one with his hand to his nose, another with the bottle to his lips, a third with a stone raised to throw at the ravens who sat, as if stuffed, upon the hedge within a yard of him'. It was as though reality admitted defeat, conceding the only element of life that Bruegel's paintings had failed to capture – movement – and everyone stayed very still.

The writer and gardener John Evelyn described the same great freeze more animatedly. In fact, the way he had it, it sounded as if the city came to life when the river slowed to freezing: the Thames turned into a carnival and there were sledges, sliding with skates, bull-baiting and coaches plying for trade. Teams of horses galloped from the Temple to Westminster and back, drawing their passengers behind. There were puppet plays and interludes; cooks, tippling and other 'lewd activities', which Evelyn called a 'bacchanalia, Triumph or Carnoval on Water'.

But the carnival on the water was a severe judgement on the land, the trees not only splitting as if lightning-struck, but men and cattle 'perishing in divers places, and the very seas so lockt up with ice that no vessels could stir out or come in'. 'Great contributions,' wrote Evelyn, were needed just to keep the poor alive. Perhaps he was thinking of the hard winters, decades earlier, when three of his own children had died, including his eldest son Richard, whose death aged five Evelyn attributed in part to the frozen roads and river, which delayed the physicians' horses.

Evelyn listed his son's truly extraordinary capabilities, at the age of 'five years and three days' when he died – his knowledge of Latin and Greek, his understanding of Euclid and the testaments. He had read Aesop, and applied morals and fables in 'strange, apt and ingenious ways'.

'Thus God, having dressed up a saint fit for himself, would not longer permit him with us, unworthy of the future fruits of this incomparable hopeful blossom,' wrote Evelyn. 'From me he had nothing but sin.'

'Here ends the joy of my life, and for which I go even mourning to the grave,' Evelyn wrote in his diary on the day of Richard's burial in January 1658. The next month his youngest son died too. Evelyn lived for another forty-nine years.

He found a kind of consolation in his garden, which became a living archive of flowers, fruit, trees and shrubs. He experimented with medicinal herbs and exotics that were thought to have miraculous properties. He gathered samples of plants on his travels around Europe and later, when the garden became more famous, he received packets of seeds in the post. He grew flora from the Holy Land and the Garden of Eden. He began to compile a garden encyclopedia. He wrote a history of trees. Even after he had leased his home, Sayes Court, to long-term tenants, he returned regularly to Deptford, particularly during bad weather, to attend the infants and delicates. There are sad entries in his diary about their blasted twigs, and how the greens and the rare plants were the most susceptible to extreme cold. Whole parks of deer were destroyed in the frost, as were skies full of birds and lakes full of fish. His oranges and myrtle trees were sick; the scented rosemary and laurel dead 'to all appearance'. Perhaps he hoped that they would wake up, like hibernating animals or fairy-tale princesses, in spring. But when the thaw finally came, it only showed him what he had lost. 'All our exotic plants and greens,' he said, 'universally perishing.'

In the spring of 1683 he started replanting. Some of his plants grew back. By the time the ground froze again in 1697, much of the garden had again reached maturity. Luckily that winter was not as harsh, though the river still froze hard enough to be turned by coachmen into a false road.

Until the water broke back through the ice, Peter couldn't go out on the river as he wanted, so he had to kill time around town. Wherever he went the anonymous crowds followed in his footsteps. Throughout the winter of 1697–8, for as long as the freeze lasted, Peter's movements could be tracked through isolated accounts from different people who glimpsed him in different places. His activities can be retraced, my grandfather wrote, by putting the various accounts set down by diarists and gazetteers, who offered eyewitness accounts and second-, third- and fourth-hand stories they had by hearsay, back together.

On one of the first nights of his stay, a large crowd gathered outside his lodgings in Norfolk Street, past midnight, many of them slightly drunk. They pressed their heads against the windows and saw four men sitting at a table eating bread and beef. It was late to dine. One of the men inside looked up and saw the faces at the windows, then nudged and nodded at another who stood, shouting in Russian, and left the room, banging the door. The people in the street could hear feet stomping up the wooden stairs.

After that, Peter travelled with a wake of followers, amateur historians and journalists, wherever he was spotted. They stuck to the tail of his caravan along with his recent purchases. He was a keen shopper.

One day he was seen by a diarist at the printer's shop at Amen Corner, where he bought a new book. Then he walked towards Smithfield with his head in it until he stepped into a gutter channelling pigs' blood and dirty water across the pavement, put the book in his pocket for later and wiped his spoiled shoes clean with a cloth.

Another contemporary historian recorded his own visit to a cabinet of curiosities in Southwark which had been seen by Peter a few days earlier. The windows of the glass-fronted cabinets were sooted up with pollution from the air, and the servants had had to unlock the doors so that the objects inside could be seen. The owner of the collection was in the country, and one of his household servants acted as the curator. The historian picked up a snakestone, then an ostrich egg, then the skull of a raccoon. He thought, as he handled each small casket, how Peter's callused hands might have held them a few days before. The weight of each object was surprising – the egg was surprisingly heavy, like a stone, while the stone was surprisingly light, possibly full of air. The toothless skull weighed nearly nothing, as if it were made out of paper. The curator showed him a picture of the raccoon which he described as similar to a badger, but that it could jump through trees.

Among many hundreds of other things, some of which were listed in an inventory compiled by an anonymous Russian envoy, and published in Anthony Cross's *Peter the Great in England*, Peter bought a geographical clock; mathematical instruments; and a coffin, which was sent to Russia as a prototype for local carpenters. The planked box struck Peter as a very convenient way to contain dead bodies – at that time Russian coffins were whittled labour-intensively out of the trunks of whole trees.

At the Turk's Head a servant told a story about Peter's visit to William at Kensington Palace. The guest of honour seemed

uninterested in the food or the wine, the collection of paintings, the expensive decorations or the company. But he was
delighted by the king's mechanical wind dial. And above all,
there was nothing that pleased him so much as the engine with
a weighted cord which was used to open and close the curtains
in the salon. He lifted and dropped the curtains, twice. The
heavy brocade parted clear of the panes, opening. Darkness
had fallen, so the window did not reveal the outside world,
but gave the room back again, slightly blurred in the warped
glass: Peter, holding the cord; behind him the king, a smile
kept still on his lips, his fingers laced over his crotch; a row
of retainers along the back; two more servants at the doors.
Candelabra bracketed on the wall lit the scene. Peter revealed
and shrouded the reflection in the window again, and again.
Twenty times, in fact, while the others politely waited.

Peter was unwilling to descend among the crowds when he
visited Parliament, so he sat on the roof instead, and peered
comically into the House through a small window like a port-
hole. The Members laughed.

Later the same day, a crowd besieged a Smithfield trader's
shop during a carnival at which it was rumoured that Peter
Mikhailovich was dressed as a butcher with a borrowed cleaver,
borrowed leather apron and genuinely bloodstained hands.

The commoners in the crowd at Smithfield, as it turned out,
got closer to Peter's person than did the members of the English
nobility, who invited him to dine again and again. He refused
each invitation because he was not, officially, there. Frustrated
by the blanks, it was said that one duke, several lords and two
marquises went one evening to Peter's apartments wearing their
footmen's coats. Standing still, the disguised noblemen looked
very well turned out, but when they moved they gave themselves
away: the Russians noticed the slopping way one man poured
the wine and another lumbered about, clattering the tureen.

Peter Mikhailovich, who was, my grandfather said, himself 'a master of disguise', guessed the conspiracy. (Herodotus, Jimmy noted heavily significantly, used the same Greek word for mask as for face.) The noblemen were humiliated when the anecdote came out in public.

On another occasion, a different crowd gathered in Smithfield to watch a conjuror. The magician, a dwarf, had a tall mute as his assistant. The mute moved the equipment, and mimed surprised reactions to the tricks. It was whispered in the crowd that the mute was the tsar, and the dwarf was the tsar's dwarf. The dwarf pushed out a large coffin-like box on a stand with wheels, and the mute set up a little wooden free-standing ladder next to it. The mute got into the box. His head and feet came out of the open ends. The dwarf took out a set of large skewer-like swords and climbed the ladder. In time with the thunder and crashing of the three musicians below the stage, he drove one of the swords through his assistant's body. The mute pantomimed great agonies, moving his feet like flippers. The dwarf climbed down, moved the ladder a little, obtained another sword, remounted and skewered the body again, this time from a slightly different angle. Again the agonies, the ladder moved, another skewer. After several swords had been stuck through different parts of his body, from different perspectives, to the greatest drum roll, the mute was resurrected. He climbed easily out of the box and folded his lanky person in half to bow – his actual body was untouched.

Almost all the anecdotes about the Great Embassy in London date from the great freeze. When the ice broke up and the river began to flow freely, Peter disappeared again, so the histories stopped.

He wanted to be closer to the water, which was why he asked to leave Norfolk Street for a house near the shipyards, in Deptford or Greenwich. With the king's agreement it was arranged for John Evelyn's tenant, a man called Admiral Benbow, to move out of Sayes Court, so that Peter and some members of his embassy could move in.

Peter had his men knock a hole through the garden wall to act as a gateway into the shipyard next door, so his retinue could pass from the house to the docks without going out in public. Nonetheless he continued to make a spectacle of himself. When sailing on the river at Greenwich, he asked to take the tiller, then promptly crashed his boat, the *Charlotte*, into the nearby *Dove*.

The high walls of the garden and the dockyard were more efficient at hiding the tall Russian than any of his disguises. It was only after Peter had left London and returned to Russia, wrote Jimmy, that the most famous story about his stay came out.

The inventory drawn up by Sir Christopher Wren and the king's gardener, George London, described John Evelyn's house and gardens as they were discovered after Peter and his people had departed. 'Severall disorders,' it said, 'have been committed.' These disorders were given in a list, divided into two parts: 'those which can be repaired', and 'those which cannot be repaired'.

The house was covered with dirt and grease and the doors removed from the door frames. The delft tiles had been levered off the walls, much of the furniture had completely disappeared – perhaps fed into a stove – and even the flint and stone on the floor were cracked and wanted replacing. Paragon, damask, silk, calico, tapestry, camblett, feather pillows, plush cushions: stained, stolen, or otherwise spoiled. The damage done to chairs alone ran to a lengthy list. Several pieces of 'walnuttree' furniture, a brass hearth, fender irons, warming pans, bedsteads, carpets, dressing tables and cornices, all ruined. Peter was not a connoisseur of art, but he liked pictures of boats; pictures of boats had been stolen off the walls. In the windows three hundred individual panes of glass had been smashed.

It was in the garden, though, that Evelyn's greatest grief was buried. 'The Zar', as the inventory called him, suffered the pathways to lapse and the espaliers to become unpinned from the sunning walls. Branches had broken off the other trees; two or three of the phillereas were destroyed, as were several hollies and other fine plants. The vegetable beds were overgrown with weeds and had not been manured nor cultivated in the due season. The gravel walks were potholed, the wilderness went uncut, the lawn 'broke into holes by their leaping, and shewing tricks upon it' – one anecdote, to which Evelyn made an oblique reference in his history of trees, is that Peter Mikhailovich, who was unfamiliar with English household implements, held races in which he and his ambassadors took turns to sit in wheelbarrows and to drive them like chariots around the house, through the gardens, and into the holly or hornbeam hedge (this could have been painful for the passenger). 'Three wheelbarrows, broke and lost.'

'What Peter did should be praised by historians,' wrote my grandfather in his notes. Sometimes, he said, we can only see things properly from a certain distance, like Orlando, who only glimpsed Sasha's true nature once, the last time he ever saw her, looking across a wide stretch of water out to sea. Orlando's affair ended when the ice melted and he looked out – through the mouth of the Thames, across estuaries and past the coastline – to see his lover's ship was sailing, to his shock, back to Russia. Apparently she hadn't mentioned it. Orlando was so transfixed by the distant boat that he failed to see the crowds floating right past him down the river: poor people who had fallen asleep while shopping, drinking and dancing on the frozen Thames. They woke up to find the ground under them had dwindled to ice caps the size of a backyard, a bedstead, shrinking to the size of a coffin when the ice, getting smaller and smaller, turned to water and drifted unstoppably out to the rising sea.

History, my grandfather wrote, is the study of missing things. 'It seems unlikely that we would have so precise a list of what was growing in Evelyn's garden if it had not been destroyed.'

After I locked myself out I waited in the car for twenty minutes or so before it occurred to me to visit William. He had invited me, leaving a half-frozen pheasant in a Tesco bag on the doorstep when I arrived, with a note: 'Come over, Will' – but I would have gone anyway. He lived in a house at the crossroads which was called Galley Gap because it was where the gallows hung until the end of the nineteenth century. The gallows had been there because of its prominent position – you could see the top of the hill for miles around – so the hanged men hung as a warning to the rest.

Will's beard had been red, and his newly white hair made his freckles jump out. He claimed not to know how old he was, but my grandmother always said that his birth in 1926 had been recorded, as well he knew, in the book at the cottage hospital which is now the old people's home, where my great-great-uncle, the previous occupant of the farm, had also been born. I always thought of William as a kind of wild man when I was little, when I used to stump around after him, wrongly thinking that I was helping him do his jobs around the farm. With his beard and the dialect which was arcane even then – he sometimes thee'd and thou'd – I didn't know his language until after I'd started school.

When I arrived and he came out of his house I felt apprehensive about what we would talk about, and London and academia and my grown-up life seemed sort of absurd; suddenly I was a lady.

There was a pile of bones crumbling apart at the joints stacked against the wall of his house, almost the same colour as the chalky stone blocks out of which the house was built and they, too, seemed to be crumbling away. I recognised two sheep skulls and several jawbones – trophies, I supposed, from the same long walk over the same fields every day for years. 'I don't like to see them rubbished,' he said, seeing me looking. He carried on up ahead. 'I can't go stopping and starting, I've two new knees.'

When I took off my boots at the porch I felt even more awkward in my socks. Perhaps he realised, because he put the radio on, Classic FM, when I came into the gloomy kitchen and the sound made us seem less alone together.

In the room he had one small table with one chair and one grimy window above the sink. The hill filled the view. There was a television on the kitchen counter, another facing it on a trunk in the corner, and a plinthed hi-fi system which I recognised – it looked dated now, but had been the first CD player owned by anyone I knew. He said he only had a six-CD Beethoven for the first year or so (and when he spoke about it he accented it, of course, like *sugar beet*).

He took two mugs down from the dresser, which were next to a framed photograph of two grouse on a moor. They were facing one another with tails up; fighting or courting. The photograph, which I had seen before, had been taken by my grandmother.

A jar of sugar went on the table and I was instructed to fetch spoons They were lying in a sheaf on the board, apparently unused, each one in a dusty clear-plastic slip. The music swelled and he had to raise his voice to ask whether the farm had been sold yet.

I told him it had not and he nodded. He probably had the sense, as long-time employees do, that he knew his workplace better than the boss. He probably did. 'It's in a bit of a mess,' was his sagacious explanation.

'Why did she let the farm go?' I didn't hesitate to ask him about the debts, assuming that he knew about it all already.

My assumption was right, and he didn't need much prompting. He should by rights, according to my impression of him, have been a taciturn man, but he was not. When he went up and down the field in the combine harvester, his mind must have been chugging with thoughts. When he was chopping wood round the side of the barn, he was otherwise occupied: forming opinions. William was a great holder of opinions and they all came out sooner or later like grain out of the harvester, like logs out of the sack.

He started long before the beginning. My grandfather, he told me, arrived at the farm in mid-August – they were doing the hay – and came into the village pub still in his funeral suit. He walked up to the tenant farmer without introducing himself and said: 'I'll want you out.' It was a proper farm at that time.

Jimmy had never lacked a sense of entitlement, and it was not difficult to imagine how he would have taken to his new position as if he had always expected it, in spite of the fact that he had never even met the relative who left him the farm, and the bequest was as good as a fairy tale. I could picture his arrival: a big group of them in the yard at the White Horse under a moon like a pink lace doily and my grandfather, a short graduate student in a hired black suit, stepping trimly out of the pub back door.

Will went on for a while about the excellence of the tenant farmer – good tidy man, took out all the hedges – and I'd drunk half my tea before my grandmother came back onto this historical-pastoral scene. It was my grandfather, he said, who had run the farm into the ground and Liv had kept up the garden, mended the fences, had the little barn re-roofed, and so on, or so he said, 'And she's up and down the roof like like a monkey while they're at it.' You would not, by the way, catch him doing that. That was in the beginning.

Then, sometime after the children were born, my grandfather ordered it all to stop. Jimmy had decided that nature would take its course. Let time have its way, he said.

Will thought it was money worries that had my grandfather stopping any work on the house and garden (Jimmy, he pointed out, was a Scotsman's name). The house fell slowly into disrepair. Liv fought to get things done, but he refused at every turn. She kept on with the animals because the animals paid for themselves, but she had no other income of her own.

'Of course, he keeps the purse strings in that desk of his.'

'Kept,' I said stupidly. There was an awkward pause. 'But it's always been a mess,' I said.

'No. She kept it very well in the beginning. You're only going back as far as you go back yourself. The world existed before you were born.'

He paused, lost in thought for once. I wondered whether he would go on, but he changed the subject. 'There's a woman calling you,' he said. 'She's after putting a bench in your low field for her sister's dying of a heart condition. She'll want to speak to you, so you know.'

I was annoyed with him for being embarrassed, and I do not like those benches. Silence fell. He shrugged defeatedly. 'I told her it wouldn't get any rest down there anyway. Kids.'

I said that the woman should speak to my uncle. Then the phone rang in my pocket – it was the locksmith, he was five minutes away.

Before I went Will disappeared into the other room. I drained my mug, and several rings of stains revealed themselves below the waterline: strata of historical teas.

He came back with a piece of paper in his hand, triumphant. 'That's your evidence,' he said, pleased with himself, 'if you don't believe me.'

It was a photograph, in colour but slightly faded – late 1960s or 1970s, I would have guessed – and showed the farm from the back garden, which extended into what is now the field behind, looking more like an allotment in the picture. Rows of small indistinguishable fruit trees, wigwams of beanpoles, literally hundreds of cabbages, lines of potatoes in neat rectangular thickets, rows and rows of vegetables (leek, beetroot or carrot) spiking out of the ground, and tufts where the lettuce would come up. It must have been late spring or early summer. Sweet peas were out but there was some blossom yet on the trees.

The house and farm buildings looked dinky and smart: rows of neat bright tiles on the roofs of all the barns. The hedges were trimmed and there were no ivies or creepers on the walls. Even the brickwork looked clean.

I was backing round in the yard when Will leaned in and tapped on the window. I wound it down. 'Brenda's calling you about that bench,' he said, 'so you know who it is.' I nodded and put the engine in gear so that he would move back from the car, and I could get off.

From the crest of the hill I could see the locksmith's neon orange van parked in the stackyard, standing out against the snow (though it would have stood out against anything). The locksmith broke the lock and let me back in, then he mended it, then I paid him an extraordinary amount of money, including an extra charge for 'inclement weather call-out', and he left.

It was getting dark outside and some of the windowpanes beside my desk were already growing frames of frost that looked like fine hair.

It was hard to tell whether William was telling the truth, because he had always been on my grandmother's side. Jimmy used to call him Man Friday, or Gabriel Oak: it was supposed to be insulting, both to Will and to Liv. I do not know the precise nature of their relationship.

It was cold, sitting still, so I wrapped a shawl around, then went back to the papers and looked through them a second time. I wanted to find the inventory of the damage done to John Evelyn's garden. Eventually I found the transcript, which had been published in *Notes and Queries* in 1956, but the search terms I typed in diverted me to a blog on seed banks which sent me, via a series of links, to an interview with a researcher from a Climate Change Institute at a university in the United States, who was talking about an ice archive.

xii

The researchers took samples of tundra from Greenland, throughout the Himalayas and the Tibetan plateau, Iceland, New Zealand, from Tierra del Fuego and across the Andes, the North-West Territories, Alaska, and on the Svalbard Islands near the so-called Doomsday Seed Bank, which aimed to store, underground in the ice, seeds and samples from every plant on the planet, in case of environmental catastrophe elsewhere. A single core from the Greenland site took three summers to locate and another five to drill – the researchers could only work there in summer, when the climate was mild and the winter ice dissipated. Once in the lab, they analysed these extracted ancient cores. They were hunting for physical evidence, in the ice, of the climate in the past.

The picture accompanying the interview, which had not come out very clearly on the site, showed a man in a fur-edged hood standing before narrow cylinders of snow which were balanced between shelving units like unpromising bridges. A team of scientists, headed by this man, had perfected the measurement of time. In his own experience, a single year measured two centimetres in the ice from the interior of Antarctica but spanned eight metres in New Zealand. The last few months could run to several precise millimetres holding their content (minerals and detritus) more perfectly than any human memories, which submerge elements of each event as soon as they pass.

These days, the melting strata were revealing artefacts from human civilisations stretching thousands of years back – as the tundra retreats, flints, clothing and the bodies of the hunter-gatherers themselves are revealed in the upper strata in Norway and Siberia. They degenerate very quickly under the sun, once released from the surface snows.

But those artefacts were the preserve of archaeological historians, the scientist explained. He and his team were extracting uncontaminated cores of ice, whose contents could be read like a tree ring: samples of ice could be selected from each overlaid storey by vintage. Ming, Biblical, Palaeolithic.

In the laboratory the ice core was melted, with the material at the centre of the core siphoned for analysis. Other parts of it, unneeded, were stored for later use. Those pristine cores, which could not be replaced, were archived in sub-zero underground storage facilities. But this was not the case for those cores which had been contaminated by contact with modern machinery during extraction. The interviewer asked the researcher what happened to these useless cores of ice, which had been taken out at exorbitant cost in money, effort and time, to reveal the past, but had been contaminated by the present, and he replied, 'We drink it.'

The interviewer then asked the researcher what it felt like to take tens of thousands of years-old ice into his own body. He asked what it tasted like, and the researcher did not have to think at all before replying. 'Clean,' he said. 'It tastes about as clean as anything can taste. It tastes very, very clean.'

I tried to stuff a load of rubbish down in the bin bag, and dropped all the documents so that they scattered out on the floor. One piece of screwed-up paper bounced across the room and began to open again, unfolding in starts. I noticed that my grandfather had drawn, on what I'd thought was the back, some notes on Antoni van Leeuwenhoek, and an enlarged freehand copy of the picture of a sperm cell, which had been published in 1684, and was drawn by one of Leeuwenhoek's former students.

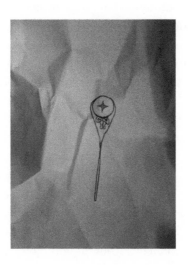

Jimmy had made notes on Leeuwenhoek's letters about sperm, in which he, Leeuwenhoek, took pains to assert that the sperm he inspected came from lawful intercourse – his own, with his wife – and was not sinful waste. A single cell, which he called an eel – he seems to have called quite a few things eels – looked like a leviathan through Leeuwenhoek's lens. He described how the world appeared to a bacterium between the teeth and from within an insect's jaws: his first publication in the Royal Society's Philosophical Transactions, in 1673, was titled 'Observations on the mouth-parts of a bee'.

He thought that whole men, in some strange form, were compacted inside every sperm cell, and he thought at times that he could pick out heads, shoulders or knee joints. Leeuwenhoek was drawn into debate with other 'preformationists', as they were known, who believed that the genesis of the human race began not in Adam's sperm but in Eve's ovaries, into which were packed – so these people thought – an infinitely diminishing series of homunculi.

Leeuwenhoek's eyesight, in combination with his microscopes, was outstanding, but nonetheless, something in the shapes and shadows he was looking at must have suggested a ballasted baby, like this one, with joints, tiny hands, and what looked like a large unknit fontanelle. The diagram shows the shape of the sperm, so the artist must have seen it – but his imagination or his memory supplied something else too. Leeuwenhoek was the first person to see the sperm cell, but he changed it when he looked at it.

Today, with more powerful microscopes, everyone has seen transmitted images of spermatozoa and we know that there is no whole baby curled inside its capital any more than there is a tiny oak inside every cracked acorn. So it was one thing for Leeuwenhoek, the first man to see the single sperm cell, to imagine the 'animalcule', but it was quite another for my grandfather to reproduce the picture. It was as if he too could change it just by looking at it. He believed that the human body was an ark, or archive, containing other minute species, but also its own kind.

'We are all his descendants,' he wrote with confidence. Not only Cain and Abel, but also Anne, Mary and Jesus; Peter the Great; Antoni van Leeuwenhoek; the Swedish sentry and the Livonian peasants; Timothy Treadwell, the original Fitzcarraldo, Werner Herzog; the two dark figures in the picture of Riga, the two dark figures in the painting of Delft; my grandfather Jimmy and myself, and you too, and so on.

iii Olaudah Equiano

i

Olaudah Equiano came up one evening when we were
walking along the field nearest the house, checking
the magpie traps. It was early summer and I should
have been studying for my GCSEs.

The traps were chicken-wire boxes with one side hinged.
We laid them by nesting a blown egg in the bottom, placed
carefully so you couldn't see, from the air, the pinhole through
which Jimmy had emptied the contents. Next to the egg we
leaned a fragile twig which propped up the lid. When the
magpie flew in for the egg, he or she knocked the twig and
the lid fell down.

I was impressed by how well the traps were hidden in the
long grass and cow parsley along the hedge, and I couldn't
help feeling sorry for the birds, who spotted the tiny chipped
blue egg from so high in the sky. They were alive and noisy
when we found them, not only black and white, close up, but
shiny pink, purple, blue and green, like spilt petrol on their
wings.

I once asked if I could keep a magpie as a pet. 'You
could,' Jimmy agreed, 'if you lived in the fourteenth century
– they called them pies at that time.' No opportunity for
historical instruction was wasted. Young ladies kept pet
magpies or starlings in cages; some taught them to talk. Pets

were taken to church on Sundays, in those days, if the local priest didn't mind. Together we summoned an imaginary church with a congregation of sight-hounds, falcons, jays and lapdogs.

The magpie was a bad-luck bird, according to Jimmy. Nonetheless he enjoyed telling generations of its myths, as he wrung an unlucky neck by holding the head and letting the body turn when he flicked his wrist. Ovid called the magpie a scandalmonger. Not black like Noah's raven, nor white like Noah's dove, the magpie was the only creature to refuse the offer of safe passage on the ark, preferring instead to sit on the top of the mast, flying off every now and then and chattering complainingly.

Sometimes we caught crows, rooks or ravens which my grandfather hung on the hedge with baler twine as a warning to the rest. There were other traps, designed for rabbits, foxes and moles, on other parts of the land, but we weren't bothering with them that day.

The magpie traps had been made by Will on Jimmy's instructions, according to Jimmy himself. I followed in his tracks through the long grass when we walked up the field. He was explaining the mechanism, which turned into telling me about his interest in the construction of contraptions, which brought him to Thomas Newcomen's steam engine (his achievement much eclipsed by Stephenson's Rocket), the Industrial Revolution and the followers of Ned Lud. He talked about Thatcher and the miners, 'like your friend Douglas'.

Doug Pugh was a Glaswegian who came to our village at the end of the 1980s after losing his job down a mine near Doncaster some years earlier. Like all the miners who had been laid off and lived locally, his former occupation warranted him a kind of mythic heroic status, and a small amount of shift work in the bacon factory. Eventually he married and settled and took over the lease on the local pub, so Jimmy was one of his greatest patrons, but nonetheless Douglas was always 'my friend' because he had been invited to speak at my primary school once, seven or eight years earlier, and Jimmy did not forget.

Douglas had been thinner then, but he was already large, wearing a shirt and tie under his denim jacket, and sat cautiously, shifting, on the corner of the teacher's table which bent noticeably under his bulk. The class heard how generations of the same families had worked together, and how he used to wash in a special shower at the end of the day. Until then, the miners we had learned about at school were nineteenth-century miners. Their wives wore mob caps, their children went crawling up the tunnels; eventually Lord Shaftesbury rescued them with his reforms. Doug began by telling us about the closure of the pits, and how the jobs, which had, in some families, been held for generations, were ultimately replaced by machines and cheap labour in other parts of the world.

'Of course,' said Jimmy slyly, 'none of this would have happened without the Industrial Revolution, which was itself brought about by the rise and fall of the transatlantic trade in slaves' – and so he rounded the subject neatly back to my own historical education: at that moment I should have been revising for my history paper.

'You've certainly afforded yourself a very elevated perspective,' was his verdict on the pictures in my schoolbooks, and he was right. The first image, 'The Slave Triangle', imagined us looking down on the earth from space. Three arrows over the Atlantic traced the clockwise rotation of slave ships between England, the Americas and the African coast.

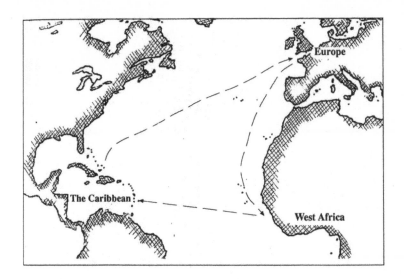

The image printed on the next leaf was also famous: the plan of the slave ship with the deck taken off, and bodies of men and women packed up against one another. A bird's-eye view, looking down on the ship's ballast. The slaves were packed so tightly that you couldn't see how they could survive the crossing.

As we walked through the top fields, my grandfather explained why he didn't like those stock images: the scale is too large, and the pictures tend to reproduce details with which the viewer is already familiar.

The real memories of real slaves, he said, were not like that. For one thing, they couldn't see everything at once. He referred to letters and memoirs of former slaves like Ignatius Sancho, Quobnah Ottobah Cugoano, Mary Prince and Olaudah Equiano, who wrote an autobiographical history of his own abduction in which he described himself standing on deck, aged eleven (he wasn't packed into the hold like in the

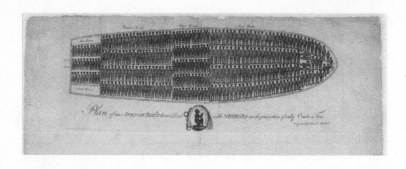

picture), while his ship pulled out of the slave port, and his 'swimming eyes' crossed the increasing distance of water to look back at the coastline. Equiano described the stifling lack of fresh air below deck. Infants fell into the 'necessary' troughs, some drowning, others dying a few days later from disease. He described the capture of one of the sharks that followed the slave ships in hope of bodies thrown overboard – the slavers sliced off a small part of its tail, then cast it back into the water so that it lost the ability to steer itself and would die slowly.

Olaudah Equiano also wrote about his early life in Africa, before he came to America, before he boarded the slave ship. His tribe, the Igbo, come from modern-day Nigeria, but historians have been unable to locate the valley he came from, which he called Essaka. When he was kidnapped he did not know where he was being taken other than that it was in the direction of the sunset – back in time. 'I had observed that my father's house was towards the rising of the sun.'

While he was still in Africa he escaped from the slavers and hid in the local woods, which were 'so thick, that a man could readily conceal himself in them, so as to elude the strictest search'. But when he heard the cries of the wild beasts, 'I began to consider that, if possibly I could escape all other animals,

I could not those of the human kind; and that not knowing the way, I must perish in the woods [. . .] Thus was I like the hunted deer.'

Back at the beginning of the narrative was his early life among his own tribe. Essaka was described as a kind of Eden – 'a charming fruitful vale'. Throughout West Africa, 'pomkins', eadas, yams, pineapples, peppers and other fruit grew 'to an incredible size'. Michel Adanson, a French naturalist travelling in Senegal, described how the Africans lived a life of 'ease and indolence' under the shade of their spreading trees.

Elsewhere, Equiano said that his tribe lived like the Patriarchs when they were in 'that pastoral state' described in the Book of Genesis, and he traced the genealogy of his people back to the Bible. Abraham was the 'original' ancestor.

Equiano could not, he admitted, help adding details to the history of his childhood in Africa. 'I hope the reader will not think I have trespassed on his patience in introducing myself to him with some account of the manners and customs of my country.' He recorded the fact that his tribe were very clean – they washed before every meal, he said, and the women purified themselves monthly. Everyone in his tribe had the same favourite colour – blue – and when the men and women went out on the land to sow and harvest the crops the village seemed empty, but the trees were full of children who climbed up to wait for their parents to return.

He recalled that the tribe rarely ate meat, and contrary to widely held belief in England at that time, they never ate human flesh. To speak the name of the tribe's God was to pollute it, so that name was never said aloud. Priests were known as 'calculators'. The houses, or huts, had no windows, just openings for a chimney and a door. Chickens went freely in and out. Equiano recounted the veneration of local snakes, which he described vividly: they were as thick as a man's leg, and the colour of a dolphin in the water, and each one 'crowed like a cock'. These snakes crept into his mother's house at night, he said, and the wise men told him to touch them.

Equiano, the former slave and author of an autobiography entitled *The Interesting Narrative of Olaudah Equiano, written by Himself,* was the main subject of the third file in my grandfather's bureau. The notes in this file, which dealt with the end of the Slave Trade and the beginnings of the Industrial Revolution, were less fluent than were the notes on the Wars of the Roses or the Great Embassy, which seemed to suggest that Jimmy wrote them after the other two. (This would also make chronological sense.) There were some disorganised notes mixed in which related to other things.

The brief biography which Jimmy wrote gave the following information.

Olaudah Equiano was surprised by the sound a watch made, the first time he saw one in the big house on the plantation. 'I was afraid it would tell the gentleman any thing I might do amiss.' There was a portrait hanging in the same room, 'which appeared constantly to look at me, and not seeing it move, I thought it might be some way the whites had to keep their great men when they died'.

At that time he was eleven. He had been kidnapped and brought to America from his home beyond the Guinea coast, with nothing on him except his name. The slave owners changed his name to Michael, then Jacob, then Gustavus Vassa.

Vassa spent much of his life on the water. After some time at different plantations he joined the navy, at first, when he was still a boy, as a slave. Arriving in England in Falmouth, at the age of twelve, in 1757, he was 'very much struck' by the stone buildings and the stone pavement of the streets. One morning he came up on deck and saw snow. He was 'surprised beyond measure' when told to take up a handful and taste it. He had thought it was salt.

He husbanded his stocks and collected small amounts of savings until he could afford to buy his liberty, and made over the right money – everything he had – to his English master, Captain Pascal, on whose boat, the *Industrious Bee*, Equiano had sailed. Pascal took the money, then kidnapped Equiano and sold him back to sea again as a slave. It was Pascal, too, who changed the boy's name from Jacob to Gustavus Vassa, after the Swedish prince who led the slaves to victory over their oppressors (it was quite common at that time for slaves to be given ironic names like 'Caesar', just like humans today give domestic pets names like Rover or Prince).

As an enslaved sailor he fought in many engagements at sea. At that time he thought he would probably die in battle, as his job was to run the length of the deck unprotected, along the line of fire, carrying spilling gunpowder (the storage crates had rotted) on his back. Other men fell, thickly, both behind him and before, and he comforted himself with the thought that he would be able to tell the story to the Misses Guerin, two Quaker sisters who had once been kind to him, at his master's house in London, if he survived.

After another skirmish he and his mates blew up their own boats, which were called the *Ocean* and the *Redoubtable*, rather than allow those vessels to fall into French hands. The view at midnight, when the *Ocean* exploded, was 'most dreadful. I never beheld a more awful scene.' The noise was louder and more terrible than thunder and the flames illuminated the midnight dark with a false light as if in the middle of night they were in day. Equiano hung over the gunwale to watch the ships burning in the distance. At the dark end of the deck he could see another, smaller light, which an Amazonian sailor, keeping watch, was using to attract insects, which he suffocated between his hands, then chewed slowly.

Gustavus grew up. He shot alligators in Georgian swamps, survived several burning boats and witnessed unsurpassable cruelties towards slaves in Jamaica and Nevis. He sailed round the world. He lived through two shipwrecks and several small miracles like that of the sailor who went blind, which must have been God's punishment, Equiano said, for a man who had often 'd----d his own eyes'.

He worked and saved until he could buy freedom a second time, then returned to London, arriving at Cherry-Garden Stairs in Greenwich in 1767. He visited old friends, supporters and abolitionists including the Guerin sisters. One day he was out in Greenwich Park, walking with some friends, when he saw Captain Pascal. He was immediately seized with a kind of panic, not knowing whether to approach or leave.

The captain held a weird, unfathomable power over Vassa for the rest of his life. Even as Equiano, in his commentary, he admitted that he didn't understand the hold Captain Pascal held over him. The former slave approached his former master walking in the park and Pascal was extremely surprised to see him, though not nearly as shaken by the encounter as Vassa. Pascal had not expected the young man, whom he had twice bought and sold as a slave, to return to London, and asked him how he had come back; Vassa said 'in a ship'; the captain replied drily, 'I suppose you did not walk back to London on the water.'

Vassa then decided to quit the sea and to train as a hairdresser (he doesn't fully explain this career move). He learned hairdressing quickly and found work in 1768 with Dr Charles Irving of Pall Mall who was famous for developing a desalination process. 'Here I had plenty of hair-dressing to improve my hand.' Vassa didn't like to be idle so he was pleased to spend his days arranging the wigs and dressing the arrangements that were done in the doctor's household. Irving was kind and good-tempered and he encouraged the young man to continue with his studies in the evening. Vassa lived in a court near Covent Garden, where the other residents taught him arithmetic, 'alligation', and how to play the French horn, which was an instrument Captain Pascal had picked out for him many years earlier, but which he had not had occasion to learn before. 'I took great delight in blowing on this instrument,' he wrote.

During the summer of 1768, he had a recurrent dream that the liquid in his veins was not blood but salt water. The worst of these dreams turned into nightmares in which the kind doctor was in the process of leeching his employee's blood by way of his patented desalination process. Vassa requested permission to be dismissed. He wanted to return to the sea.

He went down to Deptford and Greenwich again and at the docks he found a captain named John Jolly whose boat was bound for Italy and Turkey. Happily, Jolly was looking for a sailor who could dress hair.

They sailed to France, then down through the Archipelago to Smyrna, which Vassa found surprisingly ancient. The houses were all built of stone, and many of them had graves attached to them so that the whole city seemed to be a churchyard. Good wine was less than a penny a pint; the huge fruits – melon, pomegranate, grape – were the finest he had ever tasted; the fat of the lambs was rich and white. Every woman was habited as if she had been widowed on her wedding day, for they were all veiled in black silk from head to foot.

In May 1769, the ship went out again to Oporto, where she was searched by the Inquisition during a carnival in the city. Thirty-six religious laws were issued to the sailors, with heavy penalties for the breaking. They sailed home with a ballast of wine, then returned to the Mediterranean, where Vassa saw Naples, which was an unusually clean city. Fountains stood at every intersection and water streamed down the sloped streets for thorough flushing. In Naples Vassa saw two great dramas: an opera and an eruption of Vesuvius 'of which I had a perfect view. It was extremely awful.'

After surviving several shipwrecks and burning boats, alligators, sharks, the Portuguese Inquisition and a thwarted expedition to the Pole; after training as a hairdresser, mastering the French horn and officiating once, out of necessity, as a parson at a funeral ceremony, Vassa decided to write some memoirs, which he published under his reclaimed African name, Olaudah Equiano.

When he got free, Equiano spent most of the rest of his life on an extended humanitarian campaign which took the form of a lifelong book tour, promoting the *Interesting Narrative*. He travelled all over England and Ireland on an unruly, logistically inconvenient course between Bristol, Hull, Edinburgh, Glasgow, York, Southampton, Dublin, Birmingham, Cambridge and elsewhere. The point of the tour was to attract subscribers to the book, but also to tell people about the lives of the unseen labourers manufacturing the materials and products consumed in the Western world.

Equiano asked people to boycott West Indian exports, and cited the ship *Trusty*, lately sent to Sierra Leone, the free colony, with aid for former slaves. Instead of human bodies it was ballasted with 1,300 pairs of shoes. Instead of gunpowder,

Equiano suggested, other boats could send flour; instead of guns, farming tools or other implements of husbandry.

The tour was a success and the names of hundreds of men and women were added to the subscription list with each new edition, including the name of one woman, Susanna Cullen, who subscribed to the third edition of the *Narrative,* probably after Equiano visited Cambridgeshire in 1789. The Cullens were an old Cambridgeshire family, modest but respectable, my grandfather said. Susanna, who lived with her parents in Ely, was thirty years old when she subscribed.

As a historian, my grandfather found the *Narrative* interesting because Equiano saw everything from the outside: a watch, a Quaker meeting, a snowfall, an iron muzzle fitted on a house-keeper's face, a pomegranate, an opera, an eruption of Vesuvius. 'Their houses were built with stories,' he wrote, when he saw a tall brick building. He described them as an outsider – as someone who sees everything as if for the first time. This was like Ignatius Sancho, also a former slave, who described his own first sight of the sea at the point of his arrival as a little boy in chains at the slave port, where he saw the slave ships that would presently bear him away, and spoke of them as 'houses which walk upon the water with wings to them'.

Behind the biographical notes in the file was a short book with a yellow cover. *The Igbo Culture of Olaudah Equiano*, by Dr Catherine Obianuju Acholonu, lecturer in English at the Alvan Ikoku College of Education, was published by AFA Publications in 1989. The imprint gave a PO Box in Owerri, Nigeria, as its address.

Dr Acholonu begins by thanking a man who must be her husband. 'Dr Brendan Douglas Chidozie Acholonu,' she writes, 'I owe you not only my profound gratitude, but especially my deep-felt apology: a woman with the load of Destiny on her head, born to serve not ONE but ALL, could she be the country's best housewife? Thank you for all your patience and your kind heart. Forgive me for all the financial and other resources that I pump into academics. I cannot do otherwise – it is my destiny.' From this acknowledgements page it was clear to me that this was not the kind of history book my grandfather could have written.

Dr Acholonu also remembers by name all the people who helped complete this work of historical research – not only her husband, her patrons, supervisors, and friends, but also a technical crew, and Miss Christy Agoha, 'my patient secretary', who completed all the typing single-handedly. Overleaf, the introduction gives Catherine Acholonu's own autobiography at full pelt on a page and a half, from her birth in Orlu, eastern Nigeria, through her family, upbringing, marriage, emigration, children, education at Düsseldorf University, first encounter with Equiano's *Interesting Narrative*, papers given, more children, doctorate, her research interests, her other books – nine plays, six collections of poetry with epic titles like 'Other Forms of Slaughter', 'Mother was a Great Man' and 'They Lived Before Adam' – and the five languages she spoke and probably still speaks – I think she is still alive. As Equiano did at the beginning of his *Interesting Narrative*, Dr Acholonu also explains the meanings of her own names for readers who are not familiar with her culture or native language. The printer must have been out of capital 'I's at the time the preface was printed, because each 'I', in this introduction, is an 'l'.

Funded only by herself and her supportive husband, Dr Acholonu followed the route of rivers described in Equiano's memoir, and conducted an investigation into the development of native lexemes and phonemes reported in his *Interesting Narrative*. She travelled across several modern West African nations, where she discovered strong resemblances between

Equiano's portrait and living members of one particular tribe, descending, in the family tree she drew, to living relatives called Innocent, Fidelis and Oliver.

The body of the book is an account of Dr Acholonu's attempts to follow in the footsteps of Equiano – or rather, to follow his footsteps in reverse, back towards his origins in a tribe and a village in modern-day Benin, where she interviewed elders. The resulting transcripts, which were published as a series of audio, visual and textual documents, turned back to the beginnings of Equiano's life. In her book Acholonu seems to speak from within these cultures, genuflecting to the chiefs, and speaking local idiom. 'Igwe e e!' she responded, in delight (in the transcript) when congratulated by one tribal elder on the accomplishments of her research which were, he said, miraculous. The same tribal elder also remarked on the colonial British government's mishandling of native languages. They 'wrote many words in funny ways', he said, laughing.

As we walked back down to the house – no magpies that day – my grandfather told me the story about Equiano's expedition to the Arctic.

When Vassa boarded a war sloop on 24 May 1773, Jimmy said, the first thing he did was look for a bit of private space. The sailors, among whom was a nineteen-year-old called Horatio Nelson, slept in hammocks below deck, and the boat was stocked from rib to keel for the expedition. The sailors had packed themselves neat and close so that there was no spare space behind the chests in which Vassa could fit a stool and writing board. In the end he was forced to clear himself a small area hidden in the middle of the towers of boxes in the small cabin in which they kept the explosives. It was here, between crates of gunpowder, that he kept his journal.

Vassa's boat, which was sponsored by Baron Mulgrave, was

called the *Race Horse*. The accompanying sloop was called the *Carcass*. Gustavus Vassa does not appear in the ship's muster book; however, there is a 28-year-old man called Gustavus Weston, which was probably an approximation of his name. People were not so particular, in those days, about who they were.

They set sail to the north-east. Two nights into the expedition, when Vassa was writing in his diary, he took the candle out of the lantern to trim the wick, a spark tripped out and the rest caught. A minute later the whole cabin was on fire.

Equiano burned himself. His shirt and the handkerchief he had tied round his neck were on fire when he got out of the cabin, and he was smothered by the thick white smoke still pouring from under the door, like water, out into the hold. He raised the alarm but he thought that the ship was already lost, and waited for a bigger explosion.

The other sailors managed to put out the flames with wet blankets and mattresses. The journal survived. The captain told Vassa he had better not write in it any more, but Vassa found he couldn't stop.

The days lengthened, then night stopped altogether before they came in sight of Greenland. On 20 June they began to use Dr Irving's desalination apparatus. 'I frequently purified from twenty-six to forty gallons a day,' said Equiano, with characteristic precision.

The sun hung over the horizon at midnight, then rose again. The air got very cold. The boat passed towers of floating ice. Leviathans came up close and blew white fountains several metres into the air.

In a sequence that sounds surreal, Equiano described a vast herd of what he calls 'sea horses' galloping towards the ship. They neighed, according to Equiano, 'exactly like any other horses'. The sailors fired harpoons into the water but every one missed. One of these strange creatures rested on an iceberg as the boat passed by and a member of Vassa's crew shot at it. The sea horse, neither horse nor fish, dropped into the water and resurfaced with a gang of others, which attacked the boat and nearly overturned it. The sailors wounded some but captured none.

The strange animal which Equiano described cannot have been the small elegant marine creature which is now known as a sea horse – the animal which attacked his boat was too large, and sea horses do not, in any case, live in Arctic salt water. Perhaps the thing which Olaudah came upon here, at the edge of the human world, was the imaginary being which was entered by Jorge Luis Borges into his *Book of Imaginary Beings*, but also in the *Oxford English Dictionary*, where it is referred to as 'a fabulous horse-like marine creature' made of the upper part of a horse and the lower part of a huge fish, like a dolphin or shark with scales.

According to legend these mythical sea horses can inter-breed with land horses – real horses – to produce exceptionally beautiful dark ponies spotted with scales like occasional leaves of silver in their hide. The legends do not stipulate whether the cross-breed is real, like one parent, or imaginary, like the other, or whether, if the cross-breed is selectively bred with land horses over generations, their genetic composition eventually becomes dominated by the land horse's code, so that they become real. The creatures Equiano described might also have been walruses, according to the dictionary.

A few days after Greenland, the boat came to 'one compact impenetrable body of ice', where it 'stopt'. The captain decided that they had better turn and sail along the rim of this body, but his plan failed. The ship went deeper towards the uniform plain of ice which was broken only by the horizon. The ice pack was large, and growing.

The crew moored the boat on a floating piece of ice while they decided what to do. As discussions went on, Vassa measured that ice as one of his daily data-gathering exercises. In his journal, he recorded the coordinates of the boat, and the size of the berg of ice – pieces of data which mean little, if anything, unless you are navigating. The berg of ice to which the ship was attached will almost certainly have changed form by now, although it is possible that it still exists – some icebergs are centuries old – the iceberg that sank the *Titanic* still exists, although a little has been chipped off one edge.

Bright sun and constant daylight on the 'strange, grand and uncommon scene' kept the human spirit at a pitch, wrote Equiano, while peculiar patterns traced in the sky by rays and reflection between clouds, ice, light and water 'heightened it still more'. Some members of the crew were behaving very strangely. The iceberg that served instead of land as a place to moor measured eight yards and eleven inches, he concluded.

Trapped in the ice, the boat became a kind of base camp. The sailors went out and came back with small white-furred hares and foxes which they had shot. They skinned them. Then they started a bonfire and heaped the pelts onto it. The white pelts turned black. Acrid smoke rose into the bright sky, and the smell of burning skin drew the bears towards the boat. The sailors retreated to the deck where they waited with their muskets. There was a great deal of hunting and killing during these first days stuck on the ice. The slaughter, Equiano said, was universal.

They killed and then skinned nine huge white bears. They cut them open and found in their hides a thick lining of fat. But the bellies, which looked large and solid from the outside, were just pouches full of salty water.

The cooked meat was tough and chewy. Vassa found it too coarse but some of the other sailors liked it.

On the morning of 10 August the ice took in the sea. Open water around the isolated loose floating bergs froze and the ship got fastened tight. Then the crew agreed they were not going to make it to the Pole, and that they would not be the ones to find a north-east passage to India – a passage which, though they would never know it, did not exist.

The captain ordered the sailors to take out the little boats and the crew prepared for an expedition across the tundra, back to open water, where they hoped to row back, south-wardly, towards land and so return eventually to England. To do this, they had to drag the boats over miles of frozen sea. The ice shelf was increasing at that time of year, so that it seemed like each day's advance was outpaced by an increasingly distant horizon before them. They began to despair. One day they dug a hole for fishing and Vassa fell into it and nearly drowned. He couldn't swim. He worried about dying in what he called a 'natural' state, unbaptised, and finding in the ice hole a chute direct to the fire of hell. Vassa noted the effect of fear on his colleagues' faces, which, he said, became whiter than before in spite of the bright sunlight. 'Pale dejection seized every countenance.'

Then the thaw came and melted the ice and brought colour back to the water and to their faces and they reached open water and there was 'infinite joy'.

They came at last to land, in mid-August, on a barren piece of tundra, with no food, tree, shelter or shrub, where even the constant attention of sunlight for half the year could not penetrate or dissolve the ice. They refitted the boat there and continued south.

Finally they began to distinguish night from day. The sailors felt like they were floating down from the peculiar elation they had all experienced throughout the voyage.

On 10 September they sailed through a storm. Two boats

were washed from the booms, and the longboat from the chucks. All other movable things on deck were also washed away, among which were many curious things of different kinds – Equiano did not say what – which had been brought back from Greenland. As the cap melted back towards the Pole, hefts of ice the size of buildings broke off the walls which the boat sailed past. There was a deafening creak, then a huge white movement – like a lightning strike in reverse, going back in time from the clap of thunder to a sudden, illuminating flash flung off the horizon. Or like a sheet of clean linen shaken by wind. This is the process by which an iceberg is born, which is called calving, because the large white shape gives way to smaller white offspring in a process that is supposed to be similar to the way in which a cow gives birth to her calf.

iii

I have not seen an iceberg born but I have seen a cow calve. In her old age my grandmother had to be persuaded not to display the British White Cattle Society car sticker which read 'I'm for British Whites!' which she insisted would be taken in its proper bovine context by passers-by. I was not so sure. Much of the Society literature boasts about the cattle's 'pure white coat', even though white is a convergence of rays from a whole spectrum of colours, and therefore, in one sense, the most impure. It also boasts of 'direct links with the ancient indigenous wild white cattle of Great Britain'. The purpose of the strict breeding laws, which are often tightened and renegotiated, is to 'limit the introduction of non-British White blood into the breed, and to further continue the process of ensuring that the British White remains true to the type that has graced our countryside for centuries'. Six British White heifers and one bull were shipped to Pennsylvania on Churchill's orders during the war, so as to safeguard this precious pale aboriginal gene pool.

I became a member of the British White Cattle Society when I turned ten and my grandmother presented me with a calf and the promise of two more on the next birthdays. My mother wouldn't have them in the backyard of her semi, so the cattle never left the farm, but they were duly registered in my name. All the livestock has been sold now, but I must still be a member of the British White Cattle Society because they write to me, fairly regularly, with enquiries about the birth and breeding of my herd together with pamphlets containing details of semen for sale – the letters arrive like miracles through the letter box at my third-floor flat.

I remember the last time I saw one of our cows calving, because something went wrong and we had to call the vet. It was night, or at least dark on a winter afternoon, and somebody had brought an old lamp on an extension lead round the edge of the barn to the lean-to we were in, my grandmother and Will and the vet and the cow and I – I stood just on the outside of the open entrance. The lamp lit the back end of the cow, and it caught straws of gold in black shit on the floor. The cow was quiet, but every once in a while she shifted her feet agitatedly. A blue-and-brown water-fall came out, alive. The vet used a pair of huge forceps to bring it through. Then my grandmother took up a couple of handfuls of straw and used them to scrub the mucus off the calf. The vet kept turning the cow's head around and pushing it down, until at last she took to it, licking roughly at the same patch on the calf's back. I couldn't see that it was making any difference. There was still a wet pink wrinkled sheet hanging out of her back end when Will took me off to feed the others – we peeled slices off the large silage bale and forked it into the old bathtub out of which they ate. Will explained that the calf should have been ready with its forelegs raised over its head – like a man about to dive – but one hind leg had come forward, and the neck had got twisted back, so that the calf was contorted looking back over its shoulder into the womb. They often get stuck in this position, he told me. It was quiet and I could hear the cattle breathing and chewing repetitively. They were weirdly bright in the gloom, giving off a kind of reflective afterglow like bits of moon.

When we came back to fodder in the morning the calf was clean and on her feet. The mother stood in the corner, her hide hung slack as canvas over a skeleton caging a tonne of milk and marbled meat. Her little creature was bright in contrast – a slip of white dodging about the cow's underside. There was something wrong about the way the calf faltered, half kneeling, and each step was marked by a delicate, snooker-like clack in the corrupted joints. Her tongue hung from a corner of her mouth. Will said she was simple. My grandmother said she wouldn't survive. The cow, they agreed, was too old; it was wrong to have brought her to calve again this year.

We dumped a couple of bales into the metal gutter from which she fed, then my grandmother and Will went into the stackyard. I stayed behind, looking at the shining white calf, whose flank twitched as she butted against the open gate that divided the enclosure. In my mind, I could not get over the fact that the calf could be so stupid, any more than the calf could get around the gate. It would only have taken a single sidestep for her to have moved round it, but she kept jabbing her head between the bars. I was frozen there with my eyes stuck on her until she worked out the way.

That was the spring before the foot-and-mouth crisis. My grandmother had to cull the herd that summer; they were taken away in a government lorry to the nearest site where their bodies were burned in a huge ditch. Liv never got another herd. She said, half joking, that she couldn't justify the methane output, and that she was too old for a whole new family. She didn't need the money for the meat any more, she was getting by well enough with extra cash from the EU subsidies. I think she was sentimentally attached, though she didn't say it, and couldn't bear to replace them with any old Buttercup, Clover or Daisy.

By winter she had sold off a number of her sheep and all the pigs but four. We discussed it, one of the days between Christmas and New Year, when I was at the farm. Prices for lamb and beef had risen, but pork was still low and she would, she said, do better by claiming from the low stocking scheme.

'What's the low stocking scheme?' I asked.

'Paid to keep your stockings down,' said Jimmy.

Liv took in a long breath through her nose, and turned her back on him to address me with unneccessary gravity. 'They pay me to keep my livestock numbers low. I earn points for small farming.'

There was a points system, she explained, whereby she earned more cash for good conservational practice – sixty or so approved activities were set out in a list with scores beside them. 'The RSPB man, he was points.'

A man had been sent to us from the Royal Society for the Protection of Birds, as part of an initiative to influence policy and agriculture. He was an expert, a retired schoolteacher, and he came for free. Liv earned points from his visit. It demonstrated her commitment.

I wasn't there when he came, but I was there to read the written report which he sent in the post a month or so later, in which he advised Liv on how she might change her farm to prioritise bird life. The RSPB advised the farmer to cut back the historical hedgerows near the lake so that crows, who attacked the rarer wading birds, would have nowhere to land. He advised that the marsh, which was clearly marked on a parish map drawn by a seventeenth-century local antiquary, be scraped, the better to reveal appetising grubs and flatworms in the mud.

Jimmy said the man was a fraud.

Liv said that he was twenty points.

For the most part, the conservation schemes paid out by encouraging the farmer to let things be. 'Abandoning use of nitrate-based pesticide, seventeen points.' 'Field margins, ten points per metre.' 'Tree in a field. Seven points.'

'Tree in a field?'

'Yes.' She was trying to sound sure of herself. 'Seven points. Tree in a field.'

'How many trees are there in your fields?' I asked.

'Well, I've got to count them.' She picked up the forms, which were on the kitchen table, and fanned herself awkwardly, then put them down.

'First sign of madness,' said Jimmy.

Liv ignored him with all her might. 'The irony is, bloody Weston earns more than I do.'

James Weston was the owner of Ridings Farm which surrounded ours on three sides. Ridings, or its direct ancestor, was in the Domesday Book – Westons, as Jimmy said admiringly, had been farming that land since before Alfred burnt the cakes (or, in point of fact, did *not* burn them, and they weren't actually cakes). James Weston had inherited a large estate on which he farmed beet, barley and potato, intensively. He also ran 'Ridings School', where you could see dead-eyed toddlers, in fluorescent vests and hard hats, bobbing round a ring on miniature Shetland ponies. The parents paid highly for this adorable experience, as was only fair.

Weston claimed more money than my gran though, in those early days of EU subsidies, because he claimed per hectare, rather than according to right environmental practice. He had inherited plenty of land, so he could claim plenty of money, and somehow she always found out about it. Her jealousy meant that she spoke of him often, and he was a real presence in our house though we did not know him well.

Interleaved between the flyleaf and the title page of my grandfather's copy of the *Interesting Narrative* was a photograph of the actor Laurence Olivier in full costume as Othello, a part he took in 1964. On the other side was an interview with his make-up artist, who described how Olivier had his chest, arms and legs shaved, and then how the assistants applied Max Factor shade 2880, Black Liquid Satin, then two coats of a lighter brown pancake make-up. His skin was buffed with yards of chiffon, which gave it a 'mahogany sheen', and also prevented it coming off during the performance although, reviewers noticed, dark smudges could be seen on Desdemona's lips when she came into the spotlight.

Then his fingernails, palms and the soles of his feet were painted with a hard-wearing body tint. The inside of his mouth was coated with a violet dye. Last, a tightly curled black wig was fixed in place with spirit gum.

Olivier didn't complain about these discomforts because, as he said, 'I had to be black. I had to feel black down to my soul. I had to look out from a black man's world.'

The interview made me feel uncomfortable. There is still something uneasy about a white man blacking up – something weird about it – obscure and appalling at the same time. Perhaps it was a sign of the difference between my generation and my grandfather's, but I couldn't take Olivier seriously in that get-up. To me he looked less like a tragic hero, and more like a white actor in a comic costume as a minstrel, a cockney chimney sweep or a coal miner. Max Factor 2880 didn't seem a very realistic route to a black man's world.

In the last week of the summer holidays, Jimmy and I went for a walk on Weardale, and on the way back we turned off south at Stanhope and down the B6278 to Barnard Castle, where he took me to the Bowes Museum. John Bowes, the collector, was the bastard son of the Earl of Strathmore. John became legitimate a day before his father's death, when his parents married over the earl's sickbed. His mother was the maid. Young John was denied the title but he inherited the money and became very wealthy, at the end of the nineteenth century, as the owner of a corporation of north-eastern coal mines.

There were some loans from the Tate Gallery in the exhibition room, but I remember more distinctly the eighteenth-century sugar sculptures in the museum's permanent collection – in one case there were miniature ruined classical buildings and dismembered statues. In another case there were models of living things: almond paste worked to look like ripped-open figs; vases containing peonies and carnations made out of tissues of brittle sugar; and cauliflowers the size of beads in *trompe l'oeil* basket-weave panniers.

Most of the sculptures were cast from moulds made for aristocrats in France, the information said, just before the revolution in the 1780s; some of them had belonged to one of Marie Antoinette's closest friends. The sugar came from West Indian plantations. At the bottom of the placard a map drew a massive cartoon arrow originating in Barbados and landing on Versailles.

Jimmy was up ahead, at the next stand. The animals in

this last cabinet – one unicorn, one phoenix and one lion – were pure white. The mythical and the real were as still and silent as each other, lying together in a controlled atmosphere, beside the barometer in their glass enclosure.

When we left Barnard Castle we drove back down through the dales and my grandfather explained the origin of the scars on the top of the hills: they had been made by lead mines. From the top of the hills you could still see the empty mill houses, grassed-over slag heaps and bell pits, empty cottages, roads and rails, which used to run between the villages, the works and the mines but now led nowhere, or took hikers on circular routes from the car park to the peak of the hill and back. The lead mines, he said, were the dales' industrial success, though they waned at the turn into the twentieth century, then again after the Great War, after which the last mines closed.

The first miners slept out in the corners of the walled fields and inside the open-cast pits they dug themselves, which were only big enough for one or two men. On their backs they had leather sacks containing pickaxes, hammers, wedges and crow-bars. They redirected tributaries to 'hush' the cliffs, creating vigorous artificial torrents of water to split the sides of the hill and have it spill out its innards to find the seams of ore.

We passed through Grinton where, in the seventeenth century, the landlord of the public house had put it about that silver had been found at the top of the dale. The rumour was persistent, because people wanted to believe it. Within a year it found its way into several of the London gazettes. London men came up, burrowed blind into the hills and were never seen again. Miners walked from Wales with the tools they had stolen from the coal pits. Of course there was no silver, but there was highly poisonous, reasonably profitable lead.

The first lead manufacturing company in England was

founded by a man called Richard Fishwick and his partners, several members of the Walker family, who came from Hull to Newcastle to set up the transportation of dales lead downriver from Weardale and Allendale to Elswick, a foundry on the Tyne. This transportation process was almost completely dependent on the weather, partly because the Tyne froze during cold winters, but also because the farmers who helped with the transportation abandoned the boats to take in their harvests when the summer weather was good.

According to the historian David Rowe, in *Lead Manufacturing in Britain*, the Fishwick–Walker partnership was the first lead manufacturing company of any significance in the area, and the earliest constituent of today's Associated Lead Mills. Fishwick seems to have been the dominant partner, signing company letters 'From Walkers, Self and Co.'. 'He had a variety of interests and a wandering spirit,' noted Rowe, 'and a habit of bobbing up unexpectedly.' Fishwick's great contribution to the trade, which he patented, was to add tanners' oak bark to the horse dung used in burning, which resulted in a finish that was purer and more white.

In the late 1770s Walkers, Fishwick & Co. branched out from white lead into other colours, using molasses from the Gateshead sugar factories, copperas from the local mines, and other compounds bought from overseas at the port. In 1780 the company took out a lease on a building known as Paradise – not Eden, but a building called Bussell's Factory House at Benwell, outside Newcastle – it has now been absorbed into south-west Newcastle, just off the A695.

Sales of coloured lead went well, but nonetheless, in 1780 Fishwick wrote to a correspondent, 'I intend to throw off all this business except white and black at Paradise.' He went back to white lead, which was the company's original product, and was used in the seventeenth and eighteenth centuries to proof the hulls and floors of seagoing vessels. In the twentieth century, marine archaeologists discovered traces of white lead on the wreck of the Swedish warship called the *Vasa*, which was named after the ruling dynasty founded by Olaudah Equiano's namesake, Gustav Vasa, or Vassa.

The *Vasa* sank on its maiden voyage in 1628. When it was raised from the seabed in 1959 it was found to be an excellent resource for modern historians, who studied it for data about seventeenth-century society at sea, and so its name, the *Vasa*, has become a byword, in Sweden, for sunken boats of great historical importance, and of the value attached to hero-kings, warfare, and by extension, of value judgements which assess some historical periods and individuals as more important than others. This is all according to its website.

'Gustavus Vassa visited the mines,' my grandfather told me.

V

E quiano visited mines and miners in Yorkshire, Scotland
and County Durham, but the first and only time he
went down the shaft was in Wales. He went to eight
Welsh counties 'from motives of curiosity', and while he was
there he 'was led to go down into a coal-pit'. 'My curiosity
nearly cost me my life,' he said.

Equiano could hardly understand the miners, whose
language was a mixture of Welsh, English and local and technical dialects – a creole. He was surprised to find that they
simply walked into the pit through a hole in the hillside. The
tall men had to stoop but he did not.

When they got a little way the shaft opened out. The oldest
miner put out the candle in his lamp, and he motioned the
others to do the same. Equiano's was the last lamp lit, and
when he blew it out the blackness was so complete that after
only a second of it, yellow and brown folding shapes started
to sail across in front of his eyes. He had never seen perfect
blackness before. Then the old miner struck a match and a
circle of dark faces jumped into orbit.

They went on down the shaft as if they were going towards
the centre of the earth. Equiano was near the front of the
party behind two leaders who ignored him, talking to each
other in Welsh. He felt paranoid when they laughed, and

regretted refusing to take off his buttoned linen. Then there was a muffled noise like a few dry rocks detaching themselves and falling. Olaudah did not hesitate at the noise, which sounded slight, until he heard a frantic sound like shuffling footsteps up ahead. He and his companions stood still, waiting for a shout, but nothing came. Everyone went silent. The two up ahead had disappeared and Equiano was at the front of the party until another miner edged round him and they began to move forward again. They were wading in and out of puddles here; the light made a pond on the ground – a long disembodied arm suddenly stuck into it. Equiano swung back, then swinging the light forwards again, he revealed the arm again – stuck out at the elbow, somehow on end, pointing up towards where the sky should have been.

Beyond that the rest of the body had completely disappeared under one larger boulder of coal and a pile of small rocks which came across the shaft like a half-pulled curtain.

The men couldn't get round the blockage. They heard another succession of rocks falling – it sounded like someone playing skittles down the mineshaft. They turned and went back into daylight, leaving the body or bodies behind.

At the top the miners organised a rescue team, but Equiano did not go back down – from then on, he wrote, he believed that the surface of the earth was 'the safest part of it'.

vi

We drove round the back of Arkengarthdale and through into Swaledale, catching up with the evening sun which had started sinking behind the bank. I could see midges and swallows over the fields – whoever owned the farm here had an eye for the picturesque. His land was tucked into the crotch of the dale where two flanks of hill met so that the valley spread out, giving a rosy golden view back, the lines of trees along the lines of water, and irregular drystone walls running for miles until the river narrowed nearer the source.

Perhaps the farmer's eye for land was less good, though – it was an unyielding place. Later we passed him below the road, alone, cutting the hay laboriously by hand in an awkward corner of his field, which was an odd shape, and built onto the steep slope, so that the grass was coarser and sparer than in the other fields around. His tractor was abandoned on the track.

Then we drove on up into the heather, which smelled strong and waxy, like honey. On the other side of the valley the green trees down by the river looked fine-grained and detailed against the purple spreading vaguely over the tops of the hills. In the slow wind the bank of leaves lifted and fell one by one. Before the tarmac was put down it would have been cut off, here, from the nearest towns.

Jimmy had his eyes on the road and could not see any of this. From the time we noticed the scars on the top of the hill he had been, in his mind, down an eighteenth-century mine.

Although we still have some information about Fishwick and the Walkers, little is known about the miners who worked for them, digging the minerals out of the ground in the first place. Michael Flynn's *History of the British Coal Industry*, vol. 2, 1700–1830, tells us a little, but eighteenth-century writers who described miners tended to comment on only a very few aspects of their customs and their living conditions. They were wild men, who lived in remote or upland closed communities and spoke their own languages.

The miners visited by Equiano in the 1780s and '90s lived in settlements which were separated from local villages. Although they wore gold earrings, lived outside society, and had their own sets of laws, words and traditions of singing, dancing and stories, and although they were dark-skinned, the lives of the miners were very different from the lives of gypsies. The miner, more than any other, was rooted to one particular point in the earth, and the dirt from that place stuck to him wherever he went.

English travellers in the eighteenth century approached mining communities like a foreign country or a time warp. They described the alien clothing, language and customs of the inhabitants. The farmer and journalist William Cobbett, in his *Rural Rides*, noted the unexpected cleanness of the insides of miners' cottages. Another visitor to a mining village wrote about the miners' uniform: blue-and-white-checked flannel trousers, a blue-checked shirt worn with a red tie, a jacket to match the trousers, knitted stockings and square-toed shoes. Miners wore long hair tied into pigtails for working during the week. Thin strips of lead were twisted and bound into these pigtails as curlers, and at the weekend, when the hair was washed, it was let loose over their shoulders under a hat with bands of yellow ribbons. Despite the local poverty, Cobbett added, few of the cottages were without a good chest of drawers for these dandyish outfits.

Women went down the mines too, though it was not always possible to tell, from looking, the gender of any individual miner. One gentleman visitor, touring the mines, described approaching a slight boy, a putter, who was wearing a flannel shift, gold earrings, flannel trousers and overall. As he came nearer, the visitor realised to his surprise that the form beneath the loose tunic, with its hair bundled back, was undoubtedly female and, in fact, pregnant. Children were also recruited, not to hew coal from the rock face, but to perform many of the other jobs that were necessary to keep production going. As well as the hewers, there were putters, trappers, overmen, bankmen, furnace keepers, horse keepers, wailers, masons, sawyers, brick-makers and offhandmen.

The miners' customs were strange, but it was the strange colour of their skin that drew the most attention. Because they were black, their contemporaries compared them to Indians, Arabs and Negroes. One Methodist magazine of 1815 described mining communities as 'Wild as the untaught Arab's brood'; Daniel Defoe, nearly a century earlier, said that the people who worked down the Scottish coal mines were 'dejected by Poverty and hard Labour, and what with the Colour or Discolouring, which comes from the Coal, both to their Clothes and to their Complexions, are well described by their own Countryman, Samuel Colvil, as Cole-Hewers Nigri'. 'They are, indeed, frightful Fellows at first sight,' Defoe concluded.

There was no running water or pithead bath for the miners to wash in after their shifts, so they were usually dirty. Visitors deliberately conflated coal dust and dark skin, so that to be washed clean was to be changed from a savage to a civilised man. The Reverend George Whitefield, a cross-eyed minister from Gloucester who became the most famous preacher of his time, described how, as he converted an audience of thousands of miners from the Bristol collieries to Methodism, he noticed the 'white gutters made by the tears which plentifully fell down their black cheeks – black as they came out of their coal-pits'.

Whitefield wanted to take his sermons abroad, but was discouraged from missions to the North American Indians by his neighbours in Bristol. 'What need of going abroad?' they asked. 'If you have a mind to convert Indians, there are colliers enough in Kingswood' – Kingswood, which is now a suburb of Bristol, was a coal-producing region in the seventeenth century. Nowadays, gardeners in the area still find themselves cutting into the old shafts, which were surprisingly shallow and never mapped. Lawns and flower beds have been known to crack, tilt, tip like a trapdoor and pour the topsoil like sand back into the earth's crust.

Richard Fishwick and his partners were unusual in that they acknowledged responsibility for the 'dark creatures', their employees, and they tried to improve the working environment. 'The firm went to surprising lengths and expense,' wrote Rowe, 'to look after employees who suffered the disease.' ('The disease' was lead poisoning.)

Fishwick even left histories of one or two miners, who would otherwise have left no historical trace when, in his correspondence, he fretted about their health. He wrote to his London agents, about 'one of our men having fallen ill of the Lead [. . .] either through obstinacy or foolhardiness he subjected himself to [it] he has been exceeding careless of taking the necessary precautions and we fear it will go very hardly with him'. A 'skilfull Surgeon' had been paid for, 'and everything afforded that seem likely to promote his recovery'.

Another time, a group of five girls were sent from Newcastle to the leadworks in Islington, London. When they came back a few months later, Fishwick thought that they had been very badly looked after – three girls returned, 'two of them in a very distressing Condition, Grearson I think will not be long in mending but Reveley will not be stout of several weeks'.

Most mining companies were not like Walkers, Fishwick & Co. In many places in Britain at that time, miners had little or no protection from their employers. In some parts of Scotland, babies born to miner parents were bonded to the mine, making them, in effect, white slaves. The dark colour of the miners' skins was used in some quarters to justify this practice.

Equiano visited the north-east several times in the early 1790s. He spoke to the miners near Durham, who had recently gone on strike. In 1793, the year he visited the north of England for the last time, the mayor of Newcastle had to call military assistance to protect himself against increasingly violent protesting labourers in the nearby country.

After meeting the miners, Equiano took up their cause along with those of the slaves in the West Indies. He spoke at local meetings on behalf of labourers at home and in the colonies, and attended the debates in Parliament, on 2 and 3 April 1792, when he visited the House of Commons to hear the Members taking up the subject of the traffic in slaves. He saw William Wilberforce speak at 6 p.m. And then he travelled north, and a few days later he married Miss Susanna Cullen of Ely. It was a public surprise. The wedding was held at a church in Cambridge, and there was a huge crowd of guests and uninvited onlookers. Over the coming weeks, newspapers would announce the newly-weds as a touring spectacle: 'GUSTAVUS VASSA with his *white* wife'.

Mr and Mrs Equiano spent ten days together, giving some of the gazetteers an opportunity to speculate about the colour of Mr Equiano's semen (Herodotus and other ancient authorities maintained that some men have black sperm). Historians cannot look back into other people's bedrooms, but there might be some insight into the general complexion of the honeymoon from a letter the groom wrote to a friend several days after the ceremony: 'when I have given her about 8 or 10 days' comfort, I mean directly to go to Scotland – and sell my 5th Editions'.

'I am now obliged to slave on more than before if possible,' he wrote to another friend, a Scottish political agitator called Thomas Hardy, '– as I have a Wife.'

On this matter, as on everything else, Susanna is silent.

viii

Some historians have said that the *Interesting Narrative* was not a history but a lie, and not because the narrator repeatedly changes his name, his location, his beliefs, his clothes and his profession, though he does. Equiano, Olaudah, Michael, Jacob, Gustavus, Caesar, Vassa, Weston, the Black Christian and the African. Slave, sailor, manservant, hairdresser, purifier of saline, author and political campaigner. 'The evidence that Gustavus Vassa invented the African birth of Olaudah Equiano is indecisive,' decided one twentieth-century biographer. This formulation sees one protagonist of the *Interesting Narrative* as a real historical figure, and another as a figment of the imagination.

Gustavus Weston, the 28-year-old who was registered on the Arctic expedition of the *Race Horse*, was born, according to the ship's muster book, in South Carolina, America. It has been argued, on the basis of this and of other recently rediscovered baptismal and naval records, that Equiano was born into slavery on a Danish colonial plantation in the Americas, and that the African childhood described in the *Interesting Narrative* took place in a land which was completely unknown to its author.

The history, these academics argue, was an illusion which had been fabricated by Equiano so that he could maintain some distance from the condition of slavery, invent an abduction, or restore himself to his origins.

Other historians put forward the counter-argument that the records could have been misread, or may refer to another slave with a similar name, or Equiano might have pretended he was born in America to simplify an application for passage.

The accusations have a long history reaching back to 16 April 1792, when the *Oracle* announced 'a fact the public may depend on'. Gustavus Vassa, wrote the reporter, who quite openly claimed to have been kidnapped from Africa, had in fact never set foot on an African shore.

At the end of April, Equiano wrote to his friend Thomas Hardy. 'Sir I am sorry to tell you that some Rascal or Rascals have asserted in the News papers viz. Oracle of the 25th of April & the star. 27th – that I am a native of Danish Island, Santa Cruz, in the Wt. Indies.' The accusations had injured his ink-and-paper self. 'The assertion has hurted the sale of my Books.'

Perhaps it was this turn of phrase which inspired Hardy, whose letters were usually austere and political, and who ended his life in prison for repeated radical agitation, to write an unusually feeling reply to Equiano, in which he described a recent dream. Copies of the *Interesting Narrative*, roosting in a bookseller's stockroom like doves in a coop, turned on one another. The pages, torn by invisible hands, flew like black and white feathers.

Equiano asked Hardy to look out for a copy of the *Star*, which he could not find while on tour (he had an *Oracle*). 'Please buy one for me,' he wrote, 'and take care of it till you see or hear from me.' It is unclear whether he wanted to read the stories for himself, or whether he was planning to buy and destroy as many copies as he could.

It is also, still, unclear whether Equiano ever travelled to the interior of Guinea, lived among the Igbo tribe, or saw a real lion – or whether he was born and 'bred up', as the *Oracle* put it, on plantations of sugar cane and cotton.

Some historians accuse him of stealing the details of his stories from contemporary travel narratives which related accounts of life in Guinea at that time. Others, coming from the other direction, point out that details in his account are not found anywhere else in contemporary descriptions of that country. The memory of tribal life had, Equiano said, been 'implanted on me' with great care, and 'made an impression on my mind, which time could not erase, and which all the adversity and variety of fortune I have since experienced could only rivet and record.' He added a description of the simple food his tribe ate – they were unacquainted, he said, with those refinements in cookery that debauched the taste, which came from the French aristocracy. He also described the crops that grew plentifully in his homeland, which included, as well as 'pomkins', eadas, plantains and yams, wild cotton.

The mention of cotton prompted some botanical historians to speculate about the exact date of cotton's introduction to West Africa, which is unknown. There do not seem to be any other contemporary accounts of wild cotton in Benin, Guinea or present-day Nigeria, at that time. This could suggest that the narrative is unreliable. On the other hand, it could suggest that Equiano was drawing on experience rather than sources, and that the cotton near his village was a unique plantation.

In the 'imperfect sketch' which had been furnished by his memory, Equiano described balls of cotton drifting through the village on invisible currents. More cloud than cloth – like distant or very small clouds, he thought, or thicketed air. You could stretch up and close them in your fist. 'The credity which is due to this story I leave to the reader,' Equiano concluded.

• • •

After the fourth edition of the *Interesting Narrative* went to the press, Equiano had the idea of casting himself as Othello. In the fifth edition, which was published in 1792, he added a quotation to the title page. 'Speak of me as I am; nothing extenuate / Nor set down aught in malice.' The speech comes in the fifth act, towards the end of the play. This is the point at which the audience knows Othello least of all.

Before that, between the flyleaf and the title page of the *Interesting Narrative,* was a long list of subscribers who supported Equiano and the abolition movement. On the subscription pages, which lengthened with each edition, Miss Susanna Cullen was listed alongside Baron Mulgrave, who organised the expedition to the North Pole; prominent abolitionists like Granville Sharpe; and one Richard Fishwick of Newcastle, whose name was added after Equiano's visit to that city in 1793.

In the same year the *Oxford English Dictionary* credits the translation of the term 'autobiography', meaning self/life/writing, into English from Greek. Olaudah Equiano's autobiography, then, must have been one of the very first of these personal histories. Before that time, writers could only deal in memoirs, which came from the inside of their minds; or accounts, which kept outside of them. They had no particular word for recording themselves, as historians do, over time.

'For Equiano, his *Narrative*, like his life itself, continued to be a work in progress,' wrote the historian Vincent Carretta. During his life, Equiano brought up, several times, a connection between his 'dark skin' and his 'white pages'. The autobiography was a facsimile of the life, but it carried on after Gustavus Vassa died, when more documents were discovered. Historians were able to go back and rewrite the Life, and it kept changing even after it was over.

• • •

Jimmy didn't tell me about the Equiano dispute while I was doing the slave trade for my GCSEs. I didn't hear about it until later, long after the cattle had gone, when I was in my last year at school. He still liked to set his traps, and we were checking his fox and rabbit snares. Perhaps it reminded him of his telling me about the *Interesting Narrative* while we looked for dead magpies. We were walking along the hedge at the edge of the wood. It was a sunny day in early spring; I could see two chaffinches jumping about inside the bare hedge, and some small narcissi were already out. It must have been only a few weeks before we found the dog, because he didn't set his traps after that.

'Equiano should be praised for his lie,' my grandfather said when he had told the story. 'The fiction was the only available restitution – the only way to restore the exile to his place of origin, give the king back his kingdom, or the gardener his garden of Eden.'

I did not then understand what he was talking about.

'Or her,' I reminded him.

'Historically, not theoretically.' He raised his tired old eyes to heaven. 'Give the king back her kingdom.'

He wasn't speaking theoretically. As a true African, Equiano could give a first-hand account of the slave's abduction, from the inside, but he could also give a history of slavery from the outside, as an alien who had been brought over from somewhere else. 'If it was a lie, the lie was a very sensible idea.'

Olaudah Equiano, in his speeches, used to imagine a pair of giant intercontinental scales on which he weighed up the cost, in slaves' lives, per hundredweight of transported sugar. His calculations were ignored by members of the aristocracy who carried on using West Indian sugar for building elaborate confectionery architecture on impressively fragile foundations.

The aristocrats must have had to forget the origin of their

puddings, my grandfather speculated, if they wanted to carry on. 'Perhaps it is necessary not to know things. Our whole species only survives, after all, because women forget the memory of labour pains.'

I tried to protest – my grandmother had told me in no uncertain terms that this was not the case. But he had moved on.

To justify the use of humans as agricultural machinery, facts and stories got mixed up. 'The skin, which is the connection between the outside and the inside world, is the largest organ in the human body, and the most shallow. And so it gives itself to history, which is large and shallow too, and covers the whole of human knowledge, and perhaps it should come as no surprise to you and me that some of the most elaborate historical monstrosities were constructed on its thin elastic foundations.'

Nature, however, is indifferent to these constructions. Human skin will never be black and white – it comes in different shades of brown and yellow. 'Like history.' Nothing old is written in black and white. Time turns white pages yellow, and black ink brown.

According to human tradition, yellow is the colour of old skin, of cowardice, phone books, the Orient, and some kinds of butter. It was the colour of earliest memory for Virginia Woolf, who remembered lying in her cot and 'seeing through a film of semi-transparent yellow' – she said it was like lying inside a grape.

'Yellow, in particular, has been faithful to me,' said Jorge Luis Borges when he went blind, or almost blind, and he could only see a couple of colours and some fuzzy outlines through the milky haze in front of his eyes. It is hard not to read a system into his description of the colours, like yellow, that remained and those, like crimson, that had already left him in 1977 when the lecture, 'On Blindness', was given. My grandfather said a similar thing when he began to lose his hearing, and he tried to convince me (I was probably about five or six) that the hearing aid could tune into certain sounds – specifically, the frequency of bats' high-pitched communication in the barns. He heard owls in the fields, rabbits, which squeak disturbingly when they are attacked, and beyond: he lay awake at night listening to whales humming and hooting in the ocean. He was very serious when he told me this – I think that the stories were invented as much to console the storyteller as they were supposed to impress the listener, as were my grandmother's when she told me the gold back tooth was her own, grown, and it was the sun that coloured her hair yellow.

A few weeks after that conversation there was a sudden freeze and spring stopped in the middle of springing. The weather was all over the place, Liv said. Jimmy and I were doing the same walk along the wood when we found Liv's dog in one of his snares. Its body had gone hard, either with ice or rigor mortis, and it stayed in the elongated shape in which it was hanging when we lifted it out of the wire noose. It was stiff and heavy and its hair as hard as thorns or barbed wire. It may have been eating rabbits or even dead foxes out of the snares, Jimmy said – he had suspected the dogs of doing this. Or it may have run down a rabbit path and got snagged, he reflected. 'It was an old thing.'

I wasn't there when he told Liv, but I was there a few days later as she, Will and I buried the body in its basket under a pear tree down the bottom of the garden. Liv was using two sticks to walk about, so Will did the digging. He had to chop up the cold ground with the edge of his spade, hatching the surface then scraping it until he'd got a wide enough and deep enough hole.

We stood in solemn silence, as was appropriate to the occasion, until Will piped up: 'It's a waste,' he said, though whether he was referring to the dog's death or to burying the basket was not clear.

Whistle my grandfather was old and my grandmother was dead he made a romance out of their marriage, rewriting the past like Thomas Hardy (the novelist and poet, not Olaudah Equiano's radical friend, who had the same name); or like the historian Thomas Carlyle; and, no doubt, like hundreds if not thousands of other Thomases, including my grandfather. Like Carlyle and Hardy, Jimmy's marriage was bitter, but he allowed himself to be nostalgic after his wife's death. He looked back to the past and said it was better than the present, but only after it had disappeared.

I have heard of old couples who spent decades together, then died in quick succession, the survivor apparently giving up on life after his or her partner had gone. You could say that this happened to my grandmother when her old dog died – she declined rapidly and passed away only a few months after his accident. I had just started university when she had her second, fatal stroke, and had to come home almost as soon as I had left.

I drove over to the farm on the day before the funeral. Jimmy had shut himself in the drawing room with the doors, windows and all the curtains closed, except for the single set of curtains beside which he was standing, lifting and dropping the cord again and again so the landscape was revealed, then disappeared. It was a windy October day and we could see black rooks thrown about with yellow sycamore leaves in the grey sky above the brown fields. I waited in the doorway until he turned back and smiled. The smile looked horrible and out of place, like an insect landing on his face. We fetched his hat and stick and walked across the field towards the pub.

When we came down the last bit of road the thought of a drink lifted his spirits, and he got skittish – 'Ah, the Benefit of Hindsight.' It was actually called the White Horse; Douglas Pugh was still the landlord. We passed the row of council houses, now all privately owned, one of which was the house in which I had grown up. People were out, in spite of the weather – someone was gardening, his neighbour was washing his car, the next was painting a Wendy house. 'The sublime ruins of the Welfare State!' Jimmy proclaimed, not for the first time.

Doug was behind the bar when we came in. The bar room was small and he was very large, but he looked insignificant among the clutter of tiny objects around him and on him: the tattoo 'Sheffield Wendsday', spreading as his arm got fat, was the relic of an early, South Yorkshire wife. Little towels on the bar advertised Tadcaster breweries. Dimpled pint glasses with handles fruited on racks, small bags of peanuts ripened on the wall. Dusty miniature bottles of tomato juice were separating into blood and water on the shelves.

The white top of my grandfather's Guinness licked down the side of the glass. Inside it was brown and cloudy – he screwed up one eye and said sternly: 'Now settle down you.' My vodka and tonic came in a short, bulbous wine glass with a slice of lemon sunk at the bottom – it seemed impossible that this pale artefact could have grown on a tree in the African sun.

Jimmy asked Doug how business was going and Doug forecast the future of the beverage industry in gloomy tones.

He had been marrying the spirits when we came in, and after he'd served us he returned to his equipment – a plastic funnel, a clean cloth and a margarine tub full of hot water. The dregs of three elephantine bottles of peach schnapps were siphoned into a single bottle whose neck was held delicately between his finger and his thumb. For such a massive individual, the hands were small, with curving fingers like a dead bird's claws – in spite of his size I could not see him as a man who used to dig coal out of the earth.

Jimmy, meanwhile, was making conversation.

'Perhaps your heritage is Welsh, Douglas, with a name like Pugh?' He had asked him this before.

'No, we're Scots,' said Doug. After a moment's thought, he added, complacently, for politeness' sake, 'It means son of Hugh, and Hugh means sleep.'

'Oh, well,' said Jimmy dubiously.

We retreated from the bar to the corner of the room; Jimmy took off his hat and laid it carefully on the tabletop. He sat down, holding his stick between his knees in a mildly unsettling situation as he began to remember my grandmother. He drank in few, smooth draughts, and got more talkative as he felt the effects.

The first time they met, he noticed my grandmother because she was so dark. He remembered seeing her from across the room at a dance – she looked foreign and was wearing a red coat. Her maiden name was Moore, he said. He thought she was an octoroon.

The room was empty and you could hear everything from the bar. Doug cut in: 'What's an octoroon?'

An octoroon, Jimmy explained, is the white-skinned descendant of someone with dark skin. At least one of the octoroon's eight great-grandparents is black. There is no real genetic basis for the distinction, although people used to try to find scientific evidence for it. 'You can find whatever you look for,' said Jimmy.

'Like Ryan Giggs,' said Douglas, with an air of finality.

'Who's Brian Giggs?' asked Jimmy.

'Now *he's* a Welshman, plays football for Wales,' said Douglas. 'He's as white as you like, and his grandaddy's from Sierra Leone.' Doug paused, possibly wondering if he'd been racist. 'He's a good-looking man,' he added uncertainly.

'A quadroon, then,' Jimmy said. 'There were quite a few at my school, in Plymouth – because of the visiting sailors.' He paused.

'At any rate, it depends on the scale you're using. On a grand scale, we are all Africans – certainly you and I and Doug – if we go back far enough.' Olaudah Equiano, Laurence Olivier, Shakespeare, the other old man sitting in the Family Room, the topless girl on the cardboard peanut rack, the slave owners as well as the slaves.

The earliest known human remains were discovered in Africa, Jimmy explained, so everyone's ancestry comes from that part of the world. 'It is only as we breed and evolve over generations that lines and finer lines are drawn.'

Using one scale, Jimmy said, a historian might magnify the millions of tiny fish living inside us or between our teeth so that each one has the importance of the leviathan. Many of these species would survive without their human hosts.

Using another scale, he said, we might look down on the earth from space, which would dwarf any single living thing. 'From this perspective, nothing we do makes any difference anyway.' He had finished his pint, and was threatening to become mournful.

'Even the Great Wall of China,' he couldn't help adding, 'is not, in point of fact, visible from space.' He paused. 'But then again, I've never been in space.'

He wasn't finished. He spread his hands, claw-like, on either side of his pint. His were only slightly more wrinkled than my own, and we had matching thin fingers and short thumbs.

'These hands have the bonework of fossilised fins. 375 million years ago or so our ancestor –' he raised his voice to include Doug in his magnificent revelation – 'our ancestor was a fish.'

It took him several months, after Liv's death, to arrange for the removal of her low stocks of livestock.

The sheep and pigs were sent off to market where they would be sold to the abattoir. It cost money to have them driven – the slaughterhouse hired out their large truck. It accommodated a large flock of sheep and a herd of cattle, or horses. The truck had different levels with ramps between them. Our animals fitted on the bottom storey.

The driver, expecting the farmer to help, had come alone, but my grandfather summoned Will by telephone and retreated indoors, where he sat in his study, occasionally rising to the window to monitor what was going on.

It was spring outside. An audience of pigeons sat in the trees to one side of the stackyard, and, at the other side of the theatre, a crow watched proceedings from the porch roof, ignoring the decorative pottery cat which appeared to be stalking it across the slates. Crows are more intelligent than other birds, which keep well clear of the ceramic predator.

Will and I and the man from the slaughterhouse ushered the pigs from the pig ark into the stackyard, where we fanned out around them, then closed in, urging them onto the ramp into the van. They weren't much trouble, they trotted up. We closed the gates on their large pens at the back, and opened the smaller cubicles for the sheep.

The flock was penned up in the small barn, from which it would be easy to drive it into the stackyard because the gate opened onto a closed passage. I left Will and the butcher's man to it and went inside to see what Jimmy was up to.

He was standing by the window when the sheep came pouring into the arena.

'I remember the first lambing season,' said Jimmy. 'Your grandmother bottle-fed the orphans in the kitchen. I'd always thought that was a myth.'

Liv purchased her livestock before the wedding. When they got back from their honeymoon the animals were picked up, in herds and flocks or two by two in breeding pairs, from around the country. In the space of a few days living things started making noises in all directions – in the barns, over the fields, out on the roof where the new doves perched and made sexy noises and eventually flew off and bred themselves out among the pigeons.

These memories were surprising, to say the least. He went on.

During that first lambing season at the farm, in the first year of their marriage, they both rose in the dark to walk seven miles round, checking on the ewes. The sheep had already made desire lines where they tracked across the field. The sun came up while they were out (the grandparents, not the sheep – the sheep were always out). While they walked he told her about his new job, and they discussed his research. He was attempting to work out his own historiography. He talked on about Herodotus and Aesop while she delivered the lambs.

There were lambs in with the flock now. It was not a good time to be moving them. Somewhere at the back one ewe started and turned round, and they all followed suit, trickling off in different directions as they turned. Will, jogging round the edge, managed to hedge most of them back in, talking at them while he did so. We couldn't hear what he was saying through the window. Jimmy, whose eyes were glazed over, appeared not to notice the commotion.

'She even pulled their offspring out for them, as well as feeding them, and cutting their winter coats off so they were cool in summer. She dipped them to keep them clean, and kept them in out of the cold in the winter.' He turned back, away from the sheep, towards me. 'They know what they're about.'

The escaped ewe deliberately collapsed her legs. Her yellow reptile eyes rolled back. She staggered up again on to her knees, and thrust herself towards the pond. Will bellowed and the abbatoir man waved his arms in the air, running up to the railings on the edge of the pond to stop her getting further. I felt I should go out to help, but Jimmy was unabated.

The soil was clay over gravel over the Jurassic rocks, which was bad for ploughing, according to his new wife – he knew nothing about agriculture, of course, 'but she said you could sink a well anywhere on this land', if you went down far enough.

Back at the beginning, as he recalled it, the farm had been absolutely charming, and much more fruitful than it had become. They had an apiary and an orchard, and sold plums and honey before they started to rear meat.

The two men had got all the animals in by the time Jimmy had finished, and it was too late to help. I stood quietly by the window with him beside me, and did not interrupt or bother to query the lambs and plums and bees which he saw in his mind's eye while we looked at the butcher's truck disappearing at the bottom of the drive.

It seemed like all his histories involved deception, in one way or another, and while I was thinking about the strange pronouncements he began to make after my grandmother's death, it occurred to me to check the truth about the single universal family he had described in the pub.

I went online to look it up, the next morning, after I'd read everything he had on Equiano. There had been another snowfall overnight. I put on a dark blue balaclava and a woolly hat over it.

On a news website I found a story, less than a year old, which said that the remains of early men had recently been found by archaeologists in Asia and Europe. These new remains dated from the same period as the oldest previously known existing human remains, which had come from Africa: the Middle Palaeolithic. We now know much more than we have throughout our history, and archaeogenetic analysis has enabled scientists to discover a great deal about ancient human remains, but we are back to where we were before in that *Homo sapiens*, as the scientists name their own species, still do not know their own point of origin – the findings have divided us as far back as human relics go, back and back to our original point. It seemed strange that we could balance the whole of human history on these few old bones, and also that something from so long ago could have actually changed during the few years since my grandfather's death.

While I was online I checked my emails for the first time since my arrival at the farm. There was only one, and the subject heading was in a foreign script which looked like Japanese. I opened it anyway. The signature, from 'Animal Lovers', ran below a picture of a very small cat which looked very big because it was living inside a kind of glass jar. 'Please help kitty Quetta!!!!!' the animal lovers wrote. 'She is in a tight spot. Quetta is being grown inside a bottle! Please stop this cruel cruel practice!!!!' The poor cat, white as sugar inside its glass house, looked unfortunately funny, with its cute nose and alarmed blue eyes squashed up.

Around that time I seemed to get a lot of emails about these animals. They were probably sent automatically, but they didn't go into the junk file. I was never sure if the 'bonzai pets', as the email called them, were real or made up. Most mythical animals are cross-breeds which connect one species with another: a human with a fish's tail; an eagle with the body of a lion; a ram-headed God – and it seemed possible that small, cramped pets would be bred for people who live in small, cramped apartments. But looking at the picture of Quetta, who looked like a ship in a bottle, it was impossible to see how she had got there in the first place.

After a while the connection went so I closed the computer, added a coat to my outfit and went outside to put the papers I'd read in the rubbish. There was no need for the logs that were weighing down the boxes. There was no wind. The leaves which had fallen off the trees weeks before still lay in brown discs in the patchy snow around the bottom of their trunks.

I saved Catherine Acholonu's book and went back through

the last pages while I drank my tea, looking more closely this time at the grainy black-and-white photograph of a thin-limbed man with skins and weapons, not smiling, sitting on a bench which was built like a shelf on the outside wall of his home. 'We know that a year has ended,' he said, 'when we hear the rattling noise made by an unknown thing that passes through our land once a year and only in the evening, as soon as the sun sets. The noise is deafening and yet you can never see the thing. We do not know what it is. All the men, women and children throw out their old utensils and roar: "Year! Please go home empty-handed."'

This description sounded very similar to the part of the *Interesting Narrative* in which Equiano described his tribe celebrating the new year. 'We compute the year from the day on which the sun crosses the line, and on its setting that evening, there is a general shout throughout the land.' On New Year's Day the people 'made a great noise with rattles' and 'hold up their hands to heaven for a blessing'.

It was a shame, I thought, if it was true that Equiano had lied about his African origins, because it made Dr Acholonu's expedition pointless – a journey back to a place Equiano had never been. Though in a way, it didn't make any difference. Dr Acholonu was marking time like all historians, and all histories are a kind of fruitless pursuit, or misplaced enthusiasm.

At that time I took Jimmy's pronouncements on Equiano's narrative, on genealogy and skin colour, to be saying that anything could mean anything. There is no independent reality, I understood him to say. Even the codes in our DNA are selective narratives. Everything is constructed by me and you, there is nothing inside the box, except another box – a series of boxes of which the last one is empty or full of brown dirt.

Everything's relative. This was excellent news, and it helped me to write some bad dissertations. But I saw things differently after I had read the Kitchener file.

At the end of the papers on Equiano I came to the story Herodotus told about the slave of Histiaios, a barbarian tyrant. Histiaios once sent a message to his nephew, Aristagoras. Rather than writing the message on conventional writing materials, he had it tattooed, for safe keeping, on the skin of one of his slaves, who was acting as a messenger.

Herodotus, who passed this story on, did not judge Histiaios. He, Herodotus, commented very little, although he reported as much as possible, and he sometimes expressed surprise at the strangeness of things he heard from his various sources. His critics accused him of philobarbarism, loving the barbarians.

The barbarians, Herodotus said, still wrote on skin during his lifetime, though not on the skins of living men. The Ionians used to write on skins before the invention of papyrus. Herodotus was writing in what is now Turkey, more than four hundred years before the birth of Christ. At that time, the English, where they wrote at all, were writing on vellum, or calfskin, and parchment made out of other animals – perhaps the English were among the barbarians of whom he spoke. I do my notes straight onto the computer, and I try not to print them to save paper, so most of the words I write are only ever apparitions on the screen. My grandfather tended to write his notes with pencil in a notepad, before typing them up. His longhand notes on Equiano's preface were at the end of the book. In the introduction, Equiano apologised for the fact that his story wasn't very exciting. 'People generally only think those memoirs worthy to be read or remembered which abound in great or striking events,' he wrote. 'It is, therefore, I confess, not a little hazardous in a private and obscure individual, and a stranger too, thus to solicit the indulgent attention of the public; especially when I own I offer here the history of neither a saint, a hero, nor a tyrant.'

IV Herbert Kitchener

i

When he was working on these last histories, after his wife's death, he retreated further into virtual worlds. He spent all his time at his desk, in history, and more and more of it on the new computer to which he was glued, while all around him the piles of paper in his study grew like water levels rising on an incoming tide.

In spite of all this knowledge he was accumulating – so much that the room could hardly contain it – his mind was going. Outside the study he was uncomfortable, and sometimes asked plaintively where he was, and when we might go home. He had always repeated his stories, but the circuit seemed to shrink and it became slightly embarrassing; I didn't know how to respond when I heard the same thing for the third or fourth time in one visit.

The last history was set during his own lifetime, and perhaps it was too close, as he had always maintained, because it was the saddest and most mistaken of his works. After I'd read it there wasn't long left before I was due to give the keys to the estate agent and return to London. I disconnected the Internet to stop wasting time. I had decided to throw out the original notes – everything significant was on my computer, and they were only gathering dust.

I put on a scarf, hat and a pair of gloves, then wrapped

another scarf round my head. I was, I should say, voluminous by now, and when I tried to get the car keys out of my pocket I realised they were under several layers of clothing, and had to unwrap, then dress up again.

When I tried the car it wouldn't go. The tank was empty. It had started snowing again, so I moved the boxes back into the hall and stacked them carefully, like they were precious. I removed the logs that had been weighing down the loose paper, and returned them to the woodpile.

There was a number for the council on the telephone, and they put me through to a semi-automated woman. There was no one, she said, in the whole borough, who would collect large loads of rubbish. 'In fact I think you'll find it's illegal to go tipping without the council's permission, and the council don't do it, madam.' I looked across to the boxes of tattered, largely incorrect and, at that stage, slightly slushy notes, a few feet away. Lengthening tongues of water with little threads of grey dirt in it crept out from under them across the tiled floor.

'If it wants recycling, you'll have to do it yourself,' she said.

Later, when the snow had stopped falling, I transferred the papers into plastic bags and wrapped up again and set out along the lane with as much as I could comfortably carry. The fields were like white sheets spread between the hedges.

I had finished reading early in the morning. There was a muddy substance on the last papers, and the odd smudge of chocolate and leafy bits of walnut skin had got in with the work, and my grandfather's notes themselves were messy and confused. There were too many insignificant details and no sense of perspective in the piece. It began with the biography of a soldier whose ship sank in July 1916 – but not Jimmy's own father. The soldier about whom he was writing was General Kitchener.

According to Lloyd George his mind was like a revolving lighthouse, 'sometimes the beam lights up all Europe and the opposing armies in vast and illimitable perspective. Then the shutter comes round and for several weeks you get blank darkness.'

According to Asquith he was an incorrigible liar.

He astonished his physician after a skirmish in the Sudan by swallowing the bullet that had lodged in his neck and voiding it through the usual physical processes some time later. He used a skull raided from the tomb of the Mahdi for his inkpot, and at the home, Broome Park in Kent, which he occupied from 1911 until his death, he had a vast rug made from the skins of twenty-four lions, one for each hour of the day, every one of which he himself had shot.

He was afraid of the water – this was partly due, according to at least one document, to a fateful occasion when, 'owing to a gross misunderstanding', he almost drowned in the bath. He always wanted to go to Russia. There were and continue to be rumours of buggery but history rarely if ever leaves evidence of sexual activity, other than progeny; perhaps the most convincing argument is made by the sunken rose garden at Broome Park, of which he was passionately fond, and to which he added several ornaments in the form of a rococo fountain together with a suite of life-size bronze casts of scantily clad boys in 'athletic' postures.

He was an icon in the Your Country Needs You posters – then when he died this repeated story, same old story that the hero is not dead but asleep and will return. The Mahdi; or Elvis Presley for the Americans; or King Arthur who they say sleeps and is still sleeping under a stone in Cornwall or Wales, ready to come back at the right moment. Q: is the Messiah the origin or the consequence of this story? – Kitchener had a brother named Arthur.

His strengths were in battle, not rhetoric; he was a Coriolanus rather than a Brutus. He took a vow of abstinence (from alcohol) during the war – they said it made him fat and bad-tempered. They say his mind was like a revolving lighthouse – sometimes he told the truth and sometimes he lied. And was haggard and melancholy at that time, I don't know why.

The last history began at the end of Lord Kitchener's life when he was old, unfit and melancholic. In June 1916, it was two years since war broke out, and Kitchener was appointed secretary of state for war. Both the war and its secretary were losing the support of the government. Members of the House of Commons had moved to reduce his annual salary to a nominal £100 as an expression of their lack of faith in his leadership. Kitchener, who had never been good at speech-giving, volunteered to defend himself to the House. His friends advised against the idea and Prime Minister Asquith, whose first name was also Herbert, sided with Kitchener in public, but in private he fretted about what he might say. 'He's *such* a liar,' said Asquith to a friend.

The speech was scheduled to take place in the War Office, but was moved at the last minute to a committee room at Westminster, because of the crowds. Even in the committee room, people were still pressing in at the doors when Kitchener, looking tired, took his seat. It was a while before the conversation died down. He hummed and hawed for attention. His sympathisers thought that the battle was already lost. Then he began.

It was a deliberate and confident speech. Lord Kitchener explained, as to children, the tactical constraints involved in pitting strategy against resources. He gave examples, as an applicant before a board, of difficulties he had overcome. He spent some time describing the background and giving historical and strategic contexts of the current military predicament, before moving, with assurance, to his outlines for his plans for the future of his army.

He left the room 'gay, alert, elastic, sanguine', according to Asquith. Nothing short of a resurrection, the battle won.

Kitchener lunched with King George, who expressed his relief to hear that the speech was a success (he held back his surprise). The king and his war secretary were meeting – it was to be their last – to discuss the expedition which was scheduled to begin the next day. Kitchener planned to sail in secret to Archangel, travel overland to the court of Tsar Nicholas, George's cousin, who was in St Petersburg, and persuade Russia to join the war, then return, and win the war. Some historians have said that George entrusted several gold ingots to Kitchener's care over lunch that day, instructing him to gift the gold to Russia if Nicholas was wavering. Then Kitchener left, the king wishing him luck for the journey on which he was about to depart.

Meanwhile in Russia, Tsar Nicholas had promised, like Kitchener, to stay away from alcohol as long as the war lasted, but unlike Kitchener, the Russian High Commander could not keep his promise. He upset the tsarina, according to historians, by proposing a toast at dinner one evening, standing unstably and holding his enamelled goblet at a loose angle so that the wine slipped onto his plate, 'To Lord Kitchener the Great English Soldier!', in expectation of his arrival.

Within days, the history says, Lord Kitchener's supposedly secret visit was under discussion at every table at the Petrograd boat club.

The monk Rasputin was also at the dinner, according to

my grandfather's notes. Rasputin was seated as usual at the tsarina's right hand, sipping his soup, listening and saying little.

That June evening after lunching with the king Kitchener motored home alone to Broome Park, where he walked around his grounds, looking at each rose bush, and standing for a long time by the sunken garden on the terrace until the sun set. It was nearly midsummer and past ten at night.

When it was dark he went inside and walked from vitrine to vitrine, picking out, first, a very old ostrich egg, which had recently been set in a silver fretwork stand. Then an ammonite fossil which had been carved, in the seventeenth century, to look like a coiled snake. Then a china lion with emerald eyes. He held each article protectively in his cupped hand, considered its weight and confronted it with the kind of face – Your Country Needs You – that actually launches ships. He returned the objects to their places and locked the cabinet doors. Then he walked around the house alone. Light appeared and disappeared along the line of rooms. The statues in the rose garden were positioned to see his uniformed figure appear behind one window, then another, then another.

Late at night he wrote a long letter to his sister and placed it on the console in the hall. The car took him up to London early in the afternoon on the next day.

Kitchener paced the platform at King's Cross. Many of those present agreed he was acting oddly. Some of them knew about his fear of the water, though nobody really knew what went on in his mind, except perhaps his sister, but she was not present. Maybe everything was exactly as it seemed on the outside.

'The weather will be fine,' he announced, 'and anyway, I have got to be drowned' – a badly judged joke. His men laughed emphatically, then stopped at the same time and pulled on their cigarettes.

At the end of the platform civilians hurried around the holdalls, kits and trunks. Soldiers stood about in groups, waiting for their rescheduled trains to be announced. All the timetables had been disrupted for the smallest train on the emptiest platform where Kitchener stood, looking moodily out at the activity while he spoke in a low voice to his assistant, who held the detachment register which listed thirteen men. Only twelve men had presented themselves.

The list was checked. It was the youngest member of the expedition, a cipher clerk who had been engaged at the last minute to translate the Russian alphabet, who was absent.

They gave him a while. A chubby young man, not in uniform, ran up along the side of the train – but then he stopped, slightly out of puff, and hesitated, his eyes fixed on Lord Kitchener's face. Kitchener tucked his chin down, showed him the peak of his hat. 'Sorry,' said the man, and retraced his footsteps, hastening as he moved back towards the gate and retreated into the crowd.

Eventually an older gentleman emerged from the office with a telephone message. It seemed that the clerk had received an anonymous communication the evening before, instructing him to go to London Bridge station instead of King's Cross. He had assumed that the secrecy of the mission was the reason the messenger wouldn't give a name, and obeyed the order.

When he couldn't find the detachment at London Bridge he realised the mistake, and was on his way in a cab. But he wouldn't arrive at King's Cross until after the train was scheduled to depart.

The clerk's name is not given in any historical account of the story. Like historians, who put strangers' stories in their own mouths, translators speak other people's words, and end up nameless. 'Ciphers for Russia seem to have been the cause of several irritating problems,' noted the historian George Cassar.

Kitchener instructed his assistant to put the clerk on the next passenger train – he couldn't disrupt the service any longer. He climbed into his carriage and walked along the aisle between the seats, which were arranged in the modern style in two rows, and sat down heavily, on the side furthest from the platform. Then he turned and looked through the window, studiously ignoring those he was leaving behind. It was as if he was ashamed of something, they said, when the train drew out.

The harbour at Scapa Flow was full of ships being refitted after the Battle of Jutland when Kitchener arrived in rain and high wind the next day. Admiral Jellicoe, commander of the fleet, hosted him at lunch. Pink gin was served, then green soup, then lamb. They were shut in out of the storm in the admiral's private cabin, where they discussed who had won the battle.

ii

Kitchener's boat, the HMS *Hampshire*, was built in Chatham in Kent, in the dockyards where ropemakers made the rope for the London hangman's noose. The *Hampshire* could carry 1,950 tonnes of coal to stoke her six boilers. She was famous for taking four goats on board, in lieu of a ship's cat, during a voyage around the islands in the Indian Ocean. Nobody considered whether they would survive and they died of cold in northern waters, but the ship was still greeted with baas from sailors commissioned to other ships, 'interlarded with Rabelaisian allegations about the reason for the unusual cargo', according to the historian Donald McCormick. In 1914, the order was given to detach the *Hampshire* to Devonport with a Portsmouth crew, which was thought by sailors to be a bad omen, because there were rivalries between the different docks.

The *Hampshire* survived the Battle of Jutland with only light damage, and had been repaired by the afternoon of 5 June when Lord Kitchener came on board. He could hardly make the crossing along the gangway, his oversized enfeebled body buffeted by the strong wind.

The *Hampshire* shipped out as planned at 5 p.m. on 5 June in spite of the winds. She passed the Old Man of Hoy, a 450-foot stack of rock projecting from the water, which marked the start of the open sea. The little escorting boats couldn't keep up with her in the huge waves, but if the *Hampshire* cut her engines she would have been unmanageable in such high water. At 6.20 the *Unity* was given orders via radio to return to Scapa Flow, and at 6.30 the *Victor* followed her back to base.

Around an hour later those on board the *Hampshire* reported the sound of a terrific blast which went right through the ship. It sounded, said a stoker called Sims, like electric light globes flicking out. Then there was a scattering sound, like flints flung into machinery. Sims was below deck at the time, washing his hands before his dinner, when the smell of caustic fumes from the flash fire in the mess reached him and he, like everyone else, made for the deck. He would always remember the horrific sight of his mates, terribly burned, their faces obscured behind the flames leaping from their clothing, rushing towards the companionway. Some couldn't climb the ladder to open air, but Sims could and he had to leave those men behind him. When he came up he found the rest of the crew trying to launch the boats from the pitching deck before the angle at which it was tipping got too steep. The lifeboats which they did lower smashed against the iron cladding and scattered crews of men in the sea among the detritus. Only the Carley rafts, large round floats made out of thick cork, seemed to be working, and the most desperate men threw themselves in after them, hopelessly. Then they started casting overboard anything that might float. An officer jumped with an empty wooden drawer under each arm, looking like a toy angel. The explosion had taken out the ship's electrics so there was no light, and no radio contact could be established.

Herbert Kitchener didn't attempt either to jump overboard or to find his place on a boat. The last Stoker Sims saw of him, a few minutes before the ship went down, he was standing on deck.

Fifteen minutes after the first explosion the *Hampshire* executed a forward somersault and disappeared. Three Carley rafts and some wreckage remained above water. The few men in the rafts stood upright and thumped one another on the back every so often, and sang aloud all night to stop themselves falling asleep. Some survivors spoke of longing for sleep with a force they'd never felt before. Others spoke of having to whack the tired ones on the head to stop them dropping.

It was almost impossible, even for those that were cast towards the shore, to land. Most of the rafts crashed into the geos, deep narrow natural gaps running inland for some distance, where the sea had eroded the rock.

From the shore the crofters saw through the rain a great flash, then heard the explosion some time later when it came in with the wind. The storm was so loud that most of the local farmers didn't hear or see anything at all – every building was isolated by the weather, like boats at sea. They didn't hear the few dying sailors who made it to the shore and crawled up the cliffs towards the crofts like selkies or sea horses.

In the morning when the storm had cleared there were bodies on the cliffs, on the lawns, in porches, in boathouses and even in the barns.

The officers drove from house to house, telling the occupants that the navy had the rescue effort in hand. The local lifeboatmen were to 'mind their own b----- business' and to keep away from the coast. The corpses were not to be moved. The beaches were out of bounds.

All the signposts on all the roads had been removed for the duration of the war in case the Germans invaded – but in doing this, the military only succeeded in confusing itself.

Trying to find the right beaches, they found themselves driving in circles, or unable to move in any direction at all.

The men kept washing in; a few were still in uniform, but most of them had been completely undressed by the sea. The bay was full of trawlers destroying the path of mines that had been laid along the coast, several miles west of the Orkney Islands, in May 1916. The mine which hulled the *Hampshire* was laid by submarine U-Boat 75, which would itself go down a year later, with twenty-three crew members, on 14 December 1917. The mine had been laid thirty feet underwater: too deep to hit the lightweight fishing smacks and trawlers that went out regularly on that part of the coast. According to Admiral Jellicoe it was a moored mine connected by a rope or chain to the seabed. Or perhaps it had drifted westward into the path of the *Hampshire* by chance, Jellicoe later reflected.

iii

Jimmy thought not. Before they had even set out, he said, the authorities knew that the mine which sunk the boat was lying in its path. He had an idea that the mine was inscribed 'Death to Kitchener', and that Jellicoe and other commanders knew about this mine and its inscription. I was sceptical about this version of events.

History is not like fiction, in which someone has to hang on every knotted noose. Even now, there are unexploded mines from both world wars still in existence, and it seems unlikely that any single German weapon could be preordained for the *Hampshire*: the sea is too big. It seems unlikely, too, that the Germans would inscribe their mines in English – if the English had succeeded in reading it, they would have defused it and won a small victory. If the mine succeeded it would explode and never get read.

According to my grandfather's version of events, while the trawlers cleared the bay, someone else was at work in Kitchener's office in London. A junior secretary working in the House of Commons put his head round the door of Kitchener's War Office the morning after the accident, before he heard the announcement. The room looked like it had been through a storm. Every drawer was open and empty and Lord Kitchener's personal papers, mostly letters, were strewn across the desk and the floor. Beside the empty chair was a pile of hulled envelopes. The stacks of paper on the shelf had disappeared.

Off the coast of Scotland, paper appeared on the sea – after the bodies came the wooden wreckage, and after that came paper. Sheets of foolscap from what must have been hundreds of thousands of documents papering the bay were, eventually, shepherded in on the waves and flocked on the piled tideline, but from land you could not read the contents, and everyone was still banned from the beach.

Some of the paper missed the beaches and was pushed back past the Old Man of Hoy and round the headland, retracing the *Hampshire*'s route, backwards, following the path of the *Victor* and the *Unity*, back to the naval base at Scapa Flow.

My grandfather's account of Lord Kitchener's drowning seemed to come at it from the inside. He let himself in on the conversation inside the private cabin. He speculated about Kitchener's fears and his sex life. The narrative was over-burdened, it seemed to me, with unnecessary details.

The history, as Jimmy had laid it out, drew heavily on a single source called 'The Kitchener Mystery', which was published between 1925 and 1926 in a cheap periodical called the *Referee*. Its author was an amateur researcher calling himself Frank Power.

According to Power, the *Hampshire*'s fate had been deter-mined before it even set off. The history drew together a conspiracy of winds and of English, French, Russian, American, North African and Scandinavian forces, as well as the mine which hit the boat; a Mystery of no fewer than three coordi-nated plots against the soldier's life. Three widows and a tsarina, a shipment of coffins, two million pounds in bars of solid gold and several apparently miraculous incidents were, apparently, concerned. Although the official verdict was that Lord Kitchener's body was lost at sea, Power alleged that the authorities were deliberately misleading the common people. He claimed to know where the body was, and he said he would bring it back. In the post-war years, he found that there was a public appetite for this story.

The story started at Belfast in February 1916, when five Belfast dockyard workers were arrested for trying to plant several gold ingots and a bomb (an unlikely combination, I would have thought) in a strongroom in the hold of the ship.

The next link in Power's chain was the commission sent to the coffin-maker to the navy to make enough coffins for the ship's whole crew, a few days before the *Hampshire*'s departure. These coffins were hurriedly knocked together, loaded, and dispatched by boat to Scapa Flow. They arrived the evening before the *Hampshire* shipped out, so that the *Hampshire*'s crew were docked and slept innocently, on the eve of their departure, next door to their own coffins.

He described the miracle of the *Hampshire's* Orders of the Day. The papers showed no signs of ever having been wet. The script could be read as clearly as if it were fresh from the machine.

'I happen to know why,' he wrote.

The papers had been in the pocket of a man whose very existence was denied by the Admiralty. This man's name was withheld in the *Referee*, but Power said that he was a young English medical officer taking his first commission on the *Hampshire*. The officer was reported dead, and his body was never found, but some months later his family received a large parcel containing the young man's uniform. The package came from an anonymous sender. What was odd about it, the family told Power, Power told his readers, was that the clothing did not look like it had ever been wet. Like the costumes of the shipwrecked courtiers in *The Tempest*, his uniform showed no sign of having been immersed in salt water – it was as smooth, clean and fresh as if it had been but newly dyed.

Herbert Kitchener's body had never been found. There was a space, as Power put it, where the hero should have been. Power tried to fill it with details about the man: loyal and dutiful. Staunch. Cool and capable, bursting with unbounded energy. 'A real soldier's soldier.'

I couldn't really understand the account of Kitchener's death, it was too garbled. As far as I could see, the story, which Jimmy was retelling from Frank Power's articles in the *Referee*, involved three widows. The first was a Miss Elbie Boecker, a high-class German-born prostitute; the second an ageing Swedish 'hotelier' named Madame Hubert; the third was a South African Boer whose husband had died in Kitchener's camps during the Boer War. The plot also involved the mad monk Rasputin – in fact, Power said that the whole of Russia, 'with its unpronounceable names and quagmire of deceit and plots', was accountable.

When Tsar Nicholas toasted Lord Kitchener at dinner in May 1916, the monk Rasputin, seated at the tsarina's right hand, nipped out of the feast to send reports to his contacts through a pan-European network of spies and double agents. Rasputin's message gave Germany the confirmation it needed. Kitchener's journey was to proceed, and high command gave the plotters the go-ahead to set the ball rolling.

After the fact, my grandfather pointed out that the few survivors of the *Hampshire* scattered and disappeared, emigrating to India, Africa or Patagonia. One survivor went mad shortly after the armistice, killing his mother-in-law, his wife and then himself. Another suffered from nightmares for the rest of his life, and was said to have moaned in his sleep,

'Shut that bloody door – Why doesn't someone shut that door – Someone is trying to kill us.' I can't see how there can be any credible provenance for what this unnamed man once said in his sleep.

Jimmy must have been still working on this history the last time I met him, in London – he was giving a short daytime lecture at the National Portrait Gallery and afterwards was planning to go down to Plymouth. That was the only time I can remember him mentioning the Kitchener Mystery, as such. I picked him up off the train at King's Cross. He insisted he was up to the walk to Trafalgar Square. As we went along the road past St Pancras he started almost immediately to tell me about the meeting Boris Zaharoff had organised.

It was the mid-1920s. They met at St Pancras under the clock: three divers; one from New York, one from Virginia, one from Sydney; and an English gentleman in an impeccable black suit who gave the three men instructions on their mission. He would be honest, he said. It was feasible that the wreck of the *Hampshire* was booby-trapped.

Jimmy hesitated, and cleared his throat. 'I have made a false start,' he said. 'I ought to describe something of the background.'

In May 1926 a general strike was called in support of the coal miners, who had been told they would be required, in the future, to work longer hours and receive lower rates of pay. The Trades Union Congress announced a general strike for steelworkers and ironworkers, transport workers, railwaymen, dockers and printers, out of solidarity for the miners and to protest against worsening conditions for workers everywhere, universally. Action began on 4 May 1926.

Nearly two million went on strike. The government had made some preparations. Supplies were brought into London under military protection. Replacement transportation systems were slowly got up and running. Some of the more privileged members of society offered their labour, as if to show that working conditions were already fair. Undergraduates from Oxford and Cambridge were bussed down to London to work as stevedores on the Bermondsey docks, drawing the dockers' usual pay. They didn't see what the workers were complaining about, one young man said. It was rather fun.

On 12 May 1926, which came to be known as 'Yellow Wednesday', representatives of the TUC went to 10 Downing Street, and that evening it was announced that they had conceded that the strike was illegal for all workers except the miners. The general strike was called off on the 13th, but the miners' strike went on. Committees were set up by philanthropic ladies who organised shipments of clothing and shoes. The Women's Committee for the Relief of Miners' Children and Wives implored: please give money, for the miners' little children are 'running along the rough roads with broken boots or barefooted, their soft feet cut by the stones'.

'The miners didn't have any shoes during the strike in 1984,' Jimmy said. 'David Jenkins, who was the Bishop of Durham at that time, knew of laid-off miners near Sunderland who couldn't afford shoes for their children. Jenkins was laughed at in Parliament because the MPs said that the miners were having him on.'

He seemed to be losing his way. 'No shoes!' We hesitated at a zebra crossing in front of the British Museum.

In 1926 the miners stayed on strike alone, but few of them were still going by the winter, by which time many families had been brought to the point of starvation.

The strike came to a predictable end. The workers did not get what they had asked for. The government had made it clear, when the return to work was announced, that they would offer no legal protection for those who had gone on strike. Many men from all different trades went back to find their employers were offering reduced wages to do the same amount of work, or more work than before, or they found that their old jobs had gone.

We came along New Oxford Street to the Tottenham Court Road junction, where buses, pedestrians and pushy taxi drivers, whose time is money, were converging hazardously. But Jimmy was not there – he was in 1926, watching armoured cars crawl up the road with soldiers pointing guns out of them.

Virginia Woolf was very productive during those weeks, working on drafts of *To the Lighthouse* and an essay, 'On the Cinema', which was written in April and published in May that year.

Between the composition and the publication of 'On the Cinema', the general strike went on beyond Woolf's windows. She was involved with it in various ways, and kept a note of developments in her diary, alongside records of her own daily life. But she predicted that the details she got down about the political situation would become less interesting as events receded into history. On 11 May she wrote of the strike, 'I believe it is false psychology to think that in after years these details will be interesting.' The war, which had ended eight-and-a-half years earlier, was already 'barren sand'.

When the TUC gave in the next day, Virginia Woolf was very near where we were, doing her shopping on Oxford Street.

As a lady, she was intimidated by the guns and the armoured vehicles, but as a lady novelist she noticed one policeman standing casually smoking a cigarette, and thought therefore that the situation couldn't be that bad.

The next day, on 13 May, she seemed to chastise herself again in her diary for writing about the workers. 'Excitements about what are called real things are always unutterably transitory.'

We were walking down the Charing Cross Road by now. Jimmy would have been ten in 1926 and I wondered if he had any memories of the strike. 'There wasn't much going on in the backwaters,' he said. But there had been unrest at Devonport when General Haig came to unveil the new memorial, which must have been a few months before the strike. Jimmy sat on his neighbour's shoulders to see the commander on a platform which stood out of the eddying crowd like a rock out of the water. The Union Jack hanging on the memorial was sodden in the rain. Haig's speech was short, the crowd silent.

'I know you all,' said Haig, 'have suffered great losses. He may have been your husband, your father or your brother. His death leaves a hole in your lives.' He went on to talk about the names of the sailors being salvaged from the bottom of the sea. They were his comrades, he said. 'More than anything else, perhaps, I am pleased to think I am to meet a gathering of ex-servicemen today.'

The scattered applause was respectful.

After the speech St Mary's Choir took to the platform while Earl Haig walked up the road offering his thick, stiff leather glove to veterans to shake. From the vantage point, Jimmy could see him make his way along the ranks. There was only one man who did not take the proffered hand, whose spit landed on the former commander's polished boot. Then the man shouldered his way back through the booing crowd. This was about the time that the 'Kitchener Mystery' was going to print.

V

As we came down the Charing Cross Road Jimmy remembered his original line of thought, and started up the story again.

The divers met at St Pancras under the clock, then boarded a train following Kitchener's route from King's Cross to the south-west coast of Scotland where the group met Zaharoff and boarded his boat, a German salvage vessel flying the British flag. Boris Zaharoff was a German-born arms dealer, with Russian connections.

'A villain,' I suggested.

'A baddie,' he confirmed.

The divers, Zaharoff and his assistants stayed in Stromness over the weekend, a queer outfit which did not go unnoticed.

It was April and the weather was fine enough to walk along the quay without a coat on. At night Zaharoff's assistants checked and rechecked his maps, the specially designed cutting implements, reinforced diving suits and the canned oxygen. With this equipment, they would launch their assault on the wreck of the *Hampshire*.

On Monday, the captain took the boat right up to Norway, where he sailed some way along the coast as if he were heading for the Pole, before doubling back so as to come at the wreck from the opposite direction.

At 385 feet underwater the light was good enough, but heavy diving boots stirred the sand into a thick fog, so that each man felt he was alone among the wreckage.

When he surfaced the first diver reported that the guns were still loaded. The second diver said that the men had not deserted their posts – skeletons stood ready with their earphones on and their shells remained unfired. The third diver said that there were hundreds of skeletons in the forward hatch.

The first few days were spent clearing the piled detritus, silt and hanging beams, for safety's sake.

They found two old bombs which they detonated remotely, from the surface, then all three redescended.

In the murk after the explosions they couldn't see their own fingertips and one of the divers, groping along a railing, accidentally set off the final explosion which hurled all three into the mud.

Zaharoff and his assistants on the surface saw something was wrong. Bubbles were rising irregularly to the surface and the rope had gone slack. Somehow they got them back up. Luckily, the steel diving suits, which had been intended to equip them against the pressure of the atmosphere at this depth, worked like suits of armour against the bombs of a war that had finished nearly a decade before. Zaharoff took the men to hospital, which delayed the salvage operation, but it was resumed and completed later that month.

In small airtight metal caskets they brought up papers, books and between £10,000 and £15,000 in solid gold. They brought up a lifeboat and several pieces of broken furniture. They brought up clogged, rusting guns. On the final day they rigged up a set of ropes and pulleys, and floated a grand piano from the seabed to the surface.

• • •

We paused outside Leicester Square tube. People were pushing past us. Jimmy leaned heavily on his stick, looking haggard, and drew breath in an attention-seeking way, to make them give him more space.

Frank Power, he told me, took an increasingly antagonistic attitude with the authorities, after he recovered the skiff on which Kitchener had escaped (Power had forgotten to mention it earlier) from the wreck.

The small, broken boat could be seen marooned outside his terraced house in Kensington. Power interviewed the Scotsmen who were present at the time it was cast ashore, and their evidence enabled him to identify the little craft as none other than the Kitchener's lifeboat, definitely.

The very timbers that were missing from it gave mute testimony to nefarious governmental intervention, for they fitted quite perfectly with fragments of wood in the state's possession, which were displayed, flagrantly, at the Imperial War Museum. 'I long ago made a careful scrutiny, which settled all doubt!'

In 1926 Power kept the pressure up. People were still buying the *Referee*. There were protesting letters from the public published in the national news. 'I am not to be burked,' wrote Power, after the government had deferred a vote on an inquiry into Kitchener's disappearance. 'Nor is Nemesis, for those who are to blame, to be fobbed off.'

Power redoubled his claims to authenticity: the story was 'based on absolutely authenticated documents, and upon the words which have come from the very lips of those who were with the great Field-Marshal to the last'. The story was 'pieced together with much patience and after considerable research.' It came from friends and relations, from former colleagues, politicians and widows of members of the *Hampshire*'s crew. Power spoke of 'K of K's military secretary, an Old Wellingtonian' with the improbable name Archibald de Bear, 'with whom he had been at Simla'. '"We used to have great fun there in those days,"' said Archibald de Bear.'

Power was determined that the truth should be told, 'the scattered proofs marshalled together'. 'Inaccuracies, omissions and suppressions' in the official version of events would be discovered. Power claimed to have found Kitchener's body, which had been, officially, missing for ten years.

The remains had been found in a small fishing village on the coast of Norway, and stills from a cinematograph showing a pathetic funeral were published in the *Referee*. A coffin draped in the Union Jack could be seen on the back of a horse-drawn cart; a short priest with his back to the camera; and a thin crowd of locals for mourners. He said that the authorities had known all along that the missing soldier had ended up there, in an unmarked grave – they had deliberately chosen to let him lie there. Members of the public seconded Power's calls for Kitchener's body to be salvaged, redecorated with honours, sent home and interred in Westminster Abbey.

vi

At the revolving door in the entrance to the gallery we were met by a polite young man in a suit, who introduced himself as Pete, and pointed Jimmy down the stairs – the lecture theatre was in the basement. When we got there, I was relieved to see that almost all the seats were occupied, mostly by pensioners.

While we waited for the auditorium to fill up, sitting in the front row, he raced through his speech in an urgent whisper. It was part of a series on portraiture and anatomy, and scheduled to run in tandem with a talk by a historian from the Courtauld Institute who would speak, after my grandfather, on conceptual artwork and plastic surgery in 1980s New York.

Jimmy's lecture was about Henry Tonks, a surgeon who painted portraits of injured soldiers during the First World War. Tonks depicted the attempts to restore their maimed faces with plastic surgery.

Jimmy jumped about, surprisingly agile in his nervousness, conferring with the ushers, fidgeting with the microphone and fussing with his memory stick over the gallery's computer. He practised the first two slides on his PowerPoint presentation. The portrait of one of Tonks's war victims, half his face shot away, crossed the screen and disappeared, and was substituted with a face which was wounded in a different way. The first soldier had had half his jaw blown off. The second had a hole missing between his eyes, and a scar which ran down his face skewing his features.

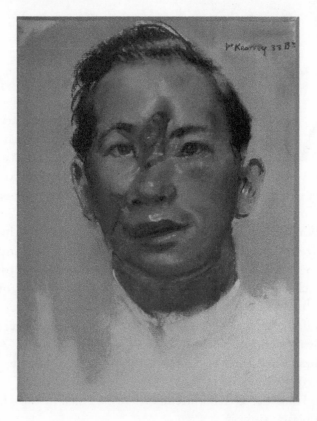

Jimmy positioned himself behind the lectern and cleared his throat. He started with a joke which I had heard before – self-deprecating and self-aggrandising at the same time: 'I'm delighted to be here today,' he said. 'Nobody seems to invite me to speak any more; I suppose they all think I must be dead.' The grey-headed audience gamely laughed.

He had plagiarised the opening of his talk from the introduction to John Keegan's book, from which he had also plagiarised the title of his talk – 'The Face of Battle'. The opening was a caveat, or perhaps an appeal for forgiveness, but it sounded almost exactly the opposite as it came out.

'I have not been in a battle,' he announced importantly. 'Not near one, nor heard one, nor heard one from afar, nor seen the aftermath. I have questioned people who have been in battle; have walked over battlefields . . . I have read about battles, of course, have talked about battles, have been lectured about battles and, in the later years of my long, my very long life, I have watched battles in progress, or apparently in progress, on the television screen.

'I have seen a good deal of other, earlier battles of the last century on newsreel, some of them convincingly authentic, as well as dramatised feature films and countless static images of battle: photographs and paintings and sculpture in varying degrees of realism. But I have never been in a battle. And I grow increasingly convinced that I have very little idea of what a battle can be like.'

Henry Tonks was a professor of art at the Slade, but Jimmy was not interested in him as an artist.

It was, Jimmy explained, what was missing from these faces in Tonks's paintings – the holes – that testified to what had happened in the war. He talked about Herodotus, who believed that the historian's job was to record conflicts, and drew on all the sources available to him to set down the stories of heroic soldiers. 'If Herodotus were writing today, he would probably be called a postmodernist, by some idiot.'

At the end of the talk the last picture whizzed at top speed back across the screen and Jimmy began to rewind the slides. He stood on the platform in silence, childlike in concentration, with the tip of his tongue just visible at the side of his mouth, silently tapping his keyboard to make the maimed men parade back and forth on the monitor. Sometimes he made the same face ping from left to right, then right to left, then back again.

There was a long moment of disconcerted silence, then someone began to applaud, and eventually the rest of the audience joined in. My grandfather seemed to pay no attention, allowing the applause to fall on him, and playing with his slides until it stopped, and then he looked up.

During the questions there were a couple of mildly aggressive challenges from a well-spoken gentleman in a brown jacket, who may have been a Tonks scholar. Jimmy reverted to the charming, patronising tone he took with non-academic audiences – 'What a marvellous idea!' – and the barbs didn't really find their target. 'I'll be sure to consider your thoughts, in the future.'

The lecture earned him a free lunch so after it was over he and I ascended in the lift to a pretentious cafe at the top of the gallery. One wall was made of glass with a view over Trafalgar Square, beyond which I could see at least six clock faces including the Big Ben tower. Each clock showed the correct time.

My grandfather ordered for both of us, trout, and while we were waiting his mind returned to the topics we had been discussing on the walk to the gallery.

It was Viriginia Woolf's idea, to bring things forth from the background. In her essay, 'On the Cinema', she had forecast the possibilities of the moving image when she complained about a bad film version of *Anna Karenina*. '"Anna falls in love with Vronsky,"' she wrote, in quotation marks. 'That is to say, the lady in black velvet falls into the arms of a gentleman in uniform and they kiss with enormous succulence, great deliberation, and infinite gesticulation, on a sofa in an extremely well-appointed library, while a gardener incidentally mows the lawn.'

The picture she described so reduced everything in the book

to a few dumb signs that it couldn't really offer any version of the book at all. 'It is only when we give up trying to connect the pictures with the book that we guess from some accidental scene – like the gardener mowing the lawn – what the cinema might do if left to its own devices.'

Jimmy paused while our two fishes arrived, surrounded on two square plates by an unrecognisable green-and-purple salad leaf that looked like feathers and was obviously some kind of shibboleth, because it was especially difficult to transfer from plate to fork to mouth. It felt almost like a triumph when I discovered, some time later, that it was not delicious. Nonetheless the trout looked like a magical bird in this clothing and that may have been the point.

Jimmy showed no signs of noticing the food.

Four years later, in April 1930, Woolf followed in Herbert Kitchener's footsteps when she took a tour of the garden and glasshouses at Waddeson, an estate owned by the Rothschild family.

She was shown round by a man called Mr Johnson, who was head gardener. He took her past rows and rows of blue hydrangeas. Hydrangeas come up pink when there is acid in the soil, and blue when the soil is alkaline. Mr Johnson remembered showing another illustrious visitor, a keen gardener, these same shrubs several years earlier.

'Yes, said Mr Johnson, Lord Kitchener came here and asked how we blued them,' Woolf wrote in her diary.

Kitchener didn't have much time to devote to gardening from 1914, after which he had to oversee strategy and tactics and the recruitment drive. But no matter what he did, his hydrangeas kept coming up with a reddish tinge.

Mr Johnson advised him with regards to the blue flowers. 'I said you put things in the earth,' Mr Johnson told Mrs Woolf. 'He said he did too.'

Virginia Woolf found herself weirdly repelled by the display of showy flowers, which she compared to the anonymous uniformed soldiers in a military parade. 'Cyclamen by the hundred gross. Azaleas massed like military bands,' she wrote in her diary. 'One flower would have given more pleasure than these dozens of grosses.'

Jimmy reiterated, three-quarters of a century later, his historiographical credo: 'A feeling for and a joy in the particular in and by itself is necessary to the historian, as one takes joy in flowers without thinking to which of Linne's classes or of Oken's families they belong.'

'Is that you, or is that a quote?'

'I'm not sure,' he said uncharacteristically. 'It might be me, or it might be von Ranke. But the point is this: the particular always stands for the universal.'

He pulled at his collar to fix the napkin which was tucked in like a bib, or perhaps it was to loosen the tie that went under it. 'They died to give us life,' he went on half consequentially. He was looking down with glazed eyes at the dead trout – a distant cousin – whose glazed eyeball looked resignedly upwards. He put down his cutlery and straightened it, carefully, on the glass tabletop. He looked out of the window. Then he picked the cutlery back up and went on with the trout as he explained.

'The important thing, she said, is to look into the background.' He pushed the tarnished scales around the fish bones which had emerged on his otherwise empty plate.

When we came out of the cafe we walked down the stairs to the hallway once again. Because the gallery is arranged in chronological order and we wanted to start in the twentieth century, at the modern end of the collection, we had to go through the exhibits backwards. We moved from recent acquisitions by the ticket hall down the stairs to a room full of Modernist artists, including Vanessa Bell's group portrait, *The Memoir Club*, in which Duncan Grant, Leonard Woolf, Clive Bell, David Garnett, Maynard and Lydia Keynes, Desmond and Molly MacCarthy, Quentin Bell and E. M. Forster sit on chairs in a living room where they met to read aloud and discuss autobiographical stories. Portraits of Lytton Strachey, Roger Fry and Virginia Woolf, who had been members of the Club but were no longer, were hanging on the wall, in the painting, behind the group. Bell painted herself into the picture too, in a hat and a dark coat with her back to the artist.

A small square connecting chamber at the end of this gallery was the area given to the war. Jimmy wanted to have a look at an original of the 'Your Country Needs You' image, but perhaps there is none – Kitchener was not there. And he wasn't in the group portrait, *General Officers of World War I*, by John Singer Sargent, which dominated the room (though Douglas Haig was in it, ninth from the right).

We stood in front of the General Officers, but Jimmy had another painting in his mind's eye. Sargent painted another picture of the war which was more famous than this one.

In some ways *Gassed* is similar to the *General Officers* – it has the same yellow and brown tones and both pictures give a panoramic view of twenty-two soldiers. But in other ways the paintings are opposites: the subjects of *Gassed* are ordinary soldiers, not commanders, and they are depicted as victims on the battlefield rather than survivors painted after the war.

Jimmy, looking at the officers, was thinking about the ordinary soldiers – he described, for my benefit, the yellow mist surrounding them. The soldiers in *Gassed* trailed across the canvas, some supporting the others. There was yellowish chlorine trailing around them in the air.

The commanders, meanwhile, had no need to be conscious of any dangers. Their pointed moustaches and the classical columns around them pointed back into old age, not forward into the polluted future.

Jimmy looked past these subjects, into the brown background. Sargent, he told me, had been disappointed with his

painting of the General Officers, in part because he had
to paint the subjects remotely from his studio in America,
and he couldn't think of anywhere to put them. He considered
a field. He considered a room. Nothing seemed right. Each
individual would have to pose alone – the whole group never
came together in real life. It was as if to make clear that his
arrangement was false, that in the end the artist gathered
them into a weird, unconvincing space.

They are half in and half out – it is like an atrium or
porch. The men are lined up across the canvas, flanked by
two enormous sandstone plinths with columns beginning at
head height to rise beyond them. It is as if they are standing
outside a temple or parthenon, or on the steps of a tomb. But
it looks like Sargent gave up on the building before he had
finished constructing it because the columns give way to walls
which recede almost immediately into what looks like clouds
of brown dust behind the backs of the subjects. Sargent said
that he painted them into 'a vacuum'.

The subjects stand in an awkwardly arranged line. The

painting is awkwardly stilted, it looks unrealistic. It looked to me as if the figures had been superimposed by computer – but that would have been impossible at that time.

The painting was considered a failure by critics too. One former director of the gallery supplied an alternative title, *Still Life With Boots* – a title which reminded Jimmy of Lloyd George's pronouncement about Douglas Haig's intellectual abilities and the rigour of his soldierly cleanliness. Haig was quite brilliant, said Lloyd George, to the tops of his army boots.

At my eyeline, their matching boots were impressive enough. Well made in soft brown leather, well painted with highlighted spurs; they were clean, unworn and still reflective, in defiance of time or dirt.

The painting had been intended to show the generals in some kind of splendour or glory, but instead they looked awkward and threatening. It seemed to have the peculiar effect of coming to show the opposite of what it was supposed to show, and I couldn't think what it was until my grandfather said, reflectively, not realising how exactly he was agreeing with what I was thinking, 'Don't they look like a firing squad?'

We moved on back through the gallery, passing quickly through the Victorian rooms – Jimmy thought the nineteenth century rather vulgar, as a general rule – and up a flight of stairs to the next floor. Samuel Pepys appeared suddenly, with a very direct gaze coming out of his frame. There were quotations from his diary printed on the information placard, which gave the impression that the man who appeared to be inside

the picture, looking out, was, in fact, standing in front of the picture, looking into it. Pepys was not a natural sitter. He didn't like being still for long periods of time, and he did not like the way he was arranged, looking backwards over his shoulder, to make the difference between the dark and the light more dramatic.

'I sit to have it full of shadows,' he said, 'and do almost break my neck looking over my shoulder to make the posture for him to work by.'

Jimmy didn't seem to be interested in the subject. He leaned in, scrutinising the corners of the image. Eventually he made a pronouncement: 'Interesting.'

He told me about the background to the painting.

Friday 13 April 1666 – an unlucky date, though as it turned out it didn't seem to be particularly inauspicious – Samuel Pepys sat for his portrait, and went afterwards with his painter, John Hayls, to spend an hour in the galleries at Whitehall Palace looking at the pictures in the king's collection.

Pepys was always, well into his old age, a keen pupil, and he had a talent for enjoying things. Hayls wanted to teach Pepys a little more discrimination – to be a discerning critic of art, he needed to learn to like fewer things. Hayls, said Pepys, 'showed the difference in the payntings, and when I come more and more to distinguish and observe the workmanship, I do not find so many good things as I thought there was'. The conversation moved naturally on to Pepys's own portrait. He decided that he wanted the landscape Hayls had painted in the background to be covered over. 'I am for his putting out the Landskipp,' wrote Pepys.

Hayls insisted that the backdrop he'd painted was well done, but he couldn't persuade his sitter. 'Yet I do judge it will be best without it,' Pepys maintained, 'and so it shall be put out, and be made a plain sky like my wife's picture, which will be very noble.'

Both sides seemed resolute. Having gone to the trouble to create a whole landscape, Hayls was reluctant to turn the setting, on a whim, into a clean sky.

Five days later, Pepys 'took coach and to Mr Hales, where he would have persuaded me to have had the landskipp stand in my picture, but I like it not and will have it otherwise, which I perceive he do not like so well, however is so civil as to say it shall be altered' – so the commissioner won in the end (he had the money), against the painter's will. After it had been changed, Pepys found, as Hayls had predicted, that his special new sky wasn't as pleasant as he'd foreseen. But he thought it better than before. He kept it as it was, repainted, with 'the landskipp done out, and only a heaven made in the roome of it'.

As Jimmy pointed out, there was no 'heaven' in the 'roome' of the picture that we saw in the National Portrait Gallery. It is unlikely to have been a different portrait, so the picture must have been repainted. Pepys came out of a dark brown cloudy background, which made him emerge the more starkly and suddenly.

All the dead go back into this brown historical back-ground, Jimmy said. 'History, like digestion, turns everything brown in the end,' just as inevitably as the good dead go to heaven, if you are religious, or into a vacuum, if you are not, unless you believe that the dead are only sleeping, and will return.

We went on back. In the Tudor Gallery we walked past Elizabeth I stamping her feet on a map of England. We walked past the Chandos portrait of Shakespeare looking like a bearded Mona Lisa, without the landscape – brown background fading to black. The wives of the kings and aristocrats were arranged more austerely in jewellery, brocade and taffeta and stood frigidly on the navy-blue walls in the windowless climate-controlled room. Two portraits, one of Edward IV and another, almost its twin, of Henry VI, were right at the front of the room at the beginning of the gallery's collection. They were surprisingly small – as small as a hand mirror – and I hadn't expected to find them in the Tudor Gallery because they weren't Tudors.

I came out of the screened entrance first, and found myself in a lit atrium at the top of a long escalator going up. A school of children in matching sweatshirts, guarded by adults at either end, was rising towards me and I had to dodge out of the way as they tided off the crest of the escalator and eddied into the small space outside the entrance to the gallery, whispering, for some reason, as if they were in a library or some kind of holy place. Retracing my footsteps towards the stairwell I realised there was a painting I had missed, which was hung on the outside of the screen at the entrance to the gallery. It was a seventeenth-century reproduction of Holbein's painting of Thomas More and his family, showing a group of Mores together in one room. Jimmy was standing in front of it.

The painting showed different generations of Thomas More's family, including More himself. 'Some of them were alive when it was painted,' said Jimmy, 'but this one and this one and this one were already dead. He did them from other portraits.' That's why some of the sitters seemed oblivious to the others, looking out in different directions.

Thomas More himself was done in this way, and More's grandmother was a portrait within the portrait, hanging on the wall behind her family.

'You probably can't see the difference of dress,' said Jimmy, 'but everyone in this picture is wearing the fashion of a different generation. They seem already foreign to one another. The young man in this portrait never actually met his grandfather, but here they are painted in together. Isn't that funny?'

He seemed confused and started towards the escalator. I had to stop him trying to use it to get down – it was going up. When I caught him he leaned in and clasped my hand and said in his conspiratorial tone, 'I think we might find the way to the Gents.'

I had not considered how exhausted he must have been, after the long journey and the walk from King's Cross, the lecture and a drink at lunch, in his ninth decade. He leaned in again, as we walked. 'He arranged the picture as if time itself did not exist!'

He was still trying to educate me, repetitiously, on the way to the toilets. 'There are several existing versions of the portrait of this family. He painted them all as if they were one family.'

ix

When I got to the rubbish dump, I found it closed
again. Remembering the ominous exhortations of
the lady at the council, I did not try to illegally
cross the barrier, to go tipping, as she called it. Why, I wondered,
was the dump always closed? – it was Tuesday morning, a
reasonable time to dump some waste. I don't know why I didn't
ask about the opening hours while I'd had her on the line.

In the village the pub had closed down and our house
had had some work done, apparently under the direction
of a man of high spirits and considerable ambition. He had
added a two-floored extension bigger than the rest of the
house, where our lean-to shed used to be and out over the
garden, and had painted the plaster on the front pink.

The old quarry was a Protected Nature Area, there was a
cul-de-sac of new-build housing in the back field, and a children's playground where one of the farmyards used to be. But
the potholes along the road hadn't been mended in the last
ten years and they were as familiar as the shape of Africa on
the map.

The post-office counter had closed, and was replaced with
a refrigerator full of Dales cheeses and other local fayre, but
Mrs Thwaite was still running the shop and she seemed to be
wearing the same slippers shaped like tiger's feet, with claws.

She hadn't had anyone asking for petrol for a good while, but she'd not mind fetching it out of the garage. When she came back she looked at me disapprovingly over her glasses.

'I remember you,' she said.

When I got back to the farm I felt like I had been on some epic pilgrimage, though it was only mid-morning and all I'd done was try, unsuccessfully, to take out the rubbish. I put petrol in the tank and went into town to carry out the research that Jimmy appeared to have forgotten.

The university is set on a hill outside the city, and the library juts out of the steepest part on a platform, looking away from the town centre out over the brutalist campus buildings, through a park to the stately home which has been absorbed into the psychology faculty which, according to a large waterproof banner, had recently been rated the second finest in the country, by an independent body.

I came through the traffic calmers to roll along the top road, and was surprised to find that all the large car parks were full. There was no reason why they shouldn't have been busy, I realised – it was Tuesday afternoon at the start of the spring term. I had to park at the bottom of the hill and walk back up.

The library was surprisingly empty considering the hundreds of vehicles outside. A sallow man and a plump white girl stood behind the desk. They were an odd couple. He was sad-looking, probably in his sixties, with combed waxed hair, wearing a grey linen jacket so well worn that it was a little shiny. She was a teenage goth. I spoke to them both so they could choose who would serve me. The man replied, in an Italian accent.

For future reference, people who weren't members of the university should seek a letter of introduction.

In the meantime, I was not to be granted access into the archives but he would take me down to the magazine repository. Without membership I could not borrow books but I could look at the open-shelf collections today, subject to a bag check.

In a side room behind the underground carrels the librarian pressed a green button on the wall and the shelves automatically shifted themselves along in a concertina motion, so you could choose which aisle you wanted to make space to walk down. He waited silently while I retrieved the magazines.

Back above ground, I went alone to the history section on the third floor, and sat by the window to read. I had also picked up some mid-century biographies of Kitchener, and Virginia Woolf's essay 'On the Cinema', from the open shelves.

The biographies confirmed what I had suspected about the Kitchener Mystery, and the magazines were unpleasant. One, apparently published by Lord Alfred Douglas, gave garbled histories tracing the entanglement of evil foreign forces with spies, battle-fixing, cahoots with brokers and moneylenders, stock-market prediction, munitions deals and Winston Churchill. In the missing copies of the *Referee* I found similar accounts: Jews, Russians, international conspiracies and, only slightly more surprisingly, Lawrence of Arabia.

The radiator next to me was turned on and blasting heat so I couldn't stand it for long. I thanked the librarian on my way out.

Jimmy had taken me up to the university a couple of times as a child, usually when he wanted to steal books from the library. Sometimes we used to feed the ducks on the lake. He had also shown me his old study, which was just across the road.

I walked along the covered walkway which had a slit

cut into the concrete, through which I could just make out the blocky outlines of the buildings beyond the fog. There was grimy snow still on the ground. Somewhere on campus, I remembered from the memorial service, there was a rowan sapling planted and plaqued in a circle of dirt in Jimmy's honour, but I wasn't about to hunt it down now.

All the doors along the corridor were closed except his, his was ajar. I paused outside, not sure whether to go in, but my approaching footsteps must have been loud because the door swung wider open.

'HULLO,' she boomed.

She was wearing a black dress with a Peter Pan collar that was, I suspected, children's wear, and a bolt of red lipstick. Her hair was short and grey but she looked young, sprite-like, even – the huge deep voice was very much disproportionate, probably deliberately so. She sat herself on a stool, like a fairy on a mushroom, when I explained who I was.

'Golly. I was one of his students.'

There was a reluctant offer of tea when I told her that I was working on his papers. This was a woman whose time was important. There were so many students, and so much history, and there was so little time, and though I was aware of all that, I still said yes. I chose white tea from the array of various health-giving teas she had on her shelf. She switched on a tiny kettle which was already full. I remembered, of all things, his beige carpet tiles.

She spoke much as Jimmy used to speak: in the practised, declamatory style of someone who gives lectures more frequently than they hold real conversations. Like him, she was not a good listener. Rather than asking what I had found in the papers she assumed, rightly, that I would want to know her story.

The woman was a Victorianist, and had written interdisciplinary books on cultures of mourning and the supernatural. This made sense of the peculiar costume, which didn't suit her.

Jimmy was the sole supervisor of the first, doctoral thesis on this subject, 'a VERY many years ago'. 'It was UNHEARD of to study anything like that then – because it was code for studying WOMEN – and they'd laughed me out of the faculty when I suggested the subject at Cambridge. (I was at Cambridge, you see, before I came here.) But your grandfather was NO OLD STIFF.'

I don't know what that was supposed to mean.

Her memories came out randomly. He hated being ensnared, as he saw it, by the undergraduate teaching schedule, and had developed a tactical habit of walking around all day as if he was just about to leave. 'He always had his coat and a little backpack on, dear, even when he was lecturing. Even when he was sitting RIGHT HERE at his own desk!' He popped into seminar rooms as if he was squeezing in an extra moment with the students on his way to the station, chatted for five minutes, then looked anxiously at his watch. 'Ah! Time flies.'

But when he left he'd pop his head in through the window set into the door of the next room. Sometimes he spent whole days doing this, 'interrupting PROPER classes'.

It was a device which worked, too, in the other direction, after he had left, when he wanted to get into, not out of, the classes, and he used to turn up sometimes and haunt the corridors as before, for several years after his retirement.

He was known, as I might have guessed, for getting catatonically drunk at staff parties – 'though he was not the worst BY ANY MEANS' – and, on occasion, in the student union, for which he was once disciplined by the dean. When drunk he held predictably forth on historiography, the archival turn and, when very drunk indeed, his father's family (my family), who were, apparently, miners from Wales.

I remembered how, in his story, his father had taken the train from Wales when he signed up as a naval cadet, and I had never thought about where he had come from.

'Of course everyone was a miner then,' she went on. 'Because we were all Marxists and everyone in the faculty had to bollock on about his working-class roots. Even when I was at Cambridge (where I used to work) it was like that. It's different now – can't afford a PhD unless you're an Old Etonian called BLOODY RUPERT.

'But he didn't talk about his old miners much. But he *did* talk about his wife a lot. A LOT. And he had up lots of pictures of her on this wall, and his whippets.'

The greasy Blu-tack spots were still there.

'Greyhounds.'

She was oblivious to the difference.

'I'm about to retire myself. And that shows what a VERY GREAT AGE your grandfather must have been!'

When I left I thanked her profusely for her time and she smiled graciously to acknowledge its value.

I was out on the walkway when the swinging door swung twice behind me and she caught up. 'I shouldn't think you know, he didn't even have a PhD.' She paused to allow this bombshell time to detonate.

She had been debating with herself about whether it was better to tell or not to tell. 'Of course a lot of people of his generation didn't, but still, he kept it on the QT.' She was flushed with the exercise. It was what was most important to her and at last she had found an opportunity to tell. Nonetheless, dear, he really was a hero in the department. A HERO!

• • •

On the drive back I thought about 'On the Cinema'. 'People say that the savage no longer exists in us, that we are at the fag-end of civilization, that everything has been said already, and that it is too late to be ambitious.' Virginia Woolf wrote this in 1926, but she could have been writing at almost any point. People are always announcing the end of history. It's exhausting to think about it.

Woolf wrote about the peculiarity of seeing, for the first time, moving images from a different time. On seeing a king, a horse and a boat move at the cinema, she said: 'The eye is in difficulties. The eye wants help. The eye says to the brain, "Something is happening which I do not in the least understand. You are needed." Together they look at the king, the boat, the horse, and the brain sees at once that they have taken on a quality which does not belong to the simple photograph of real life.'

The boat, the king and the horse, said Woolf, have become 'not more beautiful in the sense in which pictures are beautiful, but shall we call it (our vocabulary is miserably insufficient) more real, or real with a different reality from that which we perceive in daily life?'

We are seeing a world, she said, that has gone beneath the waves. 'We behold them as they are when we are not there.'

I had realised, from the conversation with his colleague and with William, and finally from his notes, that there were areas of Jimmy's life about which I knew nothing. The fact that he hadn't got his PhD didn't make much difference to me – if anything, I was slightly impressed that he had managed to deceive his colleagues in so consummate a fashion. He may even have mentioned it once, I can't remember. But the conversation interested me because it made me realise how little I knew about his real life, before I was there, or before his retirement, or before he became my grandfather.

• • •

The other library books had confirmed what I'd suspected. The Kitchener Mystery was, as I would have predicted, a lie. The people who believed in it could not get what they asked for – the soldier's return – because there were no remains to return. The cinematograph and the funeral were both mocked up. The historian 'Frank Power' was, in real life, a journalist called Arthur Freeman. I do not know if Freeman believed himself, or if he was deliberately deceiving the men and women who bought his story.

Arthur Freeman packed a Union Jack and travelled to Stavanger in Norway, where he staged the ceremony. With the help of some friends, he recorded the film at Stavanger harbour, parading a coffin in front of the sea in a horse-drawn carriage. Freeman took the part of the priest, pretending to perform the funeral rites in an Anglican cassock. Then the mourners, who had been hired to decorate the scene, were paid, and the coffin returned to the carpenter's shop, where it was dismantled and the wood recycled for the usual work refitting boats, fish carts and lobster traps.

An English journalist who was holidaying at his wife's parents' in Norway in the summer of 1926 found out the truth. The journalist made some local enquiries and was told that there had been no recent disinterrals in Stavanger, and certainly no Anglican funerals of exhumed remains. None of the local clergymen had any such thing registered in any church. A search of the cemeteries and graveyards revealed no recent graves, marked or unmarked, that could conceivably have contained the body of Herbert, Lord Kitchener.

Freeman was outraged when the story was published. He brought out the final evidence in support of his case. He had Kitchener's body! He requested that the corpse, which he would provide, be autopsied under officially examined circumstances in London.

According to receipt S-12.92271 for shipping received by Southern Railway, the double coffin, which weighed 407 pounds and was made of elm, travelled from Norway to Newcastle, then Newcastle to Southampton, before travelling to Waterloo, where the freight was collected by one Mr T. Hurry. In the station's luggage room the case was positively identified by Mr Frank Power, who knew it by a knot of wood in the packing case.

It was sent on the last leg of its journey to Lambeth mortuary where, in the presence of the Westminster coroner Ingleby Oddie and his pathologist Bernard Spilsbury, the lid was lifted. An examination of the contents was performed at night on 16 August 1926. Complete secrecy was observed. Arthur Freeman was invited, but declined, to attend.

After the coffin was opened a conference was held at the Home Office. Complete secrecy was again observed and the names of the delegates were not given. 'The case in which it was alleged were the remains of Ld Kitchener was opened today,' said the report. 'It was found to contain an apparently newly made coffin, but no human remains.'

The coroner and the pathologist could not find any trace that there had ever been human remains in this coffin, but it was not empty – inside the packing case, inside the box, inside the double coffin, there was a small amount of brown dirt.

X

'The miracle of the empty tomb is not the point,' Jimmy wrote. That was just moving bones. He left me no reassuring sign that he knew what he was doing when he wrote up this hoax as if it was a real historical truth. I tried to follow in his footsteps. Think of simple causes and effects. Be shallow. Look for mistakes.

Still, my own perspective was not as detached as I might have wanted. I could have guessed when I saw that the *Hampshire* was sent to Devonport, or by consulting the records at the National Archives or the National Maritime Museum, or at least by searching among my grandfather's papers for a telegram, which I do not think he would have put out with the rubbish.

Another researcher might have considered much earlier the possibility that the historian had some particular interest in the Kitchener Mystery, or something that related to him on board the HMS *Hampshire*, but the closer one is, the harder it is to consider the provenance of the sources and the nature of the evidence they give.

The holes in Frank Power's narrative were, to any observer with any sense of perspective, gaping. Why were people taken with this conspiracy theory? There must have been more than one cause. In Frank Power's version of events, everything had been arranged by the various powers (English, German, Russian and, yes, Frank). Someone was in control all along, and at the end, everything came reassuringly back: the rusted guns, the scrap metal from the boat and even the grand piano were winched back up from the bottom of the sea. The lost soldier's remains were found, identified and brought home.

The Kitchener Mystery is not a source of historical information about any of these things – they are all likely lies. It says nothing, or less than nothing, about Herbert Kitchener; however, it is a source of information about the unnamed people who wrote it and those who bought it, and about the figures in the background. The unidentified naked bodies washing up on the beach. The men dragging themselves to the top of the cliff, then giving up. The men falling asleep and dying in the rafts. The men jumping off the deck onto lifeboats which smashed to pieces on the gunwale. The men on fire racing down the corridor after the explosion.

After he gave his last lecture in London I helped him on his last trip to Plymouth. We walked straight from the station down through the city centre. He suggested we visit the cafe at the top of a department store where we had a pot of tea in the late afternoon looking down on the buses stopping and starting up Royal Parade, and out over the square, concrete post-war buildings – the city had been heavily bombed – which I quite liked. He gave a little speech about how ugly they were. We were at the height of the gulls swooping around over the shoppers. People never look up.

Afterwards, we walked on up the slope towards the sea. Past the memorial and the lighthouse and down to the lido, which had no water in it. We didn't go in – it would probably, he said pleasantly, have given him a heart attack. So we retreated back up away from the sea, along the steps and paths with railings that ran in zigzags along the front which went back down to the sea. The cliff was growing grey-leaved yellow flowers with tough stalks, and falls of yellow and green ivy. We crossed the road and walked back past the lighthouse again.

When we got to the war memorial, I stood with my back to the sea and read the general inscription:

In honour of the navy and to the abiding memory of the ranks and ratings of this port who laid down their lives in the defence of the Empire and have no other grave than the sea.

And their comrades of Australia South Africa Newfoundland India Pakistan Ceylon Fiji Gold Coast Hong Kong Kenya Malaya Nigeria Sierra Leone and Burma whose names are here recorded.

Jimmy was looking in the other direction, with his profile standing out against a stone lion plinthed on the memorial. He was as indifferent to the lion as the lion was to him – he was looking out towards the sea and the single grey battleship on the other side of the breakwater. I followed his gaze. Different kinds of craft – canoes, yachts, tugs and pleasure boats – beelining evenly across the flat sound, seemed heartbreakingly sure of themselves, each one on a different trajectory into open water, or back.

'Sailors, like historians, ought to be experienced before they put out. There are no stories about young men and the sea. There are no teenage mariners.' He was getting rambly, and I was not paying enough attention to him at that time. 'The sea is not the place for young men.'

The names on the memorial were arranged alphabetically and by the date of death, so all the men called Thompson who died in 1916 were together. We found his father's name that time – or, at least, we found a Thomas Thompson who died in 1916, though it could have been another man with the same name. Perhaps the copper sheeting on which they had been engraved, which was stolen in the late 1980s, had been restored. 'It's my name too,' said Jimmy. I made a flippant reply which I regret now.

Afterword

Historians can never write their own endings – the ending is always the same, the present. In a sense it doesn't matter whether I am right or wrong about my great-grandfather's death, because there were certainly real young men who died on the HMS *Hampshire*, and real people who died at sea who had pregnant wives. And my grandfather, according to the credo he developed in his old age, believed he was related to each of them, and also to the algae, fish and crustaceans that eventually ate them.

On my last day, a hand-written envelope addressed to The Occupier arrived in the post. I was still the occupier, so I opened it, but the letter was intended for my uncle.

Dear Mr Thompson,

    I am writing on behalf of my client James Weston. I believe you know my client as your neighbour at Ridings Farm. Mr Weston wishes to express an interest in extending his estate via the purchase of your farm. As you know your land lies between three Ridings fields.

    I hope you do not mind my approaching you before

time, you know it is my business to hear who is doing well and who is selling up.

We would like to propose a fair and generous deal. I do not know what you think about my client, but I will say this for him – he is buying with old money as they say, and he is not out to build a multi-storey car park. Mr Weston would be keen to continue your mother's conservation schemes, if they did not conflict. We hear they have been quite lucrative – not just a pretty face, eh? May I take this opportunity to offer my commiserations.

However, if the rumours of your selling are untrue, please excuse this letter. I am in the office Monday while Wednesday and happy to discuss future business if this purchase fails to go through.

Yours truly, John Dale

Dale Johnson & Sons

I put the letter aside for my uncle and returned to cleaning the house, which was what I was there for, after all. It made me notice tiny things I had overlooked earlier on. Under the desk I found a slip of paper on which Jimmy had copied a seventeenth-century natural philosopher's observations on thyme seeds, seen for the first time in all their miniature glory through the newly developed microscope. It may have fallen out when I dropped the notes on Antoni van Leeuwenhoek. As I was reading it the sun suddenly came out and light bounced off the newly white surfaces into the room, distracting me.

Outside, blocks of ice were sliding off the roof and water was showering from the gutter into the blue water butt at the side of the house. I was still thinking on the microscopic scale, and wondered if the tiny animals in the drops could freeze to death. In a letter to the Royal Society dated 9 October 1676, van Leeuwenhoek had described them: 'In all falling rain, carried from gutters into water-butts, animalcules are to be found, and in all kinds of water standing outside . . . They are carried over by the wind, along with the bits of dust floating in the air.' These eels make a living out of this dust, like binmen and historians.

Back at the desk, dusting, I noticed two spots of blood on the blank page of the notebook I had left open. I looked at my wrist. I couldn't feel any pain. Then a third red money spider appeared over the edge of the page and I realised what had happened. Crossing the unlined page must have been like an expedition over tundra to them, spotlit under the anglepoise lamp (I don't know if they have eyes). It reminded me of *The Aspern Papers*, in which Henry James pretended to be a fastidious scholar while he was, in fact, making up quite an unlikely fictional scenario, including a character with the daft name 'Miss Tita' (James realised that the name was too much, I think, because he commuted it to Miss Tina in later editions). James's scholar, in Venice in the summer, complained about being tormented at night by living things which made incursions onto the pages of his historical research. 'When I attempted to occupy myself in my apartments, the lamplight brought in a swarm of noxious insects, and it was too hot for closed windows.'

'Shall you study – shall you read and write – when you go up to your rooms?' asked Miss Tita later, to which the scholar replied, 'I don't do that at night, at this season. The lamplight brings in the animals.'

On 19 February 1909 Virginia Stephen described the same kind of company in a letter written to her sister's husband, Clive Bell, from her flat at 29 Fitzroy Square. 'For some reason,' she wrote at the end of her letter, 'I am tormented this morning by the image of a great brown woolly bear, which comes crawling across my page, and curls up into a ball when I touch it with my pen. It is deliciously soft, and rolls about in the palm of my hand. I think it has something to do with Clarissa. We used to be told when we were children that woolly bears could sting.'

When Stephen mentioned 'Clarissa', she meant Vanessa, her sister, Clive's wife. When she wrote about the 'woolly bear' that tormented her, she did not mean a real bear. The woolly bear is a caterpillar, the notes said, 'possibly of the Tiger Moth'.

When Virginia Stephen married she became Virginia Woolf. In 1919 she and her husband Leonard bought a house at Rodmell in Sussex, which was the house in which she wrote an essay called 'The Death of the Moth' which has become famous. It describes the final seconds of an individual moth's life. The species is unnamed. The moth does its last bellyflop on the page on which she wrote the essay – it is an essay on life and death and on the distinction between the past, the present and the future. The essay was written after the First World War, which Woolf knew, but she could not have known that it was written before the second war, which changes the essay in some ways. The page was being turned: the essay looks forward now, as well as back.

In 1909, when she was interrupted by the furry larva which crawled across her page, Virginia Stephen could not have known, either, her own future inclusion in the history books as Virginia Woolf, who would be remembered for writing pieces like, for example, 'The Death of the Moth'. When I looked her up – Woolf, Virginia – in the Merriam-Webster collegiate encyclopedia which my grandfather was given 'from all your friends at the University of Texas' (I know nothing of these friends), I found her picture on page 1,758, and under it an entry for 'woolly bear': not Clarissa or Vanessa but *Isia isabella*, which is brown in the middle and banded black at both ends. The width of the black bands are supposed to predict the severity of the coming winter. Wider bands means worse weather.

her most radically experimental work, uses interior monologue and recurring images to trace the inner lives of six characters. Such works confirmed her place among the major figures of literary modernism. Her best critical studies are collected in *The Common Reader* (1925, 1932). Her long essay *A Room of One's Own* (1929) addressed the status of women, and women artists in particular. Her other novels include *Jacob's Room* (1922), *The Years* (1937), and *Between the Acts* (1941). Her health and mental stability were delicate throughout her life; in a recurrence of mental illness, she drowned

Virginia Woolf

herself. Her diaries and correspondence have been published in several editions.

Woollcott \'wůl-kət\, **Alexander (Humphreys)** (1887–1943) U.S. author, critic, and actor. He joined the *New York Times* in 1909 and became its drama critic in 1914. Known for his acerbic wit, he became the self-appointed leader of the Algonquin Round Table, the informal luncheon club at New York's Algonquin Hotel in the 1920s and '30s, that included Groucho •Marx, D. •Parker, R. •Sherwood, and G. S. •Kaufman. He later wrote for the *New Yorker*, wrote such books as *Two Gentlemen and a Lady* (1928) and *While Rome Burns* (1934), and was the inspiration for the play *The Man Who Came to Dinner* (1939).

woolly bear *or* **wooly bear** •Caterpillar of a •tiger moth. The larva of the Isabella tiger moth (*Isia isabella*), known as the banded woolly bear, is brown in the middle and black at both ends. The width of the black bands is purported to predict the severity of the coming winter: the narrower the bands, the milder the weather will be.

Woolworth Co. U.S. merchandising company. F. W. Woolworth (1852–1919) founded his first "five- and ten-cent" store in 1879. By 1904 there were 120 stores in 21 states. In 1913 in New York, the company completed its new headquarters and the world's tallest skyscraper, the magnificent Woolworth Building. By 1929 Woolworth had about 2,250 outlets. Its stores con-

Cleaning the house, I noticed for the first time the different kinds of insect company. The house was full of living things as well as dead. On the books themselves there were dropped flies on thin grey dust. The carpet in the drawing room had an infestation of little beetles a few millimetres in length. They had tawny colouring and they lived spaced further from one another than the moths or the flies, like constellations on the floor, with a higher density like a meteor shower under the windows.

Above the window on the landing was the daddy-long-legs, which I had been told could bite. It must be a different daddy-long-legs, but there has always been one there – I don't think I've ever seen more than one – so it felt like he must have been very old, perhaps the oldest living occupant of the house. I imagine insects have short lives but I don't remember ever reading how long they live, except mayflies, which live, famously, for one day.

Cobwebs collected more at the corners of the rooms, like all light things. The flies dropped there too, not always caught by the spiders – sometimes they just lay capsized with their legs in the air. Perhaps the flies, with their light bodies, got swept up by draughts like dust.

'It appears to the naked eye, a small glistering Peal-colour'd moth, which upon the removing of Books and Papers in the Summer, is often observ'd very nimbly to scud, and pack away to some lurcking cranney, where it may the better protect itself from any appearing dangers.'

The appearing danger was the author himself. This was how he described the bookworm – not a worm at all. It was the fifty-second thing recorded in the *Micrographia*, a book of things seen under the microscope. The author, a seventeenth-century natural philosopher named Robert

Hooke, recorded its shape, tapering from a big blunt head to the point at which it tailed away – Hooke compared it to a 'carret'. Under the microscope he saw the 'multitude of thin transparent scales' with which it was covered, which he grandly called 'laminated orbiculations'.

The human eye could not then, and cannot now, distinguish between the many touches of colour on these transparent panels. The pearly effect of the light on them was caused, Hooke said, by multitudes of minute reflections. 'And indeed,' he wrote, 'when I consider what a heap of Saw-dust or chips this little creature (which is one of the teeth of Time) conveys into its intrals I cannot chuse but remember and admire the excellent contrivance of Nature, in placing in Animals such a fire.'

This appetite had made trails through my grandfather's books, some of which were quite elaborate, taking the shapes of bare branches out of six or seven pages or so. A moth fluttered out sometimes when I turned the pages – apparently the same as those that hung in my grandmother's rosewood wardrobe: silver moths the size of a fingernail. There were no actual worms. The only thing which testified that the animals had been there at all were the holes they'd made in the slightly yellowing paper. By holding the pages up to the window I could see clean air through the tree-shaped holes where the bugs had been.

When I put it in the waste-paper basket I noticed Jimmy had written on both sides of the slip of paper on which he had copied the thyme seed observations. I took it back out of the bin to have a look – the writing was spidery, he must have been very old when he wrote it down. On the back of the paper he went from the microscopic to the macrocosmic – it was a memorandum of the geological epochs. It was a lot of writing to fit on such a small space – he had crammed it in by leaving little space between the words. Precambrian, Cambrian, Ordovician, Silurian. Devonian, Carboniferous, Permian. Triassic, Jurassic, Cretaceous. Paleocene, Eocene, Oligocene, Miocene.

Pliocene, which meant more new; Pleistocene, which meant the most new; Holocene, which meant the new whole. The last age, which has yet wholeheartedly to be endorsed by the geological community, means new and human, Anthropocene.

Observation XXIX, Of the seeds of Tyme

The Grain affords a very pretty Object for the Microscope, namely, a Dish of Lemmons plac'd in a very little room; should a Lemmon or Nut be proportionably magnify'd to what this seed of Tyme is, it would make it appear as bigg as a large Hay-teek, and it would be no great wonder to see Homers Iliads, and Homer and all, cramm'd into such a Nut-shell. We may perceive even in these small Grains, as well as in greater, how curious and careful Nature is in preserving the seminal principle of Vegetable bodies, in what delicate, strong and most convenient Cabinets she lays them and closes them in a pulp for their safer protection from outward dangers, and for the supply of convenient alimental juice, when the heat of the Sun begins to animate and move these little automatons or engines; as if she would from the ornaments wherewith she has deckt these Cabinets, hint to us, that in them she has laid up her Jewels and Master-pieces.

Robert Hooke, *Micrographia*, 1665, p.153

Acknowledgements

The historian in this book uses various phrases stolen from writers and historians who probably wouldn't be seen dead together, historiographically speaking. That the historian should have a 'feeling for and a joy in the particular in and by itself' is an idea from Leopold von Ranke's notebooks, as is the observation that 'great catastrophes' arise from 'the conflict with the universal and the particular', and the precept that young people make poor historians. An analogy between history and childhood is from Thomas Carlyle. The historian who 'abandoned himself to the facts' is Borges on Edward Gibbon. 'The present, when backed by the past, is a thousand times deeper than the present when it presses so close that you can feel nothing else' is Virginia Woolf. The fishing net as a contraption for catching fish / a network of holes tied together with string is Julian Barnes on biography in *Flaubert's Parrot*. Other thefts are acknowledged as they occur.

Keith Dockray's sourcebooks *Henry VI, Margaret of Anjou and the Wars of the Roses*, and particularly *Edward IV*, have been valuable for me since I studied history at school, and I have quoted from Dockray's modern-language translation of Thomas More. I have mined several excellent books for historical details and stories about Edward York, Peter

Romanov, Olaudah Equiano and Herbert Kitchener, notably Charles Ross's *Edward IV*; Robert Massie's *Peter the Great* and Anthony Cross's *Peter the Great in England*; Vincent Carretta's *Equiano the African* and James Walvin's *An African's Life: The Life and Times of Olaudah Equiano*; and George Cassar's *Kitchener: Architect of Victory*.

John Bugg's article on Equiano (*PMLA* 121 [2006], pp. 1424–42) first drew my attention to a contemporaneous connection between black slaves and white miners.

I have adapted Nicola Twilley's interview with Professor Paul Mayewski, from Edible Geography (http://www.edible-geography.com/glacial-terroir/).

This is not an exhaustive list. The reading for this book was done haphazardly and for pleasure over several years. It is a work of fiction, and the book contains some deliberate amendments to, and conflations of, the historical account. Where at all possible, however, I have tried to acknowledge my debt and gratitude to other writers, and to recommend further material for interested readers, by crediting sources within the text itself. All errors belong to me.

Thanks to David Godwin and Dan Franklin for being so generous with their time, enthusiasm, and good advice. Thanks to Ruth Waldram, Ellie Steel, Clare Bullock and Joe Burgis at Jonathan Cape. Thanks to Sam Duerden and Rob Gallagher for comments on a draft. Thanks to David Hawkins and Olivia Smith for useful conversations. Thanks to Hannah Green, Sumi Ejiri, Oliver Courtney, Robyn Dodsworth, Vivien Harland, Nina Dunn, Will Tosh. Thanks to Charlotte Hall and Beth Vincent. Thanks to Caleb Klaces for everything.

The book is for Luke, Rosanna and my parents.